DAMAGE DONE

A DETECTIVE INSPECTOR WHITE CAPER

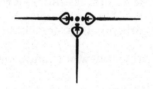

JACK EVERETT
DAVID COLES

BARKING RAIN PRESS

Damage Done: A Detective Inspector White Caper
D.I. White Mysteries, Book 4

Edited by Ti Locke (www.urban-gals-go-feral.blogspot.com)

Proofread by Hannah Martine (www.portlandcopywriting.com)

Cover artwork by Craig Jennion (www.craigjennion.com)

Barking Rain Press
PO Box 822674
Vancouver, WA 98682 USA
www.BarkingRainPress.org

———————

ISBN Trade Paperback: 978-1-941295-65-6
ISBN eBook: 978-1-941295-66-3
Library of Congress Control Number: 2017959835

First Edition: January 2018

Printed in the United States of America

DEDICATION

The Authors would like to dedicate this book to the millions of refugees displaced from their homes and countries by their government's use of military force, by the religious zealots who consider that they alone are privy to the wisdom of God, and by the people-traffickers who seek no further than to turn the misery of others into wealth.

ALSO FROM
DAVID COLES & JACK EVERETT

Damaged Goods: A Detective Inspector White Caper

Damage Limitation: A Detective Inspector White Caper

Damaged Souls: A Detective Inspector White Caper

The Diamond Seekers

1/1: Jihad Britain

The Last Free Men

Last Mission

COMING SOON FROM
DAVID COLES & JACK EVERETT

Old Gold, New Money: Fizzah Hammond series

WWW.ARCHIMEDESPRESSEUK.COM

CHAPTER 1

SPRING 2015

Aldo, as he preferred to be called, stood at the end of the Geneva airport concourse. As always, he swore it was a half-mile longer than the last time he had been there. He wandered to the car hire concessions, booked with the first one he came to and, documents complete, walked back along the hall until he reached a coffee shop.

Their meeting was hardly auspicious. Al was turning around at the side of a table, Fizzah was shuffling her overnight case under the adjacent table. They collided and showered each other with hot coffee.

"I am so sorry," and then, in just passable French. *"Je suis desolé, mademoiselle."*

The young woman was swearing in English. She collected herself enough to reply. "No, it was my fault—or perhaps both of us were careless."

Correct, grammatically, but not a native English speaker.

There were repeated protestations as to guilt but in the end, Al bought two more coffees and used a tray to bring them, together with a selection of pastries, to the table.

"This is very nice, but the coffee stained my blouse, I shall have to change."

"Where are you staying?"

"I expect at the airport hotel, I haven't yet made a booking, I am at a loose end. You?"

"Neither have I. I'm loose-endish too. I was about to motor down into France and have a look around. There's quite a lovely lake just over the border, a pretty town too."

"I suppose I will be flying back when I've booked a ticket. Beirut, I shall be returning to Beirut."

Al nodded. "That sounds like a romantic place to live."

"Romantic? Not as I see it, but it's fine, I guess. What about you?"

"I've been along to see the new Gotthard Base Tunnel—from the inside. I'm an engineer; tunnels are one of my specialities, so I'm sightseeing."

"Ah, er...a busman's holiday!"

"Exactly. You do speak English well."

"I am in the travel business...part of my job description."

Suddenly her entire demeanor changed. Frowning, she said: "Let's not do this. You are Aldo, sent here to meet Sadik, aren't you?"

"What if I am?" Surprise made him sound angry. "Who the hell are you?"

"I am Sadik's right arm—that's who, but if we are going to do business with one another you will have to understand I don't pussyfoot around." She folded her arms. "So let me ask, how do you expect this meeting to work out? Are we just going to fence around with each other or do we spend time more productively? What would you want to do with these two days, if we don't get fed up and call it off?"

Al took a deep breath, grinned, and changed the subject. "That was extremely professional, the way you made it look as if I'd bumped into you and spilled your coffee." He raised his eyebrows. "I have a hire car booked—suppose we spent a day or two together? Mmm? You could go to the wash room here and change your blouse or I could buy you one from a shop on the concourse. Then we could go see some of the sights nearby before deciding where to book rooms. Would you enjoy that?"

Fizz thought about it for a long time: the time it took to chat extensively, to start two bottles of wine—though she drank sparingly—and enjoy a pleasant meal. Eventually, she looked at her companion and nodded. "That idea of yours, about the rooms, sounds very good."

"Right, I'll see if I can find us a couple of singles."

She stood up to go, picked up her case and stopped. "You know, I enjoyed the wine and I think I might be growing to like you. It doesn't have to be two rooms."

After lunch, the trip to Talloires was quick and non-stop. No one bothered about their passports at the border as the number of people going to and coming from jobs in both countries was astronomical right now.

"What exactly is your job?" he asked, speeding up a little on the French side of the border.

"I organize travel parties. It's a few singles and a number of families moving into Europe. We have couriers who arrange permanent accommodation for them. We book the buses and take them to their destinations." She paused. "But this conversation has to be two-way. You don't just drill tunnels, do you?"

"No." Al pursed his lips. "I only included the drilling element after finishing my studies at Uni. I took it up when my father was imprisoned. After I examined my life, I thought it the only thing to do. I'll continue to do it, I expect, until he's free."

Al pulled the big four-by-four into the car park, squeezing it into a corner just as a second drove in. Finding no room, the driver backed out and parked on the street and watched as they walked to the entrance.

The light was beginning to fail and it was getting chilly; they hurried inside. A large tawny-colored cat on the lowest step was licking a paw, yellow eyes looked up at them suspiciously. Inside, though, it was warm and friendly.

The Abbaye had been built as a monastery some four hundred years ago; the interior was huge and dim except just around the reception desk. The clerk processed his booking. "You have been here before, sir?" The have was very slightly emphasized.

Al nodded. "Occasionally."

"Welcome back then, Monsieur."

Al looked round to see where Fizzah had gone.

"Hmm, you are looking for your companion, perhaps?"

Again, he nodded.

"I believe she is sitting over there, Monsieur. Part-way along the cloister."

He hung the rucksack on his shoulder by one strap and walked down the cloister, where monks had once shuffled on sandaled feet, their hands folded in prayer and their minds on matters far more sacred than the thoughts circulating in his own.

"Fizz?" he said quietly.

The woman turned her head and jumped to her feet in one quick movement. "Al." She dropped the magazine. "What a fabulous old place." Grinning, she stepped across to him, put her arms around his neck and drew his mouth down to hers.

Al smiled. What a difference a few hours could make—and he realized he was starting to warm to her. This was no silly young girl. Fizzah was a real woman, all woman.

The end of the cloister was closed off by a floor-to-vaulted ceiling and a wall-to-wall mirror. Gazing over her shoulder, Al watched his arms slide around her waist and pull her close, then he saw his hands slip downward and gently squeeze her buttocks.

"This is a monastery, you naughty man." Fizzah wriggled closer.

"I was just thinking the same. High time we chased the shadows away. " He took hold of her overnight case. "Shall we go up? It's room twenty-five."

"Been here before?"

Al shook his head. "No. It was the first phone number I called that had space. They didn't have two singles."

"Oh, dear."

"Where were they from, your customers? All Middle Eastern?"

As they took the stairs up to the first floor, Fizz replied over her shoulder. "Mainly from Eritrea, this time. I shouldn't be telling you all this, you know, I'll have to kill you now. I will tell you this, though: one stayed on in Switzerland. The Americans paid for his transport to CERN."

Al raised his eyebrows. "A scientist?"

"Yes, a scientist. He was conscripted into the army and couldn't get out. Imagine a theoretical physicist in the army?"

"Atomic bombs?"

"In Eritrea? Of course not. Anyway, we got him away. The place must be one of the worst human rights disasters ever."

"And your company rescues these people for the good of their souls?"

Fizz stopped and looked Al in the face. "These are rich people, rich families. They pay stupendous amounts to get out of places like that."

"Ah, this one."

They had come to room twenty-five just as someone came out of a room a little further along. "*Bonsoir.*"

"Good evening." Al replied.

The other smiled, looked at Fizzah for several seconds and then hurried on, saying. "Do not be late for dinner, my friends." The English was heavily accented; the accent was not French.

"That's odd." Fizzah muttered as they went into their room. "I almost feel as if I know the guy."

"I think he tried to park his car in the car park and had to leave it on the road side. Biggish one similar to ours. He pretty well tailed us all the way from the airport."

Dinner swallowed some two hours, seven courses, and an insistent sommelier who tried his best to sell them a seventy-five euro bottle of wine. When they insisted on one glass of house wine—Fizz was practically a teetotaller from habit rather than religious persuasion—the sommelier stuck his nose in the air and sniffed. Looking rather like a spaniel scenting a rich meal elsewhere, he tossed his head and stalked off.

Sometime later, they were waited on by what must have been the youngest waitress in the hotel. "Is monsieur le sommelier unwell?" Al asked her. "His complexion was quite purple."

She nodded and smiled. "Monsieur Bonjoie is a leetle breathless. He will recover. Ah, Madame, Monsieur," she looked out to the floodlit lawns, "see, it ees snowing." After she had taken their order and left, Al began again.

"Your scientist and the others. You do this sort of thing a lot?"

Fizz looked at him carefully before asking: "You really want to know?"

"I guess."

She took a deep breath. "My business is immigration. Illegal immigration, to be exact. I have worked with my present organization and on my own too. We move people to where we want them to go. Sorry, that's where *they* want to go; that's their business, not ours."

"People trafficking." Al's tone was purely interest, not judgemental.

"That's your name, not mine. And if you want to know more about me, we have occasionally moved drugs, and at least once, weapons. Does that clear up any doubts you may have?" Fizz was obviously not at ease.

"You don't have to be defensive, you know. I'll tell you this..." He spread cream on his fruit. "My father is—or maybe was—one of the biggest drug distributors in Britain. Actually, he's in prison, as you know, but he still has control of a huge amount of the trade. Sadik knows all that too. I presume that's why he sent you."

Fizz chuckled. "Sadik doesn't tell me everything. But your father...perhaps I should meet him."

"I'm planning on breaking him out soon. Takes a lot of cash though."

"Cash? That is money, yes?"

Later, they went to bed, though not to sleep.

Later still, Fizz told Al, "You sleep that side tonight. I'm not lying on the damp side."

"No problem." Al chuckled. He went into the bathroom, took a long thick towel from the rack, laid it over the sheet, and was asleep in minutes.

After morning coffee in the cloister, they went out to their gold-colored off-roader.

"Okay, my turn to drive."

"Did they put blocks on the pedals so you can reach them? Ouch, that hurt." Al massaged his arm where she'd punched him.

"Ah, I do sometimes hurt my friends when they're rude."

Fizz climbed up—and it was a bit of a climb—into the driving seat. She was gunning the engine and making the thing rock as Al got in on the other side.

"Where are we going, then?"

Fizz shook her head. "No idea. You'd better navigate." She took the vehicle out of the car lot and up the hill.

"Okay," Al pointed to a side road, "how about there? Look up there too, there are a few paragliders out, even with the snow."

Fizzah took the vehicle up the steep side road. Where yesterday there would have been sere grass and browned bracken, there was now a uniform white. Here and there, the snow was deep, levelling out hollows and hiding deep drifts.

"Hey, look Fizz. What's that?"

"I don't know; I'm a stranger."

"It's a lynx, gotta be. It's got a rabbit or a hare—a mid-morning snack."

Fizz coasted quietly to a stop and they watched the great cat. Judging from the area of blood-stained snow, it looked as though it had been playing with its catch. The animal stood up—over five feet in length—and took a great bite from the rabbit's stomach, opening it up in one tearing movement.

Crash!

A gout of orange flame erupted in the snow between them and the lynx. The animal was off in an instant, leaping across the deeper layers, running over the thinner covering.

"Go!" Al shouted, but Fizz was already going, following the lynx as it dashed for a stand of pine trees a hundred yards away. Al looked up through the windshield as another explosion, closer this time, showered them with snow and dirt. "There's a fucking chopper up there. They're not after the lynx; they're lobbing rocket grenades at us."

Seconds later, they were within the trees and Fizz braked hard to a stop, almost colliding with a tree trunk. "Out! Get out," she shouted. "They may be able to see the car from up there. It might show up through the trees."

They moved twenty yards away from the four-by-four and hunkered down behind a low outcrop. The sound of the helicopter reverberated through the woodland and branches shed their loads of snow. A car went up the road just beyond the trees.

Ten or fifteen minutes passed. "It's there again," she whispered. "Look."

A dozen feet from them, the lynx sat and licked its lips nervously, watching them.

Al licked his lips too, for the same reason. "It's quiet now. Shall we have a look around?" he almost whispered and the silence was suddenly shattered by a cross between a growl and an almighty scream. The lynx was on its hind feet and batting at something with its front paws, claws extended.

It looked down at the result. It shook its tawny fur; it looked at Al and Fizz and stalked stiffly away as though nothing had happened.

"*Mon Dieu,*" said a voice from the wreckage left by the cat.

The couple stood up and cautiously moved across.

"We know him," said Al.

"We do," agreed Fizz. "But I know him much better."

The man groaned to a sitting position and looked at them. He pulled a cell phone from his pocket and Fizz snatched it from him. "Check if he's got keys with him," she told Al. "Car keys."

Al did so, finding none. He found a gun though, a solid little Beretta which he held on to.

"Okay. Let's find his car then; it'll be up the road a bit. Can you hot-wire a car?"

"I can hot-wire anything." Al said and gently smacked the badly bitten and heavily bleeding man with the heavy handgun. "Let him sleep it off, eh?"

They regained the road in silence, both of them thinking hard.

"You said you know him, Fizz? Did he call in that chopper on us?"

Fizz nodded. "I guess so; he's the one who hired me through Sadik to get these people out of Eritrea. I recognized the voice, finally. He's, um...I think his name is Mewael."

"Been cleaning up, I guess, so neither you, nor anyone else could betray the people you brought out."

"That's about it, I think. I'll have to warn the couriers who took them on from the airport. He might not be working alone. Ah, and there's his car. I remember it from the Abbaye car park, dark gray and a white roof. God's name, you say it tailed us all the way from the airport? Let's go."

"Oh, no. We'll take his, leave ours, and wait until he comes round and uses yours to get away."

"What good will that do?"

"If I'm right, quite a lot. If you and I are going to work together you'll have to trust me."

The keys were still in the ignition of the gray Isuzu. It started up without a problem. Al cut the engine and Fizz examined the cell.

"Look at this, Sadik's number, mine. Even the text messages we used are still here. And some went to the damned 'copter."

Behind them, among the trees, a powerful engine roared into life, drowning out the rattle of the helicopter above. Al started the other vehicle and they motored up the road that led towards the heights where snow lay like a thick blanket over the rocky skyline.

The helicopter circled, then straightened out. There was a flash of fire and a long streak of smoke, followed somewhere behind them by the sound of a grenade exploding. Two minutes later, it happened again—but this time, there was an eruption of dark, oily smoke above the trees. The aircraft swept into view, buzzed them, and did a little shimmy. Al gave a cheery wave and a thumbs-up out of the window as it vanished into the distance.

Back at the hotel, Al visited the checkout to settle the bill; the manager gave him a copy which he saw was stamped 'paid'. He read the name Sadik, alongside of which rested a yellow emoticon, a smiley man. There was also a scrawled note paper-clipped to the bill:

> *Thought Sadik ought to know of your help with our friend,*
> *Mewael. He was quite interested.*
> *Bye now,*
> *Fizz*

He turned in time to see Fizz ordering her bags to be carried out. He smiled, knowing that if it had been left to him he would stay—but as busy as he was, Fizz was busier. She had told him she would contact him about future happenings and meetings at a later date. He threw her a kiss before leaving for the airport.

As Al flew home to the UK, he thought a lot about Fizz, but he worried more about his father. And how he could tell him about her? Aldo's father was not college-educated. Back in his day, a boy left school at the earliest opportunity; his place was to help put food on the table, not to fill his head with useless knowledge.

Still, Aldo recalled many of the useful tidbits that the older man had passed down to him, father to son. One of them could apply soon unless all of his plans worked out.

"If you ever have to go on the lam, son—from the police or villains—the first place they'll look is where your family lives, and then where your friends are. So,

find somewhere else. A new friend, an apartment; work away, even. It will give you a bolt-hole where they may not think to look."

That had seemed logical and wise advice, and he'd taken it at face value. Al was full of ideas for making a living, but at the moment helping his father was the only thought on his mind. He had a scheme to do that but it needed money—lots and lots of money. It also required helpers, not like Santa's little elves but young, fit people who would do anything for the sake of a challenge.

CHAPTER 2

NCA, The Headrow, Leeds

Our squads had pulled off a coup, arresting a whole gang of young teens dealing in soft and hard drugs. It was a team thing, really, but I couldn't treat them all to a "do"—I'd have to re-mortgage my house to pay for it.

So the plan was to take out my two senior sergeants, Barbara Patterson and Alec Bell. All I needed to do was find a venue—normally a task for Barbara or Alec but not this time as they weren't supposed to know it was happening.

Eventually, after a bit of tramping around, I found a place which fitted the bill in Vicar Lane, a quietish place which seemed to celebrate good food over ale, while still serving a range of single grain malts to suit Alec. Tables occupied space to the left of the door, but private booths filled all of the space to the right. The boss came out, presumably because it was past lunchtime with very few customers, and handed me sample menus. He was selling a good range of steaks so I booked a table for that Friday, for early evening.

A young lady wrote my details in her reservations book. "Have you come to us on recommendation?" she asked.

"I think I may have picked up one of your cards somewhere, not to take anything away from the place, it looks very nice."

"Oh it is; lots of ambience especially in the evening, with the wall candle lights switched on. I'll see that you get one of my best waitresses as well," she paused to look at my booking, "Detective Chief Inspector."

A girl serving entrees near the bar heard the title and jumped slightly, but quickly regained composure.

Al found what he was looking for at the Wharfedale Sculling Club. He enrolled as a member and found plenty of young, fit, drug-free, and impressionable companions. In a word, potential dupes and definitely up for a challenge—or adventure—as he suggested to them.

Al had changed in appearance since meeting with Fizz. He used a bottle of hair bleach and changed his dark brown head and body hair to something different, a reddish color he was happy with. A randomly-chosen hairdresser gave him an expensive haircut calculated to look artfully mussed-up. He completed his new look with a fake tan and a pair of tinted sunglasses. He decided he looked a little like an Australian surfer.

He estimated that he had three months before he needed to find a paying job. Selecting a team from the Scullers and organizing them into a bunch of hustlers would take quite a chunk of that time. He hoped that his initiative would both please his father and fit in with plans he had formulated with Fizz, when the time came.

The eighth boat of the day left Libyan shores. Like the previous seven, it was filled with expectant passengers looking for a new start in a place where they anticipated an easier and safer life: Northern Europe—Germany, Sweden and the United Kingdom were favored destinations. All followed the same route, aiming for Sicily, "the gateway of hope."

The earlier boats had made a successful crossing. The seventh was not so fortunate. They were in sight of their destination and had a customs vessel to shepherd them in. Many of the passengers rushed to the port side, to wave at the customs boat. The gunwale dipped close to the water; the swell and the wake of the customs cutter washed aboard, swamping the boat. It sank rapidly, leaving panic-stricken passengers thrashing about in the water. The cutter picked up seventeen. An unknown number drowned, their dreams unrealized.

Fizzah Hammad commanded the eighth boat, leaving Libya once the others were over the horizon. The one-time Merlin was an eighteen-foot speedboat that had won the Cross Channel race on three out of four years. The race official looked at the vessel, then at the diminutive captain and exclaimed, "Nom-du-nom-du-nom."

Fizzah, enchanted by the phrase, renamed the boat accordingly. Since then, it had enjoyed a very successful three more years, evading the authorities while smuggling high-value cargoes. The Nom-du-nom had finally been trapped at low-water in an inlet on an Italian sand-bank, the result of bad navigation rather than the customs' superior speed.

Sadik El Safari, Fizzah's employer, had recently bought the unstable seventh vessel at a customs auction of seized equipment. He already owned more than half the total people-carrying capacity operating out of North Africa. The loss of the boat concerned him somewhat, but only because it would trim his transport capacity for a time. The drowned passengers—the cargo—mattered not at all. They had already paid for the trip and there was an endless stream of unfortunates from every corner of the continent. He merely laughed when Fizzah reported back about the incident.

Fizzah knew what her boss wanted and was philosophical about the occasional tragedies; there was nothing she could do to prevent them. Sadik would have preferred smaller cargoes and more trips with faster turnarounds. This would reduce the possibility of his vessels being seized but such costs had to be set against the payment of crews willing to undertake the risky business. It was a financial balancing act, large cargoes with fewer trips versus more trips and the occasional confiscation of his transport.

Indeed, Fizzah herself had similar decisions to make.

She could have stopped and helped a few out of the water, perhaps a half dozen. However, her destination was the more-distant Malta, where she and three of her other passengers were due to meet a light aircraft taking them to Zeebrugge, the reason for the faster craft. That could not be jeopardized; a container ship would be leaving the following day for Hull docks in the United Kingdom.

Philosophical regrets were too expensive to contemplate.

Evangeline dug in her handbag for the disposable cell phone as soon as she heard the distinctive ringtone. She knew the caller, knew that the call was untraceable, but still went through the routine.

"Wang Tang Takeaway here. What you want?"

The silly reply still gave her a wide smile despite the exasperation the caller had caused her over the years. "Chili duck with a large portion of sugar on the side. Hey, how are they hanging, Baby?"

"This duck, she's just about done. When you comin' home, then?"

Leroy Richards grinned hugely as he pictured the pocket Venus he was speaking to. The man had always been one for the ladies, be they black, white, yellow, or any shade in between. He was black and no racist, he loved them all, but Evangeline was special. He had known her since childhood in Kingston.

"Check the book and I'll see you at seven star on Friday at nine a.m."

Evangeline knew what the code meant, but she would check it anyway in the diary they both kept. It contained numbered locations; seven star was a rented apartment in Selby, a small market town on the river Ouse where Leroy had reputedly drowned in its flood waters.

"You want any money with that duck order?" Leroy came back.

"I's fine. Just bring that pretty black backside o' yours."

"Ha, ha." And the connection closed.

She scowled at the now silent phone, though she knew it wasn't possible to keep a conversation going over a cell. Leroy was paranoid about the things since Mad Charlie Morgan had almost got to him in York. She had to admit he had good reason, though. Despite arranging a memorial service in Leroy's memory after his body had gone missing for awhile, there were still men standing around the Temple and mysterious cars parked outside her home. Those had to be Charlie's men, despite his being in jail. The bastard could carry a grudge longer than most.

———

Dressed in a black full-length coat, her face hidden within a fur-lined hood, she put the key in the lock of the Ousegate apartment. The place felt empty and she nearly passed out when two strong arms gripped her from behind and turned her round.

"Ah, Babe!" The whisper was unmistakable.

Evangeline never had a chance to speak until he finished kissing her, not that she tried to curtail the embrace. "How long you reckon it'll before we're together full time?"

He made a big sigh and then he pushed her away to arms' length, drinking in her good looks. "Oh Baby. Not long now. Still figurin' out the best way to do this last job an' then we'll be away. You know I got the house an' the papers; all we need is the money to live on an' we stop lookin' over our shoulders."

"Mad Charlie? What makes you so sure he ain't goin' to find us?"

"He thinks I'm dead, honeybunch. But I got to stay away from his boys or they'll recognize me and he'll put the word out again. Before he got put away, I heard that there was two hundred thousand pounds on my head." He grinned mischievously. "An' you can buy a helluva lot o' chickens for that much money."

Evangeline pulled her boy over to a chair and sat on his lap, arms around Leroy's neck. She snuggled closer and enjoyed the moment. It was not often they could share each other's company like this.

"An' this job you've lined up? Sure it won't get you caught an' back inside?" Evangeline cooed into Leroy's ear in her best little girl voice.

"Now hush, sugar pie, 'course I's sure. This time there's no helpers to split on me, no loose ends, no loose tongues 'cos this is between you an' me. You hear?"

"I hear you, babe. Now, let's see if'n you got any better at lovin' while we been apart."

———

I turned to Barbara and Alec and shrugged my shoulders. The party of revelers at the nearby table had turned up the volume on their argument.

We were enjoying a celebratory dinner after work, having successfully brought a child-smuggling ring to justice. The venue we had chosen, the Brown Cow, in Vicar Lane, was usually quiet and had a reputation for good food. I was busily tucking into a succulent filet mignon when they started. I made to get up, to go over but Barbara put a restraining hand on my shoulder.

"Leave it, with any luck, they'll drown themselves in booze. You don't want the hassle."

I nodded and smiled, sat back in my chair, and was about to get on with my steak when a glass ketchup bottle hit our table, breaking and showering me with glass shards and red sauce.

Looking back at the incident later, I prided myself on keeping my temper in check. The suit had been expensive—a worsted houndstooth—and it was now covered in sticky red ketchup. I picked up the pieces of glass, dropped them on a plate at the center of our table.

"Damn." I winced; one of the shards had cut my index finger. Luckily, it came out quite easily but I wrapped a paper napkin round it to soak up the trickle of blood.

I stood up, and Alec joined me.

A blond youth in his early twenties had thrown the bottle, though he now ignored us. He must have been aware of us, if only peripherally, but he just kept on talking. "...so I slipped in underneath-like and I kicked him in the cobblers before..."

I tapped him on the shoulder.

He stopped and looked around at me. "Yeah? What do you want? Go and sit down, old man before I freaking well put you down. Know what I mean?" He laughed at his big joke and turned away.

I'd intended to offer a few well-chosen words, but with the threat of violence I took out my police warrant card and held it front of Blondie's face. "You're coming with me, son." I looked at the others. "You can choose whether to join him or you can sit still."

"I'll handle this fuckwit," said Blondie, jumping up. "You handle his mate."

His size surprised me, as he must have been a good three inches taller than I was—and quick.

Still, I was quicker. I grabbed his shirt at the neck and perhaps some skin, judging by the yelp he gave.

He was still very active and I looked round for a wall to back him up to and make him calm down, but there wasn't one nearby. Then he brought his leg up and, just as he'd been describing, kneed me in the cobblers.

Excruciating pain blocked my thought processes for long seconds.

"Christ," I said as Alec helped me to my feet.

I realized the restaurant had emptied while I'd been crawling around the floor. Alec pulled a chair across and steered me into it. "Let's get you cleaned up a bit, Guv." He wiped some of the worst away with table napkins. "They've scarpered, of course, Barbara's gone outside to get a signal, she'll call Elland Road station. Give it five minutes and every squad car in Leeds will be on the lookout. They'll not get far."

But they did.

The management came out and apologized for the fracas. "We don't usually get behavior like that, sir. We're not used to it."

I nodded and assured them it was nobody's fault but the youngsters' and we left.

Around nine o'clock, a young woman came in and put a closed sign on the door, then locked and bolted it. She started to clean up the mess, first the table where the commotion started, and then the table where the police had been sitting. She carefully removed a wad of chewing gum from a saucer and wrapped it in a paper napkin. Then she picked up a bloodstained napkin from a plate, and slipped them both into her apron pocket. Then she started on the floor. Outside, in his parked car, Blondie sent out a text:

1ST STG COMP: first stage complete.

I was summoned!

Chief Constable Vance had sent me a come now message, the first time I'd ever received one. I tidied myself up, ran fingers through my hair, and headed towards the inner sanctum.

The remembered smell of pipe tobacco and Aramis still hung in the air as I entered, the legacy of the two previous incumbents. Inside, two other police officers were already seated opposite the Chief Constable.

Vance did not blink, his expression gave nothing away. "Ah, White." Vance nodded to his visitors. "Superintendent Holly and Detective Chief Inspector

Maugham have brought me information which compels me to suspend you from duty."

I frowned, I think. The significance of his words escaped me for several seconds.

"Give me your warrant card and vacate your office. I'd appreciate it if you would leave the building immediately and not return until further notice."

Slowly, I made sense of what he was saying. To say I was gob-smacked would have been the biggest understatement I could imagine, I tried hard not to stutter.

"Am I allowed to know what this is all about, sir?"

Vance glanced at the Super, who gave the slightest shake of his head,

"Sorry, White. I'm sure you know the procedure we have to follow. Suffice it to say that an investigation is in progress concerning certain offences in which you appear to be involved. Serious offences."

Vance looked again at the Superintendent, who I didn't recognize, or his D.C.I. sidekick. Where were they from?

Back to me again: "Don't leave the area. D.C.I. Maugham will call at your home to pick up your passport and as soon as we're ready to interview you, we'll let you know."

I reached into my jacket pocket and took out my passport. "There's really no need for the Detective Chief Inspector to go to the trouble, sir. "I normally carry my passport everywhere in case I'm in pursuit of real criminals." I might have emphasized the "real" just a tiny bit, and holding my passport between finger and thumb, I leaned forward and dropped it on the desk.

I walked out, trying to put as much distance between myself and the senior officers as I could, as quickly as I could.

I went via the squad room where Barbara Patterson jumped up and came towards me. I put a finger to my lips and gestured her to follow me. We reached the parking garage without a word being said, not that I could have spoken properly at the time. I felt as though I was barely breathing, as though I could hardly speak.

When we came to a stop, I simply blurted, "I've been suspended." And, finally I could breathe again.

"For God's sake, why?"

I shrugged. "As per the book of rules, I've been told nothing. There are two officers in with the Chief: Superintendent Holly and a D.C.I. Maugham who are handling the inquiry. I'd be really grateful, Barbara, if you and Alec can find out anything—anything at all—who they are, where they're from and of course, what I'm supposed to have done."

"Of course, Guv. You'll need to know everything: the whys, wheres, and whos. You want the rest of the team on board?"

I shook my head, pleased that my brain had found its way back into gear. "Best not. They'll draft in a new guy pretty quickly. They can't leave the team rudderless for long and even someone new would catch on pretty quickly. I'm asking a helluva lot of you and Alec as it is. If there's any suspicion, you'll both be for the high jump so take care. A lot of care."

"Must be something serious to suspend a D.C.I?"

"Acting D.C.I. Sergeant." I said and managed a weak grin. "But you're right."

"Well, I'd better get back. We don't want anyone catching us down here, they'd think we had something to hide." She raised her eyebrows and, considering her considerable height, they probably climbed out of my sight.

"Use your nose, Barbara. Both you and Alec. Don't mention names unless you trust who you're talking to and don't let them know who's asking. If a superior officer gets too close, just put the phone down. Okay?"

"I'll do that, Guv. Whatever we find out, we'll use our mobiles. Good luck." And she gave me a peck on the cheek.

I patted the spot. "Wow, really glad I spoke to you and not Alec."

Barbara's first call came four hours or so later. I'd spent the time gazing out of my study window without seeing a thing. I was trying to work out what I could have done to warrant suspension but really, my mind was just spinning.

"Yes?" I said into the phone.

"Hey, it's me. Don't bite my head off."

"Sorry, Barbara. Really...am...sorry." My voice was catching. "What have you got?" At least I made it a positive question rather than demanding if she had any information.

"Ah, well," she sighed. "Not as much as either of us would have liked. Maugham and Holly are both from Leeds Metropolitan, over at Elland Road."

"Well, at least they haven't had to go outside the county so it's not a full-scale inquiry. Not yet, anyway."

"No, you're right, but let me tell you what we know."

I heard the deep breath, even over the phone.

"There was a robbery at the National Bank three days ago. Horsforth branch. Six perps gained entrance; they were dressed in black ski suits with masks.

They jammed the main doors so they could not be bolted electronically before shooting out the CCTV camera over the main counter. Oh, and just as one teller was exiting from behind the counter, they shot at him as they entered. Let me see, now." Barbara was obviously checking her notes. "Not necessarily in that order, of course. Yep, that's it. Okay?"

"Yes, that's okay. But what does it have to do with me?

"I spoke to one of the DC's I knew from police training. He says—and he told me not to breathe a word of this—the SOCO team found unmistakable evidence that you were involved. Your DNA turned up in several different samples so they weren't just reliant on one."

I was knocked sideways for some moments. Had I ever been there? Certainly not.

"You still there?"

"What? Oh, yes Barbara, just thinking—trying to. There's only one thing we know. That I know." I corrected myself. "It wasn't me. I've never been there. So there's only one conclusion..."

"You've been fitted up. Framed, as the Yanks say."

"Damn right. And now, the only thing we have to do is find out is why, and by whom?"

"I've got a friend in the lab that processes our work and it also processes stuff for the Metro, since they're in the same building. I might find out some more that way, though not who or why."

"That's great Barbara, and thanks. Keep your cards close to your chest and now that we know what it's all about, I'll have something to do. Oh, I'll be staying home for the conceivable future; you've got my cell number if you need to be in touch?"

"Certainly have, Guv. Bye."

All six members of Al's team from the Wharfedale Sculling Club were tech-savvy; owners of laptops or tablets, users of state-of-the-art phones, active on social networks. Meetings were arranged, venues chosen, and dress codes established with a minimum of fuss. Sheldon would coordinate discussions and tag each directive with a code of importance varying from trivial to critical. Being paranoid over all things involving security, he used piratical symbols like crossed swords or skulls, a little childish perhaps, but he thought it would introduce a bit of fun to proceedings, and being a young group they seemed to appreciate it.

Day jobs for the members comprised IT consultant, electrician, mechanic, hairdresser, waitress, and finally himself, an engineer. What bound this eclectic group of young men and women together was not obvious. Even they had difficulty in realizing that apart from a touch of adventure, they were there because of greed, pure and simple.

The week after the bank robbery—they'd been told they were making a movie—passed without incident. As dictated by Sheldon they were now meeting for the share-out; the text message to his team included a symbol of a pirate's chest. Their meeting had been arranged to take place in a back room at the Swiss Lodge, an up-market pub on the Old North Road just north of Wetherby. The place was owned by an acquaintance of Leonard's who had originally had the idea for them all to be identified simply by a number.

Leonard had once confided to Penny that it was the old James Bond films that had given him the idea. She considered the notion worthwhile but was not greatly interested in the source. Sheldon had also liked the suggestion but had changed the idea to their having names of TV characters they were familiar with. No one disagreed. He was, of course, the only one to know the real identities behind the names.

The drinks had already been put out when they arrived, with everyone on time—another rule. Sheldon, tall, muscular and authoritative, raised his glass. "To all of us, Comrades." Then, after the toast: "Time to share out the spoils, such as they are. The amount is not important; this was our first major exercise and a test of our future capabilities."

"Hell," said Penny, "I popped a couple of uppers before the job."

"Me too." Howard laughed. "And not just a couple, either."

Sheldon dropped a bag onto the table causing everyone to grab their glasses out of harm's way. "Three thousand each. "Not bad, three grand each for a few hours' work."

"Should have been more." Howard blurted out.

"You're right," Sheldon said, nodding. "Eighteen-thousand from four cash registers and it was a Friday. There should have been a lot of pub-takings in there. But I suppose the management never allows them to get too full. Not that it is important; what was important was the way the job went down. Two of the tellers were absolutely terrified and that is realism. Just what we need in a relatively low-budget shoot like ours."

"Sheldon, you called Bernadette Bev in front of that cop the other night, in Leeds," Penny, a young woman with sparkling blue eyes, said. Why was..?"

Sheldon cut her short. "I'll be doing that quite often, calling you by names that are not ours. The coppers may be ignorant, to a point, but they aren't all stupid. Misdirection. What might Bev be short for? Beverley, a surname like Bevan? They'll be looking for the girl—or the guy—for some time."

"Great idea," said Howard. "Like the TV names too. Even if the fuzz tortured us within an inch of our lives, we can't give them anything useful."

"Let's hope it doesn't come to torture, eh? Remember this is all off-the-cuff, no one knows about the movie, not even the cops—except at the very top. Realism, remember? Now, time presses on. I've bundled your money, all the packs are the same. Take one each and then we must discuss our next outing."

CHAPTER 3

My dad had just returned to his house in my back garden, Pip was sitting on my lap having his ears scratched. His ears pricked up and a low growl escaped him. He was way ahead of the doorbell.

I pushed him off and went through to the front door, used the spy hole to see who was there. It was a habit that came naturally after the killer, Billy Jarvis, had tried his best to garrote me. This time, it was Joe Flowers, our newly appointed Chief Superintendent, a good officer and a good friend.

"Come in Joe. I presume this isn't a social call?"

Joe smiled at me as he came through the door. "The Chief thought it best that I call 'round and keep you in the picture about what's happened. Okay?"

I nodded. "Nice of him."

"And to reassure you, of course. We'll catch the buggers who framed you."

"So there are one or two who think I'm innocent? Thought I was the only one. Come on through, Joe."

Pip advanced and smelled Joe's shoes. They must have been okay, the dog backed off, just a little warily, and sat in his basket.

I gestured to the other armchair, Dad's, when he was here giving me the benefit of his wisdom. I sat down in mine.

I took a deep breath and let it out slowly. "I have to say Joe, wasn't sure who to expect at my door. I thought I'd been hung out to dry, you know. Pip wasn't any too sure, either. Growled a bit even before you reached the door."

"Wise chap." He laughed, sort of polite. "You know as well as I do, Stewart, protocol is king. We have to do things in a certain way. On this occasion, it was a sort of fait accompli; the Leeds Met boys brought a crime report over to Vance and he had no other choice but to suspend you on the basis of the evidence."

"So what was the evidence, Joe? We both know I wasn't at the bank so it couldn't have been me."

"All I can tell you is that it's DNA based: blood, hair, and saliva samples. All of it collected by SOCO at the bank. And how do you know it was a bank?"

Uh-oh. A little of my conversation with Barbara had slipped over into this one. "A wild guess, Joe. I'd supposed it was something like mistaken identity or maybe falsification of CCTV recording, but DNA? *Three* samples? That's a different ball game." I was breathing heavily. I could feel my anger rising. "This was no accident, Joe. It was a deliberate act. It's possible that I was a random choice, but it's deliberate."

Joe was nodding with each point I made. "You're right, of course," he said, finally.

"I'm going to have to prove my innocence."

"Oh, now. Slow down, cowboy. You're not going to do any such thing. What you are going to do is to sit this one out and let others sort it through. It all happened on the Met's turf; it's their boys that'll do the sorting."

"Maugham and Holly?"

"Maybe," Joe half admitted. "They won't enjoy doing this sort of thing, any more than you would if the situation was reversed. No one likes investigating a fellow officer."

He saw my fists clenching and unclenching. I said, "Well, we can't have that, Joe, fellow officers enjoying the pickle I'm in. Maybe I should resign, then I'll be a civilian. Think it might help?"

Flowers stood up, went over to stand in front of my view of the orchard, and looked down at me. I think he was a bit annoyed. "And what good would that do, hmm? You leave. they'll conclude you're guilty, and they'll let the dogs loose. Stay in your post and you'll retain the respect a D.C.I. commands."

I put my head in my hands and considered Joe's advice. "I guess you're right, Joe. I'm just feeling despondent. What I'd like to know is where they got saliva from? Blood, okay, I can understand that, but I'm not one to swap spittle even while I'm tonsil fighting."

Joe laughed. "That's the spirit. Figure out the blood and hair and you're two-thirds of the way there. Or perhaps you've already done that?"

Joe had lifted me out of the self-pity anyway, my mind got into gear again, and I began to feel better. "Hmm. Easy enough if they could access my office or this house. They'd discover I occasionally nick myself shaving. I have a hair comb at the office, and here, naturally."

I fell silent and looked at Joe, steadily. "That's me Joe, thinking about things. I can't switch onto stand-by. I just know that that pair will miss something that I wouldn't. Couldn't you arrange it so I could view the crime scene once they've finished?"

"I guess you could pretend you're interested in opening an account, but it certainly can't be in a professional capacity. It's out of the question."

"Yeah. I suppose."

"And by the way; DNA doesn't have to come from blood or hair, does it? Could be urine or vomit. Been on any wild nights out lately?"

"No, and I'm not the type to pee in the street." I shook my head but I'd be thinking even harder once he left. "Joe, I've been incredibly rude. Do you fancy a cuppa?"

"Thought you'd never ask."

"Or something stronger?"

———

The main house had once belonged to a farmer whose land occupied the whole valley, until the Yorkshire Water Authority had forcibly purchased the area and turned the valley into a reservoir. Now, the house stood in much smaller grounds with panoramic views of a lake large enough to serve most of the city of Leeds.

Leonard occupied a suite of four rooms in an extension to the original building joined by a paved and covered walkway. The rooms, like those in the main house, were large, two of them being furnished with beds and a third—his own bedroom—with a California king-size, seven-foot bed, an en suite Jacuzzi, and a four-person shower which he fantasized about filling one day. The living room and the kitchen had ten-foot sliding glass doors giving uninterrupted views over the water.

No money had been spared in his attempt to portray luxury. In Leonard's world, this meant everything. Leonard had never known what it was like to want for anything. During his growing years, he had merely to suggest that it might be nice to...and whatever might have been nice was there within hours or his father would know the reason why.

His father was someone important, someone in merchant banking who spent half of his life on the phone. Busy over weekends and holidays with no time to spare for talking with his son; no time to take part in any of his nurturing. It didn't take long for the boy to realize that the money spent was simply to keep him quiet, to save his father time. Today, a limousine had collected the father for a flight to Geneva for yet another conference. Tomorrow, it might be Saigon or Moscow, but Leonard lived his life alone. He looked forward to the day he could make his father proud, and maybe the filming might just do that.

He had just added the three-thousand-pound payment from filming the bank job to the thirty thousand in the floor safe he had had installed; it was hidden beneath a flagstone and operated like a car lock, opening and closing on a signal from his key ring. The system was known only to the odd-job man from a village workshop some thirty miles away. Money was just a way of keeping score: the more there was, the more he felt he amounted to something.

Leonard glanced at his watch. His order for lunch would be here shortly and he went into the main house to wait for the van from the Old Mill Restaurant. Their kitchen delivered most of his food, selected straight off the standard menu.

His five newish friends would be here before long, four men and two women, all members of the Wharfedale Sculling Club. It was, perhaps, an unusual balance of sexes but the women seemed to enjoy being outnumbered, appreciating the extra attention from three males, even if Sheldon seemed impervious to feminine charms.

The food arrived first and was followed within a quarter hour by the five guests, each in their own car. Their self-styled leader arrived first, spinning the wheels of his Alpha-Romeo Giulietta in a shower of gravel. He bounced rather than walked into the annex as though he owned the place, picking a small sweet pear from a bowl on the dining table.

"Yo, bro," he said, parodying the image of the west coast, college-age white boy in flip-flops and beat-up cargo shorts, hoping it made him fit in. "Food smells good," he continued, "you'll have to come over to my place sometime." An invitation as false as the "yo bro" he had started with. Leonard also understood the absence of intent but still wondered where Sheldon's place might be.

Sheldon had brought a large portfolio case, the sort of thing an architect might carry. He held it up and shook it. "Well bro, plans for our second shoot. It's a little bit different but I think you'll like it."

Leonard grimaced. "That's nice, why don't we take a drink out back? The others will be here soon enough and I want to set the food out."

"Fine." Sheldon propped his case against a chair while he poured himself a slug of Bacardi, striking the heavy glass against the auto-release ice chute in the freezer drawer. "Are we eating at the patio table?"

"If you want to, the weather's good."

The others arrived one by one and helped themselves to drinks.

"Hey, wow! Look at that."

A flock of Canadian geese was just coming in over the lake and, as if an invisible signal had been given, they came down spectacularly, plowing through the water and settling down. Penny, a natural brunette and probably the prettier of the two girls, dug in her bag for her phone and was about to photograph the flock when a hand reached past her face and plucked it from her hand.

"No photos, please." Leonard gave the instrument back. "Sorry."

"Oh, sure. I understand, sorry. But they're magnificent, aren't they? You sure a quick video would matter?"

"Maybe, maybe not. I'm not willing to take the risk, GPS tag on photos give away our location. Besides I can't have you putting me to shame. After all, *I'm* supposed to be the camera man."

"Hmm. Goose. Best served with orange sauce and crisped like only the Chinese seem to know how." Raj chuckled at his joke. It was ten or twelve seconds before Penny got it and nodded.

When they finished eating, Leonard stacked the soiled plates on a side table. He didn't notice the marked absence of thanks for the outstanding meal; in fact, he would have been surprised, not to say confused, if there had been. The group merely returned inside and stretched out on the recliners and couches.

Sheldon took center stage, spread his plans out on a low table. He found the controls and lowered the window blinds, shutting out most of the light. He poised his finger indecisively over the small console for a moment, then touched another button to bring up a bank of spotlights. "Nice, Leonard, I have something similar. Now, look at these."

Even Raj, the resident cynic, was impressed. "You do this for a living?"

Sheldon ignored the query. "These show the layout of an as yet un-named branch of a well-known bookmaker. It's located in a strip mall. Now..."

"What the hell's a strip mall?" Howard didn't like Americanisms being slipped into conversation.

"Okay, a 'parade of shops' for our more conservative members. Unlike the last time, when we went in through the front door, we will be going in through the roof. Just here." He pointed.

"How high's this roof?" asked Bernadette, the smallest of the group. "I'm not a great fan of heights. Anyway, what's wrong with front doors?"

Sheldon turned round and seized her by the ponytail. "Get used to it, kid." He was doubly annoyed at the interruption—and the criticism. "No two jobs will ever be the same. Not our numbers, not our clothes and most important, not our M.O. We're making a film in which we're supposed to be professionals, and I want the police to react to us as if we are. How would it look if all the cops smiled at us when we were filming? It has to look real. Understand?"

He let go of Bernadette's hair before looking around, studying to see if the others were questioning his actions, but none of them seemed to notice. "Listen, all of you. The police look for similarities to help them catch criminals.

Similarities mean the same criminals are at work. To make this film believable, we're not going to act like that. We're not going to use the same methods as before, nor the same targets.

He looked back to Bernadette. "Now to reassure you, my petite friend, this is a single-story building, about twelve feet high. It has a flat roof and we shall go in here, through this HVAC vent."

"HV-what?" Bernadette asked.

"Heating, ventilation, air conditioning. The fan won't be in use this time of year. We go in, slip inside the ducting which is—" Again, he pointed to dotted lines depicting air ducts beneath the roof. "Two feet wide. It's a three-person job; who wants to volunteer?"

Three hands were raised simultaneously. Penny and Leonard declined.

CHAPTER 4

Dad had moved in eighteen months ago after I had a chalet home built in my back garden. After my suspension, I had assumed we'd see a lot more of each other. I had assumed wrongly.

Four days had passed since I'd been put out to grass and, apart from one breakfast and a late supper, I'd seen neither hide nor hair of him. I guess he'd been spending a lot of time with Margaret. *Well, why not,* I asked myself. They were the same generation, laughed at the same things, liked the same TV shows, and they had had plenty of time to spend together. It made sense.

My dad had been born in Bloxwich, a small town just north of Birmingham, where he was introduced to rock-and-roll. I've heard him tell and retell his "Butterfly" story so many times that I know it off by heart. Before my suspension, Margaret had us over for dinner and he'd recounted the tale for her. While thinking about Margaret's cooking I had dozed off, dreaming his story word for word.

> *The local Cooperative Store had opened their upstairs room to hold a "jive-night". The noise had been deafening even across the street, the old floor timbers were given such a pounding that they flexed and bent. Downstairs, the ceiling cracked and spread plaster all over the shop. He listed the groups whose records had blasted out from the sound-system: Bill Haley, Danny and the Juniors, Little Richard and so on, legends now, of course. He reached the high point of his story. The DJ played "Butterfly", the version by Andy Williams. Dad was just about dancing solo in my sitting room when Margaret clapped her hands. "That was my favorite, too, only it was Charlie Gracie I loved. Boy, could he play that guitar?"*

The phone rang and woke me up. I was so desperate for the sound of a real human voice that I nearly suffocated myself in cushions trying to get to it.

"God!" I said aloud. "Four days and I'm stir-crazy."

"It's only me, not the big feller in the sky. Sorry to disappoint."

It was Barbara, my faithful sergeant. Lucky she hadn't come in person, I might have grabbed her and kissed her!

"Getting well rested, I hope?"

"Something like that." I laughed at the thought. "But not very. What have you got to tell me?"

"Well, it's as we thought it would be. Maugham and Holly have taken over the investigation but there is absolutely nothing coming out of their office. It's like they've had a DA4 notice served."

I grunted. "And nothing else of any import?"

Barbara grunted too. "Only that Joe has had to bring in an Inspector Grainger to fill your boots."

"And is he okay?"

"Not a he, boss, a she. Melodie Grainger, formerly of Wakefield C.I.D. Bloody keen to make something of her chance."

"You don't sound terribly keen yourself, Sergeant."

"Can you tell? The pin boards have gone from the walls and she has made it known, in no uncertain terms, that a clean desk policy will be maintained."

"That's bloody stupid. None of you'll be able to find a thing."

"Exactly. And the amount of time we're spending on tracking stuff and polishing the place and filing and..."

I took a deep breath, audible down the other end of the line. Disappointment at my patented folder and stack system being discarded was heavy in my voice. "So there's nothing else going on except polishing, then?"

"Well, there was another robbery last night. Actually only three perps involved and their methods were a bit different to our last lot."

At least this was interesting. "Well, tell me about it, Barbara. Please."

"Just coming to that. Seems they climbed up a supply pole then, somehow, scooted across the electric cable. You know, they hang off another wire overhead."

"Yeah, a catenary supply, much stronger wire than the electric cable."

"If you say so. Anyhow, they must have gone over at night, unscrewed the vent fan and crawled into the ducting. Guess they hung out there—maybe they took a nap—and waited for the safe to be opened."

"Money left in the safe? What do you mean?"

"Ah, sorry, Guv. It was a bookie's. Either very lucky or they'd studied the place very well; they hit the manager's office and waited for him to come to open the safe. They knew somehow, that the manager left money in the safe after night meetings. Perhaps he thought this to be better than carrying it in a car to a bank's night safe."

"How did they get into the office?"

"Through the air grating. I'm guessing but it was probably on push-fit lugs, something like that. Again, good planning or even better guesswork. Sorry I can't be more explicit but without being allowed full access we'll never know."

"Of course, I understand. Well, well. Who's handling it then and, come to think of it, how did you find all this out?"

"You may not believe this, but it was my predecessor, Shelly Fearon."

I got as far as "Shel..?"

"I heard some gossip and called the Metro for information. They just put me through to her without a word. She'd been the attending officer. Small world isn't it?"

"Is Shelly still handling it?" I asked hopefully. It would give me the chance to talk with her later.

"No, sorry. She'd had to hand it on to C.I.D. but I can tell you this...it hasn't gone to Maugham and Holly."

"That's good news, anyway. Any CCTV?"

"There was but we're out of luck. Shelly never saw it, C.I.D. was too fast."

We both fell silent for a few seconds. I was trying to think of anything else to ask her, she was probably waiting for me to speak. Then she remembered something. "The only thing she said after that was that whoever did it had to be bloody fit. The cable they crossed on was twenty feet above the ground and was a helluva way from post to roof top. Were they tightrope walkers, she wondered? If not they must have been strong enough to do it hand over hand."

"Wonder why they didn't use a ladder?"

"I asked that too. No access at the back of the place, apparently. If they had used one, they would have had to leave it in the street. That would look a mite suspicious to the beat bobby."

"Mmm. They could have taken a fourth person to move it away or even lifted it onto the roof."

Barbara giggled. "We shall never know."

"No, just thinking. It's probably nothing to do with our crew at the bank. M.O. is different, as you said. But..." I scratched my chin—maybe a hunch struggling to surface. "Hey, never thought to ask. How's Alec Bell amid all these new office processes?"

"Gone. Told me he had at least six weeks accumulated leave and was going to take them—full stop. Of course, it could be something to do with his muttering about the office getting to look like Paddington Station and women officers should stick to running hospitals."

"Coincided with Melodie's clear-desk policy?"

"How did you guess? To the minute."

"You wouldn't know where he's gone, would you? He and I could have spent some time throwing ideas around. You know the sort of thing."

"Not really. We girls just don't do that, you know. He said he'd gone off somewhere but I don't know where. Do you want me to ask around?"

"If you do make contact, you could let him have my address and cell number, if you would. Please."

I think there was another grunt from the far end but I wasn't certain. The line went dead. Was that a touch of jealousy? Because I hadn't asked her? She had said that girls didn't do that.

Raj was playing the latest computer game on Leonard's newest toy: a computer hooked up to a video wall. Sheldon ignored the game and walked straight across to stand in front of the wall.

"Time for that later," he announced. "Business first."

"Leonard's still sorting out the food." Raj complained in his baby-voice. Sheldon looked at him until the boy turned away. Despite being the youngest by no more than six months, Raj did seem to be significantly less mature than the others. He had some regrets in recruiting him, although he had done a good job the night before.

"Leonard will have no interest in the payout. He took no part in our last job, so his pay goes into the general pot."

The atmosphere changed immediately. This pronouncement came out of the blue and everyone's attention was on Sheldon. They had supposed that all payouts would be shared equally and on a weekly basis.

Sheldon continued. "The job went to plan, for which we have to thank Raj and Bernadette. They exhibited a fair amount of patience. Sitting in the duct work for hours wasn't easy, and making their way along that electric support line demanded a good deal of perseverance.

Those singled out for praise grinned at each other.

Howard spoke up. "We could all have done that. Scooting across the cable would have been no problem at all."

Anyone watching would have guessed instantly that all in the room were athletes; even relaxed, the way they moved and the sculpted appearance of their bodies was associated with training. The girls could certainly have matched any of the male members of the group.

"This is favoritism," Penny continued. "There's no other word for it. We should all have a wage."

Sheldon laughed. He felt like saying that was how the cookie crumbled, but he didn't. Instead, he said, "I chose one for her size and the others because they probably won't be on the next job. That will belong to you, Howard, but mainly to Bernadette and Penny.

"And just so you all get it right, the money will not be going to anyone not participating. I will divide as I see fit after paying out for food and any materials, etc. But I'm aiming at getting you a minimum of two grand a week. Just don't forget that we are only playing at this."

The others looked perplexed.

Sheldon said, "We really can't keep it all. After expenses like your pay, we have...I have to give it back. I mean, we're not real criminals, are we?"

They appeared to understand, but were obviously uncertain of there being real impartiality. They would go along with it for now.

"The next job will again be split between three of us. Three shares will be paid out, three will go into the pot." He looked at the group, seconds stretched out. "Anyone who doesn't like that can vote with their feet. You walk away, leave the group. But if anyone does that, I have to warn you, the rest of us may have to kill you."

Sheldon smiled but it was in no way a reassuring expression, even when he added: "Of course, I may be joking."

He threw three bulky packets to the three who had gone into the bookmaker's offices. "Careful what you spend it on and where. We don't want you drawing attention to yourselves."

Leonard started to clean up and Sheldon went on to make his last point. "Now, ladies, want to know what I've got lined up for you? I'm sure you'll like it, a chance to dress up?"

Howard scowled. "Dressing up? Just what can a girl do that I can't?"

"She can flounce around in long curly wigs, struggle into skimpy underwear, and walk along a catwalk."

The room went quiet.

"Can you?"

Later, from his car, Sheldon texted a message:

2ND STG COMP

Then, on the car's Bluetooth, he called a number in Turkey. It was a message box used solely by himself and the woman whom he thought he might love.

Hi, Fizz. Job two went just as planned. Two more and with your share, escape will be carried out. Suggest we meet soon in Gib.

I was in a sour mood that morning. I think I was missing the human contact at the office and, of course, not seeing anything of my dad. The weather didn't help either, the rain was coming down so hard that my orchard was invisible, and the noise on the metal roof of Dad's bungalow drowned out the TV news.

When the front door bell rang, I was very thankful. I hurried down the hallway, worried that whoever it was might be drowning in the downpour. By the time I got there, I was convinced it must be a travelling salesman. Whatever, I had my best grin on when I opened the door.

"Are you just glad tae see me or did someone tell ye a joke?"

Sergeant Alec Bell usually seemed the dour Scot at work but over the past year, I had learned there was a lot more to him than appeared in first impressions. He was, in fact, a likeable character when you pried the crustiness off.

"For God's sake man, get yourself inside." Alec leapt up the steps as if he had springs in his heels and dripped steadily on my front door mat. I closed the door. "And is that a gun in that brown paper bag or something of a more thirst-quenching nature?"

"Morning Stewart." He handed me the brown paper bag. "Unless ye'd prefer tae keep the formalities in which case, Good Morning, Chief Inspector."

"Get your coat off and hang it up, unless ye've just called to sell me a bottle of Ballantine's."

He hung his disreputable mackintosh on a coat hook. "Certainly not sellin' ye anything. I just thought ye'd care to share a dram or two unless ye have other places to go." Alec's accent was getting thicker by the minute.

"Nae, I hav'na." I replied. "You go down the passageway there, sit anywhere you please except the brown leather chair and I'll get a couple of glasses from the kitchen." I resolved to stop copying the man's accent; he might well take exception to it. So when I brought the two heavy tumblers into the sitting room, I had the speech under control. He was sitting on my old couch with the coffee table placed between us and he was just cracking the top off one of the bottles.

"Water?" I asked, pretty sure the answer would be negative.

"Not unless you think I should wash ma hands. I dinna care to adulterate guid whiskey."

"Suits me. Slange," I said as I lifted the generous measure of spirit he had poured and took a drink. The sensation at the back of my throat reminded me why I didn't normally take spirits neat or drink first thing in the morning. I put on a brave face. I took another small sip, as much to clear my throat enough to speak as for any other reason. "So, is this just a social call, Alec?"

"Not exactly, Guv—er, Stewart. Barbara told me you were at a sort of loose ends and seeing as I've taken no holidays for years, I decided I'd take some extended leave. To be frank, I reckoned you'd need a hand to find out who's been framing you."

I smiled, warming to the sometimes cranky fellow, "You're prepared to accept it wasn't me then?"

"You?" Alec's eyebrows zoomed upward. "Ye reckon I'd doubt you? There is'na a bent bone in your body."

I laughed. "Thanks, Alec. That does me good."

"A few funny bones maybe but certainly no bent ones." He sported a grin like the Cheshire Cat's, a pretty unnerving expression for someone who rarely smiled.

"That's very kind of you Alec. I'm touched. But without resources I don't see what we can do."

At that moment, the doorbell rang and Alec jumped up. "I'll get it. That'll be brunch."

"Brunch?"

"I ordered for us both. I haven't breakfasted yet, don't know about you."

"Well, actually..." I hadn't eaten either. With Dad not being at home, I'd just let things slip a bit.

"I'll get some plates out," I called after him.

I carried the empty glasses through to the kitchen and laid plates and cutlery out on the table. I was just about ready when I heard some sort of commotion in the passage: doors slamming, wheels clattering on the wooden floor. What's he done? I wondered. Pizza on wheels?

I went back to the living room to tell him I'd set the kitchen table and stood there, amazed. I came face to face with someone I had always thought was one of the loveliest women I'd known. Shelly Fearon had been one of my sergeants when I had first come to Yorkshire; we might have had something going had it not been for one major hiccup. She usually smiled at me but now, her expression was serious, perhaps doubting; certainly questioning, awaiting some reaction.

"Hey, Shelly! To what do I owe this pleasure? Have you and Alec been plotting? It's a long way to come just for brunch."

"No, Guv." She was obviously relieved. And just like that, it was back to old times, when she used to work for me, even though it had been nearly a year since she'd been promoted to inspector.

"I prepared the brunch, it's in the cool box down there." She pointed. "I brought you some other goodies too."

"Goodies?"

She grinned, and Alec did too. "Like Alec, I've got lots of vacation time owed. I suppose we're all the same, no family, work sort of takes its place. I didn't believe you'd been involved in a crime, so I decided a bit of help would go a long way."

"Shall we eat first or chat?" Alec put in, still doing his Cheshire Cat impression.

"I'd quite like to know what the goodies are."

"They're outside: a mobile incident room with a projector and screen, a dedicated laptop and router, several whiteboards, one or two other things."

"Which are?" I asked, grinning as much as Alec.

"A Skype circle. We're planning to bring in Barbara Patterson and her feller, what's his name, Levy? There's also Jake Hartley, one of my trusted lads I'd like to add to the team."

It might have taken as long as five seconds to organize my thoughts. "You put the food out, here, in the kitchen, and I'll put the coffee pot on, should just be big enough for doubles all round. Are we expecting any more surprises?"

I was babbling, trying to cover up my feelings and wiping away a persistent tear from my eye. I was more than cut up by this show of solidarity from my fellows.

We ate huge dry-cured pork sausages in toasted brioche rolls with fried sweet red onions as a topping. "That is going to put five pounds on my hips," Shelly said when the last crumb had gone from her plate.

We settled back with second cups of coffee—a brand I'd brought back from Florida that had been in near-freezing storage in the icebox until now.

Shelly took a sip of coffee and opened the conversation, "Holly and Maugham run C.I.D. at Leeds Met. Normally, bits and bats of info make their way through to our offices and we can keep track of what's going on, but not at the moment. They're playing their cards abnormally close to their chests."

"So...we still know only that the job I was supposed to have been involved in was carried out by six unknowns in ski gear. No trace of them? No joy with identification?"

"That's what I thought. But there has been another job my guys were looking into. There was a DVD recorder, which somehow got copied on to my laptop."

"Ah, the bookmakers?"

"Well, they prefer to be called Turf Accountants."

"Yeah. Posh."

"It was a wee bit audacious, going in through the roof fan and along the ducting."

Shelly patted the back of Alec's hand. "And why at that time of the morning? Surely there'd be more cash around at the end of the day?"

"These boys must have done some homework," I pointed out. "The robbery took place after a night meeting. That right?"

Shelly nodded. "Right."

"That night was well chosen. There'd been Friday night racing at Lingfield?"

Again, she nodded.

"The punters would be watching on large screens at the bookies—sorry, the Turf Accountants—because they'd just been paid. Lots of construction sites just round there, paid cash in hand, they'd be throwing money around as if it was going out of fashion. The manager, of course, would be used to this and he obviously doesn't fancy taking the money in his car to a bank's night safe."

"Absolutely," Alec muttered. "Nay bank accounts for those laddies. The robbers would have acted before the banks opened so that it was all in the manager's safe and before an armored truck could arrive."

"The place would be swimming in money and only three involved—rich pickings."

"Let's finish up breakfast and get a screen set up. Then we can all take a look together." Shelly's suggestion got instant approval.

CHAPTER 5

The picture on the six-foot roll-out screen was clear. A door slammed open and people looked up, suddenly stiff and scared. Three slim forms in black track-suit bottoms, black hoodies, and plastic masks came through, brandishing guns and—it seemed a little incongruous at first—aerosol paint cans. Then they sprayed the camera lenses and that was the last we saw of them. Audio continued, but apart from the rustle of paper (probably bank notes) there was just a deathly silence.

"That's it?" I asked. "Not a lot to go on at first glance."

"More than you might think," Alec said. "Compare these three with the ones that hit the National Bank. They're very similar. Masks are different but the perps are the same shape and size."

"Could be part of that gang, then? Changing the numbers involved would be quite a nifty idea—and the choice of target."

Alec nodded. "Maybe. Still armed robbery though, good enough to send them down for fourteen years."

I nodded "True, but let's not get too excited. It's a theory, a good one but still a theory and we've no proof as yet."

Shelly was a little more upbeat. "Not sure that this helps but it's what I want to show you. We need access to Holly and Maugham's copy from the bank robbery. Look at this." She moved round to sit at one of the laptops and clicked a thumbnail. It bloomed large on the screen and she expanded one part and clarified the result. "I took this still from the DVD when I had the chance. There's a glint just here on this guy's wrist, and even though they're wearing gloves, this one's wearing an identity bracelet."

"Hmm." I stooped over the screen and pointed my pencil at a particular spot. "Looks like a small stone. A diamond; maybe a sapphire that's set into the gold."

"Eyesight's better than mine." Alec said.

"Whatever, it could be." Shelly agreed.

It was a minor cause for celebration, something to go on, no matter how small. But what Shelly said next had us thinking. "I know we haven't had a chance to see the CCTV images from the bank job, but don't you think the descriptions are similar? All in black, with hoods, and those tight track-suit bottoms, similar body types."

I thought carefully before I answered. "We have to tread pretty cautiously before coming to any conclusions, let alone putting them to anyone else. Those outfits are the clothing of choice for many thieves."

"Childhood memories of Robin Hood?" Alec asked and nodded to himself.

"Likely, I suppose. In this instance, though, it could be deliberate copying of what they'd picked up about the bank raid. But..."

They both looked up.

"That bracelet Shelly noticed, that was good work. Very good. Let's explore all the avenues we can find before we go any further down that one."

"But what else do we have to go on, Stewart?" Shelly was obviously a bit downhearted despite my encouragement. "What is it they really have on you?"

I'd forgotten this was all about the connection to me. "We know that our esteemed colleagues have three DNA samples. We've no idea what type, or where it came from. Could be hair, blood, saliva, skin, even urine."

"I heard one was from chewing-gum."

"That so, Shelly? Thanks for that. Where did they find that? I mean, if there was hair then it could have come from my comb or a hairbrush. Blood? How could they have come by that?"

"We could do with a look at their pictures." Alec tapped his finger on the table. "Of the crime scene."

"It would be great, wouldn't it?" Shelly spoke in a ruminative tone. "Trouble is, Holly and Maugham have it locked up tighter than a duck's...tighter than the Tower of London. No way to see it until they decide to bring charges."

"Oh, don't let that get you down. What I'm wondering is how old the samples are. We know the scene-of-crime boys gathered them after the crime, but they could have been collected originally at different times and places."

It was Alec's turn to sound thoughtful. "That tech guy. Bet he'd do it for you, heard him mention your name, you know."

I frowned. "What tech guy? None of our technicians could get hold of C.I.D. records at Elland Road."

"Not you, Guv. Inspector Fearon."

I laughed.

"You mean...oh, what's-his-name...Fletcher?" Shelly asked, ready to take offense. Then she remembered.

"He could have a point there."

I let it go. Snooping around like that didn't sit naturally with me. "No, guys. Apart from asking people the same questions as C.I.D. has already asked, to people who work near the bank or cleaners on the premises, we don't really have access. And that sort of activity would soon get back to our friends, Holly and Maugham."

"So what we want," Shelly tapped the files which held what we knew about the two jobs, "is another job and get there first."

Alec squeezed my arm. "I have tae agree with the Inspector."

Shelley smiled and said, "Oh please, it's 'Shelly' here in Stewart's house. We're all friends."

Alec melted. He gave her a genuine smile, not the Cheshire Cat one he'd been favoring me with, and said, "Thanks—Shelly. What I was going to say was that Stewart can't go anywhere near another of their crime scenes, assuming they're connected. It's just what C.I.D. will be waiting for. One lot of DNA is one thing, two lots, Stewart will be wheeled into a dungeon while CPS writes his case up and sips from champagne glasses."

This time Alec's over-the-top scenario brought it home. It was an illuminating thought, but I wasn't about to get anywhere without my friends. After that little lesson in depending on one's friends, we set up the equipment and the whiteboards. We easily filled them with lists of the little we knew and what we needed to do next. When we had finished, my living room looked like a station crime scene office.

Dad was going to be just a little surprised.

"Is that you, Asmin?"

Sergeant Ranjit Patiala, now serving under Superintendent Clive Bellamy at the NCA, recognized the voice on the phone instantly, even with no more than the four words spoken. But he did need a little thinking time to recall his old undercover name. "Yes," he replied after a moment. "But this can't be who I think it is, can it? You're supposed to be dead, isn't that so, Leroy?"

"Well I guess I deserve that." Leroy Richards admitted. "But Mad Charlie had me in his sights, man. I just had to die."

"Ah, yes. I remember that badass. Fought him to a standstill but it wouldn't have stopped him from chopping you up into little bits and feeding you to the rats under that building, would it?"

"Yeah, yeah, yeah, I know all that. But listen, I'm a changed man. I've kept my nose clean. Even thinkin' of makin' an honest woman of my girlfriend but

I can't do that now. Someone's framed me, man, and I can't go anywhere until I get that cleared up. "

"What do expect me to do about that?"

"Well Asmin, I just thought you know a lot of people in Leeds and maybe, one o' them might be able to help me."

"You'd better explain what you're up to, Leroy."

"I hear the Police have my DNA even though I ain't been in Leeds since long before you picked me up at Askham Bryan. Closest I's been is Horsforth, way out west."

"Thought you lived at Selby."

"I did, my girlfriend's place—but that ain't Leeds, neither."

"Hmm. You know what sort of DNA and which police?"

Leroy shook his head, then remembered he was talking into a cell. "I got a sort-of contact in the Leeds Met boys. Sample came from inside a bank, if you'll believe that."

"You done a bank job lately?"

"Don't do stuff like that."

The words bank job had a familiar ring, but he could not pin it down immediately. "DNA's funny stuff, my friend. Who'd you know that could do this?"

"No one, Asmin. No one. Mad Charlie, maybe, but he's been put away. He's got ten years or more, I think. Besides, he thinks I'm dead, like everyone else."

Ranjit thought for a moment longer then. "Give me a few days, Leroy, and I'll see what I can find out. You'll be on this cell number?"

"Sure, and Asmin...thanks. I owe you one."

"Yes, you do, my friend."

All of which, now that Ranjit thought about it, begged a couple of questions: who was Leroy's "sort-of contact" at the Leeds Met—and how did Leroy get put straight though to Ranjit's phone?

Harold Nicholson's "Festival of Design" was a biennial event. It took place inside the large department store, the largest store of its kind outside of London, and was attended by wealthy and famous stars of stage, screen, and television. The event lasted three days, although only the first held any interest for Sheldon. On that day, Prince Abn-el-Rahim, a crown prince of the Saudi Arabian royal family, would be there with his entourage.

Sheldon's father had once had a friend who sold and fitted high-quality Axminster carpets in middle-eastern palaces. It was a bit like taking diamonds to South Africa; and often he'd taken Sheldon along as a fetch-and-carry gopher. He'd seen that this particular Prince carried an enormous wallet with him and paid cash for everything. Rewards for servants, craftsmen, and tradesman who gave extraordinary service were of the gold watch variety, carried somewhere in the Prince's voluminous robes. Even the friend of Sheldon's father owned a gold Longines dress watch earned by merely being in the right place and, appropriately enough, at the right time.

It was not Sheldon's intention to steal the Prince's cash, a foolhardy and risky idea where open gunfire from bodyguards might well lead to casualties among his team. Rather, it was his intention to try something far more inventive that would not involve anyone from the Prince's entourage.

Sheldon had performed his usual meticulous groundwork. He intimately knew the backstage layout and construction details. He had gotten himself employed by Harold Nicholson on several occasions between drilling jobs: as a clerk, as an after-hours cleaner, and as a stockroom trolley man. Each time he had worked for the organization, his appearance had been different. His skin color varied from pale to deeply tanned, his hair was long, short, blonde, brown, reddish, shaggy, buzz-cut. His clothes also varied with the jobs he did: scruffy, neat, ultra-smart.

He knew where all the passages led, on what floor the various goods were stored. He noted that rooms adjacent to the display area, normally used for storage, were converted to dressing rooms for the show. Staff toilets were of particular interest as they offered temporary hiding places. He saw where keys were required and had taken steps to have copies made.

It had taken him a year to create his final plan, now he needed to train his team. They were learning slowly, experience needed to be built carefully so that each one came to understand the skills Sheldon wanted them to learn and use. Victims had to be coaxed into jumping at the right moment, in the right direction, and only practice would lead to the perfection he envisaged.

Today's job required three of his team, and him. At nine-thirty Raj would drive Penny and Bernadette to the store. He would sit and wait for the girls to come out when the job was done. Sheldon had already started work, intending to join the other employees as a shelf stacker. He wore a store uniform that had been issued just before Christmas when he'd gotten himself hired as seasonal help and never returned.

The other members of his team had no idea they were red herrings. Bernadette and Penny thought they were doing a background work for a future scene in the movie. They had agency permits which identified them as specialist plus-size models. They had both laughed uproariously when they learned this, both were lean and fit, though a size twelve was "plus-size" in the industry. They had been hired to flatter the Prince's wives, who were somewhat more amply endowed than the girls.

Thanks to Sheldon's tutoring, they could now strut along the runway with the aplomb of seasoned models. Both had had extremely short haircuts, they could wear wigs and hair pieces with colors very unlike their own.

On his arrival, Sheldon walked the store intently, checking that no last-minute changes had been made. Finally, a swift examination of the changing rooms and the temporary cashier's office left him satisfied that nothing had been overlooked.

CHAPTER 6

It had certainly been a while since I had last been woken with a tongue in my ear: a voluptuous woman working her way across my face. But the last few moments of the dream brought me down to earth as the caresses turned out to be the affectionate embrace of an eiderdown mattress topper and a duvet.

I woke up quickly enough when my dad's voice interrupted proceedings: "I'm cooking breakfast, that all right with you?"

And that's when I discovered that there *was* a tongue in my right ear—Pip's.

I answered my dad, discouraged the dog from slobbering all over me while still managing to fuss over him, and was soon washed and dressed. Pip followed me to the stairs and raced ahead to wait patiently at the bottom step.

"Margaret gave me a lift home last night," Dad said. "She didn't stop. Saw your car but the lights were out so I didn't come in to say good night."

He brought a pan to the table and lifted tomatoes, bacon, sausage and an egg as large as a coverlet across the rest. "Dad, I'm going to die from a heart attack if you go on feeding me like this."

"Nonsense. Look at me, I'm as thin as a rake."

"You've got the genes to survive, I'm not so lucky. Anyway, yes. Had an early night last night." I forked some sausage and bacon and began to eat. Although my Mum had tried to teach me not to speak with my mouth full, she had never been very successful. "I had some guests here most of yesterday, you remember Alec Bell and Shelly Fearon?"

"Sure. I saw you'd been playing silly devils in the living room. More like an office than a place to sit. Shelly, did you say? What's she doing back? Thought you two had broken up."

I grinned. Nobody else could ask such direct questions but that's what dads do. "You get your own breakfast and mind your own b..." I stopped as I realized what I'd been about to say. "We're working, okay? I need some professional help; it's the only way I can do this."

Dad put the coffee pot down in the center of the table and sat down. I'll give him his due, he didn't push.

"Where do I start?" It was my way of pushing the boat out but he was right in there.

"The beginning of course, normally the best place."

So I told him about the bank robbery, my DNA being recovered, and my suspension. I told him about how my team had got together to support me and the fact that we had a tiny clue: the identity bracelet. "Apart from that, we've got exactly less than nothing."

Dad drained his coffee cup and poured another. "Top you up?" He nodded when I put my hand over the top of the cup. "Fine kettle of fish, isn't it? What's the point of suspending you?"

"Protocol, Dad. They have no choice in the matter."

"Oh, come on, they know you're one of the most dedicated men I know. Your job's always come first. It's obvious isn't it?"

"What's obvious?"

"It's a bloody frame-up. What you need to do is find out why. Not how, *why*."

"Actually, you've hit the nail on the head. Why? No one else has asked why and if I knew that I'd be halfway to catching them."

"Well what sort of DNA have they got? Does it come in different sorts? Do you know that?"

"They've got hair, blood and saliva samples, I believe."

"That's ridiculous. You'd have to be tearing your hair out, cutting yourself and spitting—all in the same place. Ridiculous. Or, maybe you were in a boxing match, eh? And, by the way, I noticed how you very neatly dodged that bit about Shelly, What's the score there?"

"Dad..."

"Okay, okay but just let me say this. She's intelligent, she's beautiful and, clearly, she still has feelings for you."

I snorted. "That chicken's been fried, Dad. She was here as a friend to help in solving how my DNA got mixed up with a robbery. No other reason."

"No spark still there then?"

I didn't answer at once, poured a second cup of coffee while I considered the idea. "Don't know. Since Connie stayed in Florida and clammed up...with Shelly, I'd have to take it very steady."

"Well..."

I held my hand up. "That's all I'm saying."

If my dad had brought a black girl home when he'd been my age, the family and the neighbors would have been combing eyebrows back out of their hair for days. And his dad would have had more than a word or two to say. In fact, Dad did open his mouth but closed it when he saw my expression.

We were still sitting at the table an hour later. Dad had started the coffee percolator again and we were enjoying our third cup of the morning as we heard the sound of a car turning into my drive. Alec and Shelly were suddenly standing on the doorstep. Shelly, in particular, seemed anxious to get something off her mind, but I got them both to sit down and finish the fresh coffee. Dad filled their cups while he exchanged a weird sort of smile with her.

"Okay, then," I said at last. "Tell me what you're dying to tell me."

Shelly looked at each of us in turn. She was as serious as I'd ever seen her. "Not a word of this leaves this room, ever."

We nodded and promised.

"My job's on the line if Holly or Maugham ever find out."

We were all pretty serious. Dad would deny everything even if I told him to spill the beans.

Shelly nodded and began. "I have a tech guy at Elland Road, in C.I.D. I stopped by first thing this morning. I returned some files as an excuse and let it slip that I was working on the National Bank and the Turf Accountants incidents and he said that there was DNA evidence from both crime scenes that matched."

Dad was looking at each of us in turn; his forehead looked like a piece of corrugated cardboard.

"It means that at least one of the perpetrators was present at both places," Shelly finished.

"Not exactly," Alec said. "It just means that someone—not necessarily a perpetrator—could have been at both places. Say, a punter and a bank customer."

I nodded. "That's so, Alec, but pretty unlikely. They are miles apart."

"Well yes, but I didn't want anyone building up hopes just yet."

"Sure. So we start our white wall. Mark X's for the six goons we know of, show the venues. Hmm, we need..."

"A street map of Leeds. Working on it," Alec said. He opened the laptop, which must have been on standby since yesterday, because it started up immediately. "Maps, Leeds..."

Shelly chuckled. "What've you put in his coffee? I don't remember him ever being this gung ho."

"Ha! He took a shot in the shoulder a little while ago when we were trying to catch a drug gang. You often get this sort of reaction from lead poisoning. Or maybe it was the single malt whiskey I took him in hospital. Been a changed man since then."

Alec clicked the button once the map had loaded and the printer started to churn it out.

"I think we're going to need him, Stewart," Shelley said. "And even then, I don't think we're going to cut it."

"Shelly..."

She bit her lip. "Without the back-up of a team, uniformed officers for the legwork and access to the feedback that H&M have, we'll be damn lucky to do anything."

"H&M, the fashion people?"

"Holly and Maugham." She laughed. And punched me on the shoulder.

"Well, you could be right, Shelly. But what's the alternative? Let them make false assumptions, maybe? I'll say this, I hate my name being dragged through the mud but with people like you and Alec on my side, I'm a whole lot happier."

Alec interrupted us. "Look at this, you two." He'd marked the two locations in red on the map and pinned it up on a whiteboard.

My cell rang. It was Barbara checking in, wanting to know what she could do to help. "Barbara, thanks. Do this for us, contact every snout you can dig up—not just ours, but those who our colleagues use. Someone must know something. Offer them inducements, help with offencees, money, whatever it takes. Get everyone in on the act; maybe Melodie Grainger can give you a few names."

"Mel...? You are joking aren't you?"

"Doing my best, Sergeant. Doing my best."

The two with me got the message as well, I think.

———

The Prince came at nine-forty-five, along with at least sixty staff and hangers-on. The women were dressed in conservative clothing. Most wore the less-strict abayas, mostly black, with a sprinkling of colored fabrics paired with hijabs. A few wore burkas, but they were in the minority on this occasion.

Sheldon had positioned himself as near to the main seating area as possible. He had found that a person who looked busy was less likely to be asked to go somewhere else. He occupied himself with hanging and re-hanging garments on the racks, looking busy while keeping his eyes on the activity around him.

Some eleven or twelve of the Saudi males were not in the viewing room. Presumably, they would be on security duty somewhere. The rest were listening more-or-less attentively to the women they were escorting, ready to signal store personnel when a garment might be of interest. With the cheapest of the designer outfits being around four thousand pounds, it would not take long for the coffers to fill when the models paraded along the runway.

Other celebrities—minor, for the most part—wandered round the edges of the seated customers: John Walker, the *Yorkshire Post's* fashion correspondent with a photographer in tow, and Penny le Tour, who edited the same press group's fashion magazine. Bernard Craven, who starred in a Yorkshire-based soap opera, chatted with the leading lady from a sister soap over the far side of the Pennines. A seat had been reserved at the end of the front row for the Leeds Lady Mayoress; rather obvious plain-clothes police tried to blend into the background.

Someone came to the center of the stage and spoke, there was a brief applause, and then the show was on. Along the elevated walkway the models came, striding like cowboys stalking into a saloon in the Old West, glancing at the audience with a hauteur that suggested they were beneath their notice. Sheldon watched closely, noting the gestures from the Saudi women, the nodding of their men-folk or minders, and the signals to the Harold Nicholson staff, who would hurry away to mark the chosen garment. He also noted the bundles of currency passed to other staff who wrote receipts and took the money away.

From his chosen position, Sheldon could see the notes going into special satchels as they were tallied on a calculator by the store's accountant. The wads of money from the Prince himself, Sheldon noted, were going into a separate bag, presumably because these included large amounts of high-denomination notes.

The fashion show had been divided into four sessions: Winter, Spring, Summer, and Fall. At the end of each segment, the money bags were sealed and taken by bodyguards away from the area.

Sheldon would like to have stayed for the final "Fall" segment since this was where the girls, Penny and Bernadette, would be parading. But he had to follow the money. He grabbed an armful of summer dresses from the nearest rack and walked to the storerooms. Back here both male and female security staff walked the same corridors.

No one took the slightest notice of him. Someone with such obvious familiarity with the layout was virtually invisible. He moved along the passages, around sharp corners, further and further from the applause. He exchanged his armfuls of dresses with another rack of garments that he could wheel along.

He parked the rack in front of the temporary cashier's office, timing it perfectly with the brief hiatus in the buying as the models changed clothes for the final time. He stamped on the clothing rack's brake to make sure it was immoveable, and stood on tiptoe to look through the door's half-window. Two people were inside, unloading money from the leather satchels, consulting lists, typing information into laptops.

Sheldon gently tried the door, expecting it to be locked. It was. He grinned and moved to the next door along—this room had once been used by security staff for coffee breaks. The wall of the two rooms was nothing but a thick layer of compressed paper: soundproof, insulating, and about as useful as a security barrier as blotting paper. He kicked at the partition: once, twice, three times, and opened up a man-size hole.

The two occupants were just opening their mouths in shock as Sheldon straightened up on their side of the wall. He reached the table and had begun to scoop money into the largest bag.

"Here, what—" was as far as one man got before he saw the gun that Sheldon was pointing at him.

"Sit down," said Sheldon quietly as he waved the muzzle towards a chaise-longue in the corner. "And don't make a sound."

He put the gun back on the table so it pointed at them and calmly finished filling the bag with bank notes. The tellers sat rigidly as he left the same way he had come. It was almost twenty seconds before the woman in the money office unlocked the door to find the heavy clothes rack blocking the way.

When two more people came along from the show-area with the last of the money bags, there was no sign of Sheldon.

Alec Bell was taking a turn at brewing coffee in my kitchen when I heard his cell phone buzz. Moments later I heard him respond: "Hold on Ranjit. You need to tell this to D.C.I. White himself. Just a moment." Alec nearly tripped over his own feet as he came through to the living room, holding the instrument at arm's length, "It's Ranjit Patiala, Guv. Leroy Richards is alive."

"Ranjit?" I said into the cell, "Or would you prefer Asmin?"

"Whichever suits you. Joking aside though, I need a face to face. I have information that I prefer not discuss over the air waves."

"About Leroy?"

"In one respect, but there's much more. I need to make one or two house calls first. Could I see you at three o'clock in your office?"

I laughed. "At the moment, Ranjit, I don't have an office. I'll give you my home address, got a pen?" I gave him the address. "Come as soon as you like, my ears are starting to burn already. Oh, and I would appreciate it if you didn't tell anyone in my office that you're coming to see me."

At two-fifty precisely, I heard a car pull into my gravel drive; I had asked the others to squeeze their vehicles together to give Ranjit enough room; thank goodness my father didn't drive. It certainly seemed as though my home was steadily turning into my office.

Ranjit's handshake was warm and powerful and he gave Alec a hug which suggested a far closer relationship than I had been aware of. The Alec that I knew was fast disappearing to reveal a more rounded person than I had imagined.

I introduced him to Shelly, who was obviously dying to know who the Sikh was—and what information he had.

Finally, just as we had got everyone sitting down, Dad breezed in with Pip darting ahead to sniff this new stranger.

Dad provided us with a choice of mixed drinks. Ranjit looked at the tray and paused for a moment. "Ah, could I just have water? Would you mind?"

Dad obliged and Ranjit thanked him.

I explained the set-up to Ranjit. "These are all friends, Ranjit; they're giving their time to help me with a project which I'll make clear later."

Ranjit's face grew serious. "Well, you may be able to add a detail here and there but I think I know most of the situation already. I've spent most of the day in your office and at Leeds Metro. I've helped their inquiries on a number of occasions and so they've explained the circumstances to me in this case. Let me start by telling you what I have: Leroy Richards did not drown."

"No, he's surfaced again." Alec collapsed in a fit of giggles. "Wisht, must be the drink."

We all grinned at the joke.

"He contacted me this morning," Ranjit continued.

I put my hand up. "Can I just ask if he still knows you as Asmin?"

The other nodded. "Asmin Singh. Yes. But more interesting is the fact that he and you, Stewart, are suspected of working together. Superintendent Holly at Leeds Met confirmed that DNA traces from both of you have turned up at the scenes of an armed robbery in Leeds."

I winced. "Both of us? The soup is getting thicker. Does he know this? Richards, I mean."

"He knows about his own supposed involvement but not yours. He contacted me, once he found out, to ask for my advice and help. He was adamant that he had had nothing to do with it, and, in fact, had not been mixed up in any nefarious activities for a considerable time. Police records back up his claim. He maintains that any evidence the police have has been planted."

Ranjit held up his finger. "Importantly, from my reading of the man, he's telling the truth."

I looked at the others with raised eyebrows. Then, to Ranjit, "So do I, because it's just what happened to me and it's why we're here, trying to find out why. While we can't take Leroy at face value because of his past, if they won't believe me, they aren't going to believe him."

Ranjit nodded and said, "Well, I have what you need—time and access to resources. You're welcome to both."

I reached across to offer a handshake. "Good to have you aboard, Ranjit. What would be most welcome is a look at the forensic reports on the crime scenes. But for now, I think an early tea and then a brainstorming session. Dad, can you get the kettle boiling?"

Dad got to his feet. "If I'd known we were having guests, I'd have got something in."

"That's defeatist talk, Dad. What would Mother have said?"

"Um. We'll make do with what we've got."

———

Sheldon had a Plan A and a fall-back Plan B. However, Plan A went exactly as he wished.

A fire exit route between the first and the fourth floor provided a fast ascent to the third. There, double doors in the outer wall led to an industrial suspended track where stock could be transferred to and from the warehouse across a street. Clothes hung on a rack, shoes, purses and other items travelled in bins below.

The two-way track was in continuous motion during the working day and it was a simple task to drop the heavy bag of money into a bin and to step into the next. He still wore his uniform and was, to all intents and purposes, still invisible. In the farther building, he stepped off, transferred his ill-gotten gains to a waiting cart, and took the elevator down to the ground floor.

Just outside the vehicle access doors to the warehouse was a white van. A white van gave complete anonymity: six out of every ten vehicles in this part of the city were white vans.

Sheldon drove away, observing speed limits carefully. Somewhere behind him, a still unknown fate had befallen the two girls from the team. Rather than taking the money north to Leonard's home as had been agreed, he headed out of the city towards Selby. His plans for the haul of cash did not involve any of the others.

Sheldon gunned the engine a little as he left the city limits and grinned. Phase two of his plan was about to be implemented. He pressed the send key on his phone one-handed to transmit the prepared text:

STG 3 COMP

Fizz got the message in microseconds; it was quite some time before his father also saw it.

CHAPTER 7

It had become a habit of mine to leave one of the twenty-four-hour news channels switched on when I was at home. While I was going over the brainstorming session we had had earlier, with one or two good suggestions to be followed up, a news item caught my attention.

> "...the robbery was well planned. It took place during a private fashion show at Harold Nicholson's for a wealthy middle-eastern family. It is understood that the police have made several arrests although the man thought to have absconded with the money has not yet been apprehended..."

Scenes from the department store were shown, reporters speculated on how the money was spirited away, but the amount stolen was never mentioned.

Almost automatically, I reached for my phone and rang Barbara's home number. "I've just heard about the robbery at Harold Nicholson. What... pardon?"

She sounded half-awake. "This is the first time I've slept for days. Let me get up and make some coffee. I'll ring you back. Okay?"

I perhaps should have felt guilty about waking Barbara but I needed to know what she knew. Seventeen minutes later the phone rang and Barbara sounded more awake.

I apologized for waking her up and repeated what I had said earlier. "What can you tell me?"

"Right, here's what I know so far. We think there were four people involved. Two female, two male. The Met have three of them in custody. The girls are nineteen and twenty, they were there as models, or at least that's what they say. The guy was a little older, he was their chauffeur for the day. The chap who got away...got away with about half a million pounds. Cash. Have a feeling that's an understatement."

"Ouch! Do we have any names?"

"The Met have them locked up; I presume they have their names."

"Is there any connection with our other, earlier robberies?"

"Nobody is saying that. The Met are questioning them, obviously, and they seem to be cock-a-hoop."

"Given that they haven't got the money, I wonder what they're cock-a-hoop about. How did they catch them?"

"Something one of the security types said. 'The two girls were not the typical model body type, curves in all the right places but were exceptionally well-muscled, like athletes. And they asked more questions than they should have.' Further questioning by our friend Holly, no less, revealed the two were under orders from a mysterious guy, someone they know only as Sheldon. They said they were employed by this guy to work as models for the day. That was when their lawyers turned up and told them to close their mouths."

"Nothing to suggest they were a part of the team we're interested in?"

"Not that I can see. But there is something odd. The girls called themselves Bernadette and Penny; the one outside was there to pick them up and, as I said, they mentioned a Sheldon. Suggests a gang, doesn't it?"

"Sounds as though your ear's been pretty close to the ground, Barbara—for which I admire you. But a gang using familiar names...what's familiar about them? Am I missing something? And how did you come by this information?"

"Pure luck. I'd taken some evidence requested by the Met over there and they brought these two muscular young ladies in. David Morris—did I ever mention him?"

"Not that I recall."

"He had a thing for me once. He was with the girls but went into the observation room and I followed him in."

"A bit reckless. Won't Morris say something?"

"Doubt it. Sort of gave me a squeeze and suggested it was about time we got together again and..."

"And there's no law against raising your eyebrows and smiling?"

"Absolutely. Anyway, they're locked up and questioning will continue in the morning. Oh, and the reason their names might sound familiar: they're using the names of characters from a popular American comedy show, *Big Bang Theory*. I'll bet anything the other guy is calling himself Howard, and if there are other gang members they're probably code-named Leonard and Raj or Amy. "

"Glad you know that. Pop culture isn't my forte—although you're right about one of the others. They have a Raj in custody, he was to be the girl's getaway driver. And that brings us back to the original six then? Interesting." I was really thinking out loud but delighted by the depths to which Barbara could sink to get information. I doubted if I would use an old girlfriend merely to get information. I commended her initiative. Still, her answers really only raised more questions and there was no one else I could ask. I thanked her sincerely, wished her a very good night and told her to get back to bed.

Sheldon settled into one of the three flats he rented in the Garforth area. Three, because he could come and go at odd times without neighbors becoming used to regular hours or consistent visits. And the location gave him access to the motorway routes, to east-west and north-south destinations. Within two minutes, he could be out of the area; within a half-hour, he could be out of the country, and the souped-up Alpha Romeo was a match for most police cars.

Sheldon left most of the money from the store robbery hidden in the car's trunk, in removable side panels. He took some spending money into the apartment and switched on the TV news channel. A Bacardi and coke later, he was sprawled out on the settee. He put down a second drink when the phone rang. It was Leonard.

"You made it okay, then?"

Sheldon snorted. "By the skin of my teeth," he said, steering clear of the truth by a wide margin. "Someone must have tipped the real police off pretty fast, the store was overrun with them."

"And the money?"

"Had to drop it and run. Still, it will save me having to give back what we don't use. Have to admit I hate that part, but there'll be other days."

"You haven't heard about the others then?"

"Haven't heard what?"

The Police have Raj, Penny and Bernadette in custody."

"Oh, that's bad luck." Sheldon hoped his grin didn't affect his tone of voice "No, I hadn't heard that, but they won't keep them long when they find out they were genuine. Have they been in touch?"

"Who, the others?"

"No, no. The police. Did our lot tell them anything?"

"No, but then, I wouldn't expect them to blab, certainly not as soon as this."

"You never know, my friend. People can let details escape accidentally. For all you know, they may have your place staked out, just waiting for one of us to turn up."

Leonard grunted and was silent, thinking. "Look Sheldon, are you sure these jobs are what you say they've been? On the level, I mean. And got any suggestions as what to do next? You usually do."

"I'd stay at home and out of sight as long as possible. I know we're on the level, but I haven't actually got anything by way of proof. Anything you need, have it delivered. I think I'm going to drop off the radar for the time being, too. I'm going to stamp this phone into little pieces now. Wait for me to call you; I'll do that as soon as I know we're in the clear."

"At least you saw to it that our guys have some good lawyers."

"That's right, I did. See you." He switched the phone off and as promised, used his heel to grind it into bits.

I took Pip for a walk before breakfast along the riverbank that we both enjoyed so much. I made a mental note of a deep hole in the river that I hadn't noticed before. It was opposite the end of a dried up stream bed: a likely place to find big eels and barbel.

An idle walk like this was often a good way to run through the thoughts in my head. Some people preferred to discuss things with others but I worked better in isolation. I could explain stuff to Pip, he always listened attentively.

My dad was cooking breakfast in my kitchen when we got back. I was pleased that I'd had a bit of exercise by then. Dad was never one of the "eat sparingly and fill up on fruit and nuts" brigade. He believed that bacon and eggs and fried bread with sausages and tomatoes were what nature intended a breakfast to be. I was less certain, but there were plenty of days when I ate alone and hopefully reversed the artery-hardening effects of Dad's meals.

I also had to hand it to Dad; he had a deft touch with the coffee percolator. The aroma of Arabica was a convincing wake-you-up.

"Ah, there you are. When Pip didn't wake me I guessed where you'd both be. Did he get any rats? Boy, he loves catching those varmints."

"Well, he's a Jack Russell, isn't he? But nope, today he just made a lot of noise and scared off a load of sand martins."

"Oh, yes. The banks opposite Green's Farm are honeycombed with nests."

"Green, eh? How do you know the owner's called Green?"

"Because I probably spend more time down there than up here. Get to meet people, chat a while. Margaret likes it too."

Until he came here, my dad had been a confirmed townie, a guy who thought that the world stopped at the city limits. He didn't take rambling walks among the trees or talk to strangers. I grinned and patted his shoulder. "If you enjoy it, that's all that matters."

He served the food straight from pans to plates and we both sat down. "I've not asked much before, Stewart. Are you in trouble with this business? You've been spending a lot of time at home."

I knew as soon as he used my given name that he was serious. I really ought to have explained fully before, after all, he'd been in the meetings with my colleagues.

"Not what you could really call trouble. There are some nasty guys who've carried out some robberies, and for some reason they've tried to lay the blame on me. I'm suspended while it gets cleared up because those are the rules."

"Well, I can see you aren't taking it lying down."

I laughed. "My father didn't raise me to take things lying down, or to be idle when there's work to be done. Of course you've noticed several colleagues are volunteering their time to help. We'll get there though, you'll see."

"Hmm. Now about that pretty girl, Shelly? The one you were keen on."

"Dad, you're an old devil. She's a damned good copper who also happens to be a lady."

Dad shook his head slowly. "She's more than that, she's a whole heap of woman. If I was you, I'd slap a lead on her before someone else does."

Fortunately, the arrival of the said Shelly brought an end to that embarrassing conversation. I waved her through to the lounge and squeezed an extra cup of coffee out of the machine. As she reached across to take it from me, our hands brushed together; our eyes met at the same time.

I got quite a charge out of those few moments. I didn't know if it was mutual, but I just couldn't stop myself. I asked her, "When this lot is over, how about you and me spending some time together?"

The perfume she was wearing seemed to overwhelm the coffee when she smiled back. "I'd like that Stewart, but actually,"—my heart hit bottom—"I don't see there's a need to wait that long."

My heart started up again. Heavens, I was like a teenager. "Sorry, what was that?"

"I said that I'd been hoping you might say something before this."

I bent forward and our lips touched together. I'd never dreamed she would taste so good. And through the kitchen door, I saw my dad get up from the table with a mischievous grin on his face.

Leroy put his phone down just as Evangeline walked past. He reached out and pulled, dumping her into his lap. "Now, you come here, Sugar, and give your daddy some loving."

Evangeline put her arms around his neck. She really did believe he loved her, loved her with every bit of his being. Out loud, she said: "I don't go handin' it out willy-nilly, you know. What you done to deserve it, boy?"

Her words might have discouraged some men, but not Leroy. He knew what his lady liked and he knew what she didn't. "Just been checking wit' some of my..." He stopped, searching for the right word. "My contacts. Now, seems like I ain't the only one who's been set up with planted evidence. Remember my old sparring partner? That Detective Inspector White? They found some of his stuff mixed up with mine and I haven't been near that man in years."

The more serious Leroy became, the less of a black boy's accent he had.

"So that kind of confirms my innocence. Wouldn't you say?"

"An' how do you find that out?"

Leroy snorted which turned into a short laugh. "Not all those police men work just for the police, honey. Some of them work for me as well. Info is key, Sugar. I have to find out who is doing this."

"And you're the man with a plan, I s'pose?"

"Not yet, not yet; but I buy info from a man who does. He's called Asmin."

"I know about Asmin. Where you keep getting all this money from, Leroy? These..." she paused, "these contacts must cost a pretty penny or two."

"It's what comes around, goes around, honey. I pay boys who are good to me with money from the boys who want me to be good to them."

As if to compensate for Leroy dropping his accent, the more confrontational Evangeline became, the more she lapsed back to her Jamaican patois.

"Leroy Richards, you talk in riddles. Time's come when I want straight answers. Like who is this Asmin, really, and why do you trust him again, all of a sudden? Not long since you was callin' him everythin' from a pig to a donkey. Seems to me he ran away pretty damn quick when you was hidin' out at that place near York. He never come back to help me when the cops was buzzin' aroun' like bees roun' a honey pot."

"Well," Leroy slowed right down. "Guess he knew it would do him no good, nor you neither. Get you both banged up and, you believe me, Sugar, neither of you would want that. I know!"

"Well, okay. But you promised me you was finished with all that. This mama will not sit aroun' waitin' next time you go 'way fo' a long time!"

"Now don't you worry, honey-chile." He smudged the tears that were running down Evangeline's cheeks with his thumb. "I think the po-lice will be on my side this time. It's why I called Asmin—he's a go-between an' he'll go 'tween me an' the po-lice. Soon as my contacts point the way," he made a gun with two fingers and a thumb, "I'm firin' him like a bullet. You wait an' see."

The phone call that Al had been waiting for came that evening. He had dropped the name Sheldon as fast as he had his little gang.

"Hello, Aldo. Everything okay with you?"

Despite knowing his father would say exactly that, Al winced. He had hated his given name since he had been old enough to recognize it. Calling himself Al improved things a little, pretending it was "Allen" was even better, and he had continued with the fiction ever since.

"I'm fine, thanks. Doing a bit here, a bit there, like you do. And you?"

"I'm good. Life's always good when you can pay for what you want, you remember that. And when you can't pay, you got to learn how to take. Catch my drift?"

"Oh, I follow you. Can't say too much but I'm busy making plans. One of these days, I might just surprise you."

The older man chuckled. "Just so long as it's a good surprise, I hate the bad ones."

"If all goes to plan, this one will be a doozy."

"When you coming to visit me?"

"I will, I promise. But, I'm like two hundred miles from you and my old banger just isn't up to it."

"Sorry to hear that. Hope these plans of yours include getting yourself some new wheels."

Al grinned into his phone as he thought of the Alpha Romeo parked in his garage and lied comfortably. "Just thinking about that now, as a matter of fact. Couple of jobs to do first and I'll be trailing round the showrooms."

"What are you interested in, then? You don't want nothing flash, you know. The coppers pull up the flash ones as a matter of course. Fords are good, don't turn anyone's head and they've sold more cars in the past year than any other maker."

"Well, could be. Depends on money and what the best bargain is at the time. Actually, though, I quite like these Japanese cars. Nissans and Hyundais."

"Thought Hyundai was South Korean?"

Al cursed under his breath. "You're right, slip of the tongue." Even after all these years, his dad was still getting the better of him.

"What about women? Any of those on your radar?"

"Women? Don't have much time for them yet. Wasn't it you said they were costly items? Don't bother 'til you can afford one?" Aldo did not mention Fizzah. Dad knew about Sadik but, as far as he knew, nothing about Fizz.

"Hey, you do pay attention to what your old dad tells you. That's good. You keep listening and you won't go far wrong. Now don't forget to come and see me. It gets lonely in Brixton."

"No, shan't forget..." He realized he was speaking to a dead phone.

He looked at the clock; five minutes exactly and they'd switched him off. His mind took him back to the only time he'd ever visited Brixton prison in London. There might have been more forbidding places on this earth but he had never been to one. The gray stone walls, covered in soot and towering over everything around them, gave only the merest hint of what lay inside.

Al licked his lips and lifting his glass, emptied the dregs of the Bacardi and rum. He would kill himself first. Brixton, a place of nightmares where his dad was serving a ten to twenty, but not for much longer.

Later, a fresh drink to hand, he called his sister. His twin, but as different from himself as chalk and cheese, black and white. When their parents had split, she had gone to live with her mother and he with his father. There had never been much affection between them, but he supposed that he did love her in some crazy way. Why would he call her, otherwise?

"Hi, Mel."

"Hi Al. Dad just called me, said you'd had a chat."

Al wondered how the older man could call them both when he was allowed only five minutes. He might have raised his eyebrows but kept the thought to himself. Maybe he was buying another inmate's minutes?

"You managing all right without the old feller? Eating okay?"

"I'm doing fine, thanks, and you know I don't eat that much. You still trying to do the stick insect thing?" He added a laugh to take any sting out of the remark.

"Something like that. See much of Mum?"

He shook his head then looked at the phone and raised his eyebrows. "Can't do that no more, Mel. Just kills me to see her, like that home she's in, it's no place to be. She doesn't know me, doesn't even remember she's got a son. Best to remember her how she was."

"I can see that, but I think I'd still visit even if I did have to come all that way."

"You still at the same address?"

"What?" She suddenly sounded a little startled. "You thinking of coming to see me?"

Why would she should be so taken aback? "No, no. If I had a strong enough reason, I'd call you and give good notice."

"Oh. Right. Well, in that case, I have moved. Across to Stepney; it's closer to college, and I finish my masters this year. Anyway, you can always get me on this number."

"Fine." Al couldn't think of anything more he wanted to say, he nodded, knowing, as before, she couldn't see him. "Nice talking to you, Sis. Keep yourself safe." He closed the phone before she could reply.

He put the phone down, his chores for the evening complete. He reached over the top of his drink and picked up an iPad from the table. One of the apps kept track of his accounts, showing what monies he had and where they were. He needed ready cash for his longer term plans as well as more immediate things: the next chopper flying lesson, the upgrades he envisioned on his next car, and one or two trips abroad.

"Ah!" He put the tablet down and checked the digital recorder for any cryptic messages that his dad, in particular, might have left. There had been no hints in their conversation but it was best to be certain.

Satisfied, he turned on the television news channel. Sky TV reported the robbery at the Harold Nicholson store; the reporter mentioned that the police had interviewed three suspects but there was nothing more than he already knew. He guessed that nothing had been said about the others in the team which pleased him, despite the fact that he had already broken ties with the little organization. Of course, given time, they could—and probably would.

Al finished his drink and prepared for bed. Tomorrow, there were bigger eggs to fry, including dumping his beautiful Alpha Romeo Giulietta, a job that would break his heart. The only thing that made up for that was his getting together with Fizz; if she needed his dad's contacts as much as she seemed to, she had to keep Al happy.

CHAPTER 8

Shelly didn't stay the night, although it was discussed. We felt that with the house currently being used as an office, and with all manner of coppers passing through, embarrassments could too easily occur. When she did leave, however, it was with the promise of good things to come.

Ranjit and Alec turned up later—and together. I hadn't caught up on the ins and outs of that situation yet, but no doubt, I would. Whatever it was, I was intrigued. Today, Alec was grinning even more than recently. He seemed happier than I remembered him ever being.

"You just happy?" I asked him. "Or do you know something I don't?"

"Well, both actually. I'm happy because I can see the wind changing. It's been blowing in our faces since this business started but now, I think we've got a following wind."

"Sorry Alec. You've lost me somewhere."

"I mentioned to Ranjit that we knew the Met boys had video recordings of interviews and how nice it would be if we could take a look."

"Aha."

"You're jumping to the wrong conclusion. What he said was there was no way he could help, but didn't Barbara have a connection across there?"

"Hmm, I know about a David..."

"Morris."

"That's the one, but if he took a video out, he'd be in front of a firing squad so fast his feet wouldn't touch the ground."

"Exactly. But Barbara mentioned an identity bracelet and look at this." Alec handed me a really clear snapshot of an identity bracelet—*the* identity bracelet, I had to assume—with a single stone set into the surface. It could have been a diamond, sunk into the nameplate.

"Now, you'll be telling me this is the same as the one we have that was taken..."

"Yes, the very same," Ranjit said, looking over my shoulder. "It's proof that this man was present at the store robbery and the one at the National Bank. In this interview, he's been saying that he had just turned up to drive his girl-friend home."

"Wow!" Then the thought turned a bit sour. "This is information that we can't hold on to. It will mean wholesale resignations if we do." I explained further and their faces fell. It was a bummer, and they nodded reluctantly.

I called Flowers and told him that I needed to see him. He sounded pleased and was ready to drive out to my house. That would have proved a bit difficult as I would have had to get the others out of the place first. He agreed to meet me at the Merrion Center Coffee Club.

I left straightaway and Joe was already sitting there when I arrived. He was wearing a plain raincoat over his uniform; it was a nice thought.

"Morning Joe." A waiter brought me a coffee and a croissant. "Thanks." I said to the waiter. I turned to Joe, "Thanks to you, too."

He snorted. "My pleasure." He seemed to be in a bit of a hurry and waded right in. "So what's set your tail alight?"

I held up a finger and took a quick gulp of coffee. "Bit dry, sir." I put the cup down and leaned closer, over the table. "Now I'm going to ask you to listen to me and don't attempt to reproach me before I've finished. That okay?"

He nodded.

"Okay. Being framed for a crime or crimes is not something I ever expected to experience; if my father knew the whole truth, he'd be mortified. Now, I know you said I should leave the whole thing to the Met and D.S. Holly, and I did that for a few days, but I started to worry about them missing things."

Flowers nodded. "That's natural, but it's still the best way."

"Well, when I thought about the DNA you told me about, I had this idea that they'd consider it proved and not bother any further. I'd be guilty. It would be the easiest thing to do." I looked across at Joe and took another mouthful of coffee. "Mud sticks, Joe, wherever it comes from."

The chief super put his hand on my arm and gripped it. "Of course, that's all understandable but you do not—I repeat, you do *not*—have to worry. The two chiefs are in close touch with this case. Nothing will get by them; they go way back."

I nodded as he sat back and took an envelope out of my inside pocket. "A few friends and I have been busy chasing favors and we've come up with some information they might have overlooked. We've found out, for example, that there are six members in this group. They've been clever, changing out the number of people involved in each crime, along with their modus operandi."

"Each time?"

"The National Bank, the Turf Accountants and now, Harold Nicholson's. They don't use their own names; they refer to each other by the names of characters from a television show: Raj, Howard, Leonard, Penny, and Bernadette, and we think Sheldon. He is the one we're unsure about, but the Met have Raj, Bernadette and Penny in their lockup..."

"Hey, hold up a minute. You're saying those three are connected?"

"They are. And Leonard, Howard, and the one we think is going under the name Sheldon They're all still out there."

"You're going to have to tell me how you know all this."

I sighed. "I hoped you'd cut me a bit of slack on this. If I answer that fully, it could be very harmful to some loyal friends. Still, you or the Chief could let the Met know that it would be a good idea to go through the interview tapes again—the store and the bookies—because what I'm going to show you will prove I'm right." I opened the envelope and took out the two photographs and laid them in front of him. "One of those we believe is of a person who got in through the air duct at the bookies. We think the same person also acted as the getaway driver at Harold Nicholson's, who probably escaped with the one called Sheldon and the money. He's known as Raj."

I tapped one of the photos. "This is from the interview with him after the store job. This one," I tapped the other, "is from the tapes recorded at the bookies job—although we could be mixing him up with Howard. It would help if we could get their real names."

Joe put his glasses on and looked.

"Same hand, same bracelet. If the lab blows them up, they'll find the same slight damage in each one. I found that out by examining them under a low-power microscope. Check the pictures against the interview tapes."

He picked them up and looked from one to the other and back again, then he turned them over.

"The notes on the back are merely a resumé of what I've just said," I assured him. "Any good interviewer should be able to screw a confession out of the guy before lunch time today."

"We'll start now," Joe said. He pulled out a rather impressive new smartphone from his pocket, took several shots of my photos, and sent them off. Then he typed out a text. When he'd finished, he nodded slowly and said, "Happen to know that our chief and theirs are in a meeting about now." He glanced at his watch. "Or soon will be. I've sent the gist of what you've told me to *my* boss and I think fireworks will start to fly."

"That's good, Joe. I'm pleased we had this talk."

"Another thing you may not have realized is that if all three jobs are the work of the same group, then it all comes back to us. We may be NCA now, but we're still hot on organized crime, and mark my words, I'll be back to you post haste."

He leaned in close and spoke very quietly. "It's very good that Inspector Fearon, Sergeant Bell and Sergeant Ranjit Patiala are all able to give you a bit of help. The fact that they all happen to be out on holiday makes them free to do whatever they want, doesn't it?" My boss tapped me on the shoulder and was gone before I had time to say goodbye.

Crafty old sod, I thought to myself as I drove home. I was still chuckling when I turned into the gate. My mood changed when I got into the house, though. There was a letter in the postbox with a US stamp on it. I opened it before going through to where I could hear the others talking and laughing.

I thought I'd recognized the handwriting: large and ornate. It was from John Merrick, the Florida sheriff who had helped with the Cleghorn case.

> *Hi Stew,*
> *Thought you probably should know about this. Hope to see*
> *you again one of these days. Keep the beer in the fridge in*
> *case I should turn up.*
> *JM*

Enclosed was a cutting from the Sebring newspaper. It announced the forthcoming wedding of one Constance Cleghorn. *Connie.* There was a photo of the couple. She looked beautiful and happy.

My eyes filled and spilled over as I climbed the stairs quietly so the others wouldn't know I was back. Maybe Connie didn't blame me for the death of her brother, Robert, after all. That had been nagging at the back of my mind all along. Maybe there had been someone else all the time. Or maybe she'd just decided to move on. Regardless, it brought the curtain down on any romantic thoughts that were still flitting around my head.

And perhaps, it was for the best.

Superintendent Holly and Detective Chief Inspector Maugham had both reached that stage in the interview where they had become fed up with asking the same questions—albeit, in different ways—and listening to the same damned answers. They were both about ready to give up for the day; in fact, Holly had already closed his folder up.

At this point, their Chief came in to the observation room and spoke into the mike. "Any progress?"

The other two looked up and each gave a barely perceptible shake of the head.

"You'd better come in here, then."

In the observation room, the Chief raised his eyebrows.

"A dead end," muttered Holly.

"Brick wall," Maugham added and went on. "They plead innocence; the girls were doing a modeling job, the lad was picking them up."

The Chief Constable handed them a stapled sheaf of papers. "Look through these, go back in there, and bring me a confession within the hour. All right?"

The pair of them scanned the sheaf slowly, desperately trying to grasp the details of the photos and the fact sheet that the CC had handed them. Holly grasped the import first, followed a scant second later by Maugham's sudden intake of breath.

"Aye, sir," they said in unison as smiles broke across their faces.

"And who do we have to thank for this?" asked Holly.

"Keep this on the QT, Superintendent, but a certain Chief Inspector on leave has proved invaluable, I understand."

"White!" said Maugham. "How the hell did he get his hands on this, I wonder?"

"I never mentioned any names and it's not up for discussion. It involves a state of trust between one's fellow officers. Suffice it to say, you've been given the weapons—now go and fire them."

Holly and Maugham headed back into the interview room where Raj sat picking his nose. They didn't even bother to sit down.

"Patrick Henry Kelly of twenty-seven Cambridge Street, Meanwood, Leeds," Holly began, "also known as Raj—we intend to charge you with certain crimes having to do with robbery. The actual severity of the charges will depend upon your cooperation. The choices open to you range from armed robbery, breaking and entering, grievous bodily harm, aiding and abetting criminal activities, to upwards of a dozen more that I haven't thought of yet."

Holly drew a deep breath, and then he and Maugham sat down.

The young man began to splutter and stutter; his mind raced, out of gear. "I already told you that I only came to pick my girl up."

Holly opened the papers the Chief had handed him, put them on the table, and arranged a photo on top of the stack. "This is a photograph taken from the cameras at the National Bank in Horsforth two weeks ago. This covers the period of the robbery." Holly lied deliberately; the camera at the bank had been shot out and they had no such photo. He pointed to the second photograph. "This came from the camera at James Allan's, the Turf Accountants robbed five days ago. The bracelet looks remarkably like the one you're wearing." He then told his second lie with a malicious smile. "I expect Sheldon and Bernadette to confirm this to us shortly."

Raj knew he was beaten. If they knew about Sheldon and the others, he was living on borrowed time. "But we were really only making a movie. With realism," he said dispiritedly. He made his confession before his lawyer came back from the washroom.

The girls lasted even less time than Raj. They had all been identified by this time, and as soon as their real names were mentioned, and the crimes they could be charged with spelled out, tears followed.

"Jail?" DC Holly said to his colleague.

"Don't you think so?" Maugham replied in the affirmative.

The girls began talking between big gulps for breath. The police officers had their confessions in no time, despite their lawyer frantically trying to get them to remain silent. Holly and Maugham let them assume Raj had ratted on them. The girls turned tears off—and the fury on. Leonard's supposed address came out, as well as the make and color of Sheldon's car.

"How do you spell Giulietta?" Holly asked.

"Italian name," Maugham pointed out.

But try as they might, they got nothing else from the two girls, except that they thought they were making a movie. They genuinely appeared to have no knowledge of anything else. Before the three detainees were taken back to their cells, however, a plain-clothes detective, whom Holly did not recognize, met them in the corridor.

He offered his warrant card and told them he was peripherally involved with the case. "My superior wondered if you might ask them about the DNA evidence collected at the bank," he said. "You can tell them we know it was placed there as false evidence, and we'd just like to know how it was collected in the first place—and why it was left there."

"We asked that," Holly said, "but they had no idea, and said we should ask Sheldon. And—I know I've seen you around here, but who is your superior?"

"Ah, did I not say? He gave me this to pass on." Ranjit Patiala gave him a hand-written note. "Chief Superintendent Flowers. The note says what I mentioned but I wanted you to know immediately rather than have you read it later on."

"Strike while the iron is hot."

"Precisely, sir."

―――――

Cameras set into the gateposts at the top of the half-mile-long driveway picked up the movement. An alarm attracted Leonard's attention to his security monitor and to the cavalcade of police cars entering the gate.

He acted immediately. Two bags with changes of clothing were always at the ready. He simply picked them up, and took his money from the safe before passing through the glass doors onto the patio. He was down the outer stairs before the vehicles were more than halfway down the drive.

He went under the decking and through a wooden door into a low-ceilinged workshop. There were racks holding scores of small power and hand-tools. None of these mattered; the only thing that was of importance was the kayak, which moved gently with the low swell coming through the narrow channel to the reservoir outside. Strapped to the kayak's decking was a fold-up bicycle. Leonard stowed his gear, slid into the seat and urged the little craft through the narrow opening out onto the water. Behind him, the door hummed shut.

Leonard directed the craft along the bank with powerful thrusts of the paddle. Within minutes, he was out of sight of the house, just close enough to hear a voice amplified through a police loud-hailer. But then, that too was gone.

His escape plan had been in place since he had taken up with Sheldon. He had almost expected to employ it with every job. When he had heard the girls had been apprehended, it was a foregone conclusion that his location and name would be revealed. Just in case he was spotted, he moved along at a steady pace, forcing himself not to hurry or to look back—both were signs of guilt. He made his way around a small headland beyond which twigs and other flotsam collected by the currents crowded along the narrow beach.

He drove the kayak up among the debris. He stepped out into ankle-deep water and deliberately turned the craft on its side to fill it with water. Minutes later, it was stable and covered with bracken and sticks.

Leonard reckoned it had taken him five minutes to get this far. He unfolded the bike and climbed the reservoir bank to a cycle track which circumnavigated the water. The path intersected with others which, crisscrossing, led steadily away from the lake into the Yorkshire countryside. His panniers held his clothes and the money, while his kit and the kayaking helmet were a near-match for the hundreds of other cyclists on the path.

He was now invisible.

CHAPTER 9

Chief Constable Vance arrived at my home at about a quarter before seven. The waft of "Blue Yonder" cologne—in keeping with his blue uniform—preceded him through the door. I had been forewarned of an early visit but I was expecting my chief super, not the big cheese himself.

"Morning Stewart. Absolutely wonderful day, isn't it?" he said, as though we were old friends. "Any coffee on the go?"

"Won't take long, sir. Come through into the living room, why don't you? Bit of a mess, I'm afraid, it's being used as a working office."

"I guessed as much," he said, loudly enough to hear as I went through to the kitchen. "You've even improvised your own white evidence boards. Impressive."

"That's right, sir." I returned, having turned the kettle on to boil and made no mention of the others who had done such sterling work for fear of implicating them. I just hoped that none of them would arrive before the Chief left.

I heard the kettle doing a jig and excused myself for a minute. My cafetière held three good cups—just right for unexpected visitors. I put the coffee on a tray with milk, sugar, and three mugs—an extra one for my dad in case he came in.

Vance was sitting on the settee where he could see out into the orchard. "I can see why you bought this place." he said as I poured. "Delightful."

"Help yourself to sugar and milk, sir."

"Black as the ace of spades, thanks, and as bitter as it comes. Any fish in that river?"

"Oh, yes. Chub, pike, barbel, everything you could wish for. Not that I usually have much time for it, the odd hour or so."

"That's good. We'll have to have a private match one of these days. River fish are stronger, don't you think?"

I nodded. "Oh, sure. Stronger muscles, pound for pound..."

"And this coffee's excellent." Then, suddenly, he was all business again. He took out a leather case and I recognized my warrant card. "I hope you can take this back with no hard feelings, Stewart. I can only apologize for the rules that dictated the way we had to act."

I took the offered case. "I understand. Still, I'm a little bit puzzled. The matter of the DNA seems to have been resolved remarkably quickly."

"Ah! Well, Joe Flowers texted me about the probability that all those three robberies were the work of one organization. If true, then they would become our business as the local force on this sort of job, and that put a new face on things. It was your knowledge of the gang members going by alternate names, and also you recognizing the identity bracelet. It all helped to exonerate you."

"Unless I'm a member of the gang? Maybe I'm the one we think is called Sheldon." I laughed uproariously to show that this was a joke. Even so, the Chief Constable's chortle was not quite as amused as it might have been.

"Well, again, we had a stroke of luck. A fellow police officer from Bellamy's lot also happened, by chance,"—he winked—"to be around when they were re-interviewing the suspects."

I made a wry grin, more worried than expectant. There was a lot of play-acting going on here.

"There was tomato ketchup mixed in with the blood traces. Very odd. Ring any bells?"

Thoughts of blood and tomato ketchup whirled though my mind. I shook my head. I said, "No idea..." Then I remembered the melee at that café a few weeks earlier, the broken glass and a ketchup bottle on the table.

"Well, of course. I do remember—"

"Sergeant Barbara Patterson remembered it for you already."

"And there were six of them at the restaurant, I think," I answered. "I nearly arrested the chap who had thrown the bottle; it might have prevented all this if I had."

"As easy as that." Vance said.

"How many did they catch, then? All six of them?"

"Three. Two women, and a male driver. There are addresses for the ones they call Howard and Leonard. Sheldon is still a mystery we're working on." He cleared his throat. Now, I wondered how soon you wanted to come back and whether you'd want to take the case."

I don't know what reaction the Chief expected, but I paused before saying yes.

Noting my delay he said, "Well, if you'd return to work tomorrow morning, it would be good. Really good. The business of taking over a case from the Met needs some careful diplomacy. I know how I'd feel if I'd just made a great breakthrough and then had the case taken from me."

I nodded. " But there might be a solution." I rubbed my chin. "Suppose we could leave the investigation with them, and me and my team be allowed access to their notes? I can't see the Met being antagonistic if we pursue Sheldon and Leonard. They may already be outside the Leeds Met's jurisdiction by now."

"That's good, Stewart. Diplomatic, as you said, and there'll be a little less of our budget being spent if we share the case. I think I can win with that. Tell me though, why did you suggest we go with just Sheldon—and not Howard and Leonard? I doubt it was budget considerations."

"It gives them something to hope for," I chuckled. "If they can find these two before we do, right? Mind you, if we're looking for Sheldon, we might also be able to implicate Leonard and Howard. That would be their tough luck."

Vance stood up and tugged his uniform into place. "Tough luck, hard cheese, whatever. So, welcome back Detective Chief Inspector. See you at the office tomorrow, then?"

"Depend on it, sir."

———

Alec and Shelly were delighted when they heard my news later on.

"Thank God," said Alec. "I was really getting to miss ma auld captain's chair." He began taking down the notes and pictures on the white boards and bundled them up.

Shelly nodded towards the kitchen; once there, she said. "Stewart, I'm really happy for you. Would you be okay for dinner, say, Saturday? Here? I'll either bring it or cook it here."

"I don't remember being this happy, Shelly, ever. Dinner sounds very, very good."

I didn't know how long it would last, but I could enjoy it while it did.

CHAPTER 10

Returning to the office was a little like a hero's return home. The reception committee was vast, dozens and dozens of people—many unknown to me—blocked the elevators, lined the entranceway, the stairs, and the passage to my office. A wave of clapping preceded me from parking area to office level. Somewhat humbled, I nodded and smiled until I reached the team office. Here, although there were fewer people, it grew worse, in a way. The Chief, Joe Flowers, and Barbara Patterson led the others in adding cheers and whistles to the cacophony.

Like all the chiefs I had ever met, Vance loved the opportunity to make a speech. He kept it to a few words of appreciation for the team's efforts before turning to me.

I was dazed by it all. It was only when he had finished and left us that I got my breath back. My sixteen guys and a new woman of around thirty whom I belatedly guessed to have been my replacement, or to be kind, my stand-in.

"Wow!" I said at last. "Thank you all for that most riotous of welcomes, my ears will be ringing for a week. And, to show my appreciation and thanks, you are all invited to the White Horse cocktail bar after work where the drinks will, of course, be on me."

There were laughs and more clapping and eventually almost everyone had returned to their desks and chairs. That left Barbara and the stranger waiting for me.

"Guv, may I introduce Inspector Melodie Grainger?"

"Thank you, sergeant."

I offered my hand and we shook. "My stand-in from Wakefield?"

She nodded in a non-committal way.

"I need to speak to the inspector in my office before anything else," I said to Barbara. "When we're done, can you come along, please?"

Entering my own office should have been a pleasure but it was an alien place. So many things were missing and many other things stood in their places.

Inspector Grainger saw me looking round. "I just moved some stuff to make the place more efficient for me, sir. I can soon put them back."

I nodded. "It's perfectly understandable that you wanted your own space. Where are my files?"

"In the storage cupboard. I didn't want to touch the contents unless authorized. It seemed the best thing to do."

As she talked, I moved around. I put a painting Dad had given me of a heron diving into blue water back on the center wall, and checked the printer for any messages. I looked into the bathroom and noted the array of feminine toiletries that filled the single shelf and the back of the wash basin.

"I understand that you made my team empty their desktops?"

She nodded. She might have thought I was going to compliment her. "Yes, a tidy desk shows an organized mind."

"We differ on that one." I sat down and looked up at her. "I did much the same when I was first appointed Inspector. Like you, my thoughts were on efficiency and good work management. I started by telling the guy with the most stuff on his desk—most of it looked like rubbish to me—telling him to clean it up, which he did." I smiled to take any malice out of my manner.

"I was mistaken, Inspector."

"Maybe a bad first choice."

"No. I was wrong and privately, I apologized to that man and told him to use his own methods."

"Not a good move, sir, in my estimation. Never apologize, never..."

"Never explain. Yes, I heard that one too. Another thing we differ over, Inspector. Well I'm sure things are different in Wakefield and you'll be happy going back there?"

Grainger had her mouth compressed into a thin red line.

I wrapped up quickly. "Now, I'll leave you to it and you can put your own things together. Let me know when you're ready to go and I'll arrange transport back to Wakefield. I'll be in the team office. Call Sergeant Patterson. And I sincerely want to thank you for all of your efforts on behalf of myself and the teams."

Inspector Grainger was ready to go inside ten minutes, far sooner than I had anticipated. Alec Bell had also returned to duty at the same time as I had. I gave him the job of helping the lady carry her stuff down to her car and returning her whence she came. Before I signaled Barbara to come through, I stood at the door and raised my voice. "I hate to see so much wasted desktop space. I want efficient desks, not tidy ones."

I left before the noise level rose too high.

Paul Leduc, also known as Howard, had been between jobs when he joined Sheldon's team. His share of the money from the cat-walk job had been stored in the trunk of his ten-year-old Vauxhall. He had considered spending it on another car or using it as a deposit on a house, but when he saw the report of the arrest of the two girls and Raj on the television news, he was suddenly pleased that he had done nothing irrevocable. Thanks to Sheldon's insistence, no one in the team knew the identities of the others and in his own case, that included his address, so the police had little to work on—which was probably why they let him go.

That said, who knew what trivial clues he might have left behind? But still, somewhat panicked, he decided he'd better disappear.

He had already packed all his worldly possessions into his car, and decided to head south to Burton-on-Trent where a former friend lived. His friend worked—or had worked—in one of the several breweries which dominated the small town.

As Paul tore down the M1 at a barely legal speed, he tried to sort out what to do next. He had a passport if he needed it, although a few European holidays had left him unenthusiastic about foreign parts. However, his savings of eighteen grand, which included the film pay, was not going to last him forever. He either needed a job, or needed to pull a job. Adaptable and very fit, at twenty years old, with a medium height and nondescript features, he was open to any suggestions that might come his way.

The journey took an hour and a half and, at a quarter before six, when Brian Yarrow returned from work, Paul was parked outside his front door. He grinned as the other stared through the windshield and raised his eyebrows. They had met as very young teenagers, both on holiday with their parents. At the Butlin's holiday camp, they had smoked their first cigarettes and choked on pilfered red wine from Brian's mother. Despite being roundly rebuked by both sets of parents, they had laughed about it together and became good friends.

Brian was surprised to see him, but quite pleased about it. They sat in the front of Paul's car and recalled past times. However, when Paul carefully raised the matter of staying over for a few days, until he found a job and living space, his friend made a face. "My dad's a miserable old sod, so I can't help you there. But, I've a mate who might be able to. You could see him. Um, got a notepad?"

"I've got a phone." He logged the address of Brian's friend and a few minutes later, set off.

The friend was Henri, a young Frenchman who worked as a waiter. He shared a room with two others: Biel, an East European, and Sanjit, from the Indian sub-continent. They offered him sleeping space on a couch in the main living room but, although he took the offer gladly, after the first two hours of tossing and turning, Paul promised himself to find something more comfortable the next day.

The following day, he thanked them and left to drive into the town center, looking for rooms to let and a job. He found both at the Silver Wheel casino, which catered to anyone with pounds to spare, most of which inevitably wound up in the establishment's coffers. Even so, there was a never-ending line of patrons willing to chance their cash. And there were rooms on the premises for the late-night staff.

The casino boss was a Macedonian named Matto who had finally given up on recruiting young, attractive female dealers. He had wanted the girls to offer other services, but the number of job applicants dwindled as his dubious reputation grew in the city. Paul learned the rules of blackjack in a single sitting; he seemed to be a natural and spent his first shift relieving punters of enormous amounts of cash.

There were smoke breaks throughout the night, and during one of these, he remarked to a more experienced dealer that he was surprised that credit cards were never used.

"Credit cards leave records; cash doesn't," the other dealer said, and within moments Paul had conceived his great idea.

He allowed the takings to accumulate rather more than was recommended and in the men's lavatory, hid the bank notes around his person before making a fast getaway. Paul had not noticed the CCTV cameras peering into each cubicle, however, and bouncers were on his trail almost as soon as he ducked out of the rear door. He led the chase into the multi-story parking garage, where he feinted a sprint to the third floor, then doubled back down to the ground floor. He even made use of the casino's security pass to open the barrier, and was away before the bouncers realized their quarry had fled.

Paul broke several speed limits on his way to the ring road, looking for a place to lie low for several hours. He had driven as far as Lichfield before he found a safe haven.

Once Stewart White's name had been cleared, Ranjit decided to cut short his time at Leeds. The day after he attended the Detective Inspector's celebration party, he called in at the Met Offices on Elland Road before returning to his office at the National Crime Agency in East Anglia. He was at his rooming house packing his clothes when his phone buzzed insistently.

"Hello, Asmin."

It was Leroy Richards once more. "Hello, young trouble-maker," he replied. "What can I do for you?"

"Asmin, that's not kind. I've got information that D.C.I. White might find very interesting."

"Very well, boss. And what is that?"

"Well, I understand that he works at the Ridings Regional Squad. That right?"

"More or less. It changed its name a while back. It's now a part of the NCA."

"Whatever. You might pass this on—"

"Why don't you just call them yourself? Good intel is always welcome, whatever the source."

"Ah. We have history, Asmin. Stewart White an' me. He might not forgive me for going over the wire at Askham Bryan prison."

Asmin snorted and tried not laugh outright. Askham Bryan was a class-three prison where old lags and relatively unimportant prisoners were held close to the end of their sentences. He had been working undercover and had been the one to pick up Leroy that night and drive off with him. "I seem to remember you only had a six month sentence to serve—not a hard job for a man of your experience."

Back then, Leroy thought he had hired the Sikh as his driver and right-hand man—something he could not have been more wrong about. But Ranjit liked to keep up appearances. "You know I could go back there, or a much more severe place with extra time, unless D.C.I. White puts a good word in for me."

"You want me to act as a go-between?"

"Yeah, that's right. You do that an' I'll send you this stuff on the phone right now. Some damn good pictures, too."

"Well. Might I ask what this info is, since it'll be my neck on the line?"

"Hmm. Fair 'nuff. Think I told you 'bout my DNA bein' planted at a bank job and maybe a bettin' shop too?"

"You did."

"Well, these pictures are the guilty sons-o-bitches that set me an' him up. They run in a gang o' six—well, this one called Paul did—but some of his mates had their collars felt."

"Okay, and you know all this—how?"

"Because one o' my informants works in a casino in Burton-on-Trent and this guy, who goes by the name of Paul Leduc, ripped the casino off—no more'n an hour gone—an' he is one big dummy. Never cottoned onto the fact that they had cameras in the restrooms, looking down the stalls and taking pictures of yo' ass and all. Every-bleeding where—"

"Okay. Got the picture. Where is this prize idiot now?"

"Headin' south like the Devil's after him. Drivin' a green Vauxhall Vectra an' if I tell you any more, I might as well fetch the boy in myself. Now your friends can do it better and that's goin' to help me."

"Fine, Leroy. You send me the pics and I'll get back to you as soon as I hear anything. There'll probably be a reward in it for you, too."

"You keep it, Asmin. I'll do this for old time's sake. Sending the stuff now."

Ranjit—Asmin—got through to Stewart White, passed on the information, and told him the source. Stewart, with his eyebrows still up near his hairline, passed the information onto his own team before examining the picture of Paul, formerly Howard. He shook his head in puzzlement and made a return call to the Sikh.

"Ranjit? Stewart White. Why do you think Leroy's doing this? Has he got himself involved with this gang and he's getting out before we find out?"

"I don't really know, Stewart. My best guess is that he's keeping his nose clean and he's making sure it stays that way. The prospect of going back to prison for two more years is not appealing to him, even if you were going to be there too."

"Me?"

"Joke, Stewart, joke. He's in the same boat that you were."

"Yeah. Well this is all very welcome and he got it to us fast enough to be of some use. I guess the casino will report it to the local police—"

"I doubt that, Stewart. I doubt it very much. The casino will want to handle this themselves, I think. If they catch him, he probably won't walk again. Leroy called him an idiot and he's absolutely right."

"Sure. I can see that."

"It might be a good time for you to seek assurances from the CPS that Leroy's sentence isn't going to be extended. You can tell them that he's already provided invaluable information and you want to officially make him one of your snouts. Of course, that's only a respectful suggestion, sir."

"And Leroy wants this?"

"I believe so. I can arrange a safe phone for him or a secure meeting point. What do you think?"

I couldn't give Ranjit any immediate assurances, but promised him I'd get straight back to him.

I knew my way around the Crown Prosecution Service and spoke to someone with whom I had had dealings with before. My contact listened to my story and said that if I could get my request backed up by my chief, it would probably go through. That was good news and before I had time to dial the Chief, Barbara tapped on the door and came in with more of the same.

"Couldn't call with this—you were on an outside line. This Paul Leduc, it got immediate results on the instant call-back line. Seems like The Green Man Hotel in Lichfield wants to ingratiate themselves with the police in general. Leduc's booked himself in a room there and paid with fifty-pound notes tagged with a certain casino's mark. Hotel staff wonder if they should lock him in his room?"

"Remind me why we should want to interview him when Leeds Met has been given the go-ahead to catch him? He's the one called 'Howard', and since we now know four names, maybe they can lever some more information out of the guy."

"It appears The Met did question him, but obviously hadn't got enough to hold him."

"Well, they have now. Can you take care of it? I've got an urgent matter to take up with the Chief."

The Chief, when I got to see him, positively beamed at me. "Well, Stewart, knew I could rely on you. How did you locate him?"

I told him about Leroy Richards and how it would be useful to add him as a senior officer's snout. Then I asked him if he would be prepared to back the application to have his remaining sentence quashed, as it could be a little embarrassing for him to finish off his stay at Askham Bryan.

"Leave it with me, Stewart. Daley Ward at the CPS owes me one, we'll put him on probation. Does that suit you?"

"Absolutely, Chief."

"Leroy Richards—that the name?" And he wrote it down.

A little later, I contacted Ranjit and passed on the news of Leroy's change in status. I also mentioned how much the idea appealed to me and that we should set up a meet with the guy.

"One other thing, Ranjit. Can you find out what Holly learned from the girls when he let them know that Sheldon had walked off with half a million pounds while leaving them behind?"

CHAPTER 11

Leroy agreed to meet me at a truck stop café between the town of Garforth and the old A1, a road now superseded by more modern highways. At the time I arrived, it was packed with truck drivers eating thick bacon sandwiches and drinking tea from heavy mugs.

Leroy came in a few minutes later: I still remembered his angry face from the courtroom. I stood up then moved sideways as a huge, bearded truck-driver also got to his feet, speaking some mid-European language. Leroy saw me and joined me at the little corner table.

"Morning, Leroy. Been a while."

This time he grinned at me. "Surely has, Mister White. I see you came by yourself."

"Been checking?"

"Second nature." His eyes were constantly on the move, checking for other policemen—or perhaps, from pure habit.

"Well, sit down. Fancy a breakfast?" The smell of bacon, sausage, and fried onions was getting to me. "Full English?"

"Never say no to an offer like that, Mister—"

"Call me Stewart, unless we've got company."

"Stewart. When I came to England to find my dad, a 'full English' was the first thing he bought me when we got together."

"Been a few years, I guess."

"Hell, yes. Must be...oh, twelve years, I reckon."

Considering the look he had given me in that court, when they'd taken him down after sentencing, he seemed pretty friendly right now; an infectious grin, affable—likable even.

"I'll order, won't be a minute." I noticed he watched me all the way to the counter and all the way back again. Likeable maybe, but shrewd. I'd ordered one coffee and one tea with the breakfasts. When it came, I asked: "Tea or coffee?"

"Tea for me. Ta. That okay with you?"

I passed the mug of tea across and kept the coffee for myself. "Anything at breakfast time so long as it's wet and hot."

Leroy grinned at me and I felt myself grinning back. "So, was that gossip I gave Asmin useful?"

"Asmin?" I was at a loss for a moment or two, "Ah, Asmin. Yes, it certainly was. The young man you fingered was in our lock-up at Leeds within two hours."

"Hey, not bad considering he was in Burton when I called."

"Well, actually, he was in Lichfield, but it was your info that let us put things together."

"How come a young punk running off with cash from his work is interesting to you?"

"Because he was one of the six that robbed the National Bank in Horsforth, Leeds, and left my DNA there to incriminate me. But you already knew that. Now, how come a young punk running off with cash from his work interested *you?*"

"Ha, ha. You got me, Stewart. 'Cos they left my DNA there too. So, maybe we're both of us cleared?"

"Maybe we are, but why would they want to implicate you?"

"That I don't know."

"You know the bank?"

"Course I do. It's *my* bank. My branch. I use it 'cos it's about the farthest from my home that I can reach easily."

"Maybe you dribbled then, or maybe you spat—"

"Come on, Mr. White. I's a big boy now."

"We'll find out. Oh, and apart from being cleared of a connection to the bank robbery, I've some even better news for you."

I stopped as our breakfasts arrived in the hands of a Polish girl. She disappeared and I started again, only to stop once more when she reappeared with condiments.

"News?" Leroy inquired, reaching for the ketchup as I went for the mustard.

"You're off the hook as far as going back to Askham Bryan."

"That's sublime, Mr. White." His voice rose like a kid's. "Sublime."

"And you're on the payroll if you want to keep sending us useful information."

Leroy was dipping a piece of fried bread into his egg yolk and stopped, eyes wide open. "I'm workin' for the Po-lice?"

"If'n you wanna." Not a very good copy of Leroy's Jamaican accent, but then, I am from the Midlands.

Leroy swallowed the rest of his tea. "So, no prison extension, huh? No going back?"

I shook my head and cleaned my plate up. "Not as long as you keep your word. We could put you in touch with a beat cop that you could report to but that's likely to draw attention to you, which is not a good idea. We can provide you with a safe phone that will come straight through to me. That would be better, I think. If any of Charlie's thugs come calling, just holler, okay?"

He nodded. "Good thinking, Mr. White."

"Stewart."

"Stew."

"Stewart. Now, where are you located?"

"Where do I live, Stewart?"

I nodded.

"Not too far from you, but just far enough so we all stay happy."

"I need an address, Leroy." I passed a pen and my notebook across. "Write it down."

We finished up and stood to leave. Leroy offered his hand and we shook on it. "Thanks, Mr. White," he said in a small voice.

"Stewart."

Then, uncertainly: "I did spit, Stewart."

"Sorry?"

"At the bank. How long ago was this? A month or so?"

"About that."

Leroy pulled a bunch of paper from his inside pocket. He held a battered check book. "Look at that, Stewart. Pay-in stubs around that date."

Puzzled, I looked. A stub covered in ink showed up just before the date, and the one after it had fingerprints all over it.

"Bloody pen broke, din'it? Should've used one of their cheap things 'stead of mine. Spat on a tissue to wipe it off. Then licked my fingers and wiped them again." He tapped the table. "That's where they got it from."

"The burglars?"

"Nah, the police."

"Makes sense, Leroy. Makes sense."

But I would follow it up and check the evidence.

Shelly was coming over tonight but at five-thirty I was still catching up on the reports from my team; they had not been idle during my enforced leave.

My guys had agreed with me and chosen not to take the three cases from the Leeds Met even though it could be argued that they came under our aegis.

We did have recordings of the interviews and copies of the reports. Earlier, I had tried to follow the interview of the one we knew as Raj, but my mind kept wandering off to other aspects of the case, and I could not give it the attention it needed.

The inspector from Wakefield—I could not bring myself to think of her in any other way—had trashed our squad system of working. My officers told me that she had declared it "too American." No one knew what that meant. It worked, it produced results, and I was grateful that I hadn't been away longer.

She must have been pretty sure I wasn't coming back.

I looked at my watch: six o'clock already. I could spare another half hour, I supposed, but I also wanted to pick some wine up on the way home. Shiraz for me and chardonnay for Shelly, and that needed chilling.

Guilt won out and I quickly read through some more reports: a family homicide (a wife stabbed her husband after she caught him cheating in the matrimonial bed), several robberies which might or might not be the work of a single group, and a drug-running incident. And there were East Europeans selling fake documents, others selling fake passports and credit cards. I was suddenly very tired of European problems and I swept all the stuff into a drawer and locked it.

I stood up to go, deciding to come into the office tomorrow and start afresh. Five minutes after my deadline I was away, although the usual twenty-minute journey was delayed where the road was being re-surfaced. I picked up the wine I wanted and when I arrived home, Shelly was already there trying to explain to my dad what jerk chicken was. Dad was shaking his head; he was incredibly set in his ways and thought that curries—any spicy food, in fact—were the work of the devil.

"Look," he was saying, "these things are used to hide the fact that the meat is bad." He looked across at me for confirmation.

I shrugged. "Don't look at me, oh-wise-one. I'll eat anything that this lady prepares."

Shelly giggled and I could hardly believe my ears when Dad took a forkful and chewed it slowly. "That's very tasty, my dear." He took another. "Absolutely delicious. Write the recipe down for me, will you? I'll go and get my wife's recipe book."

Then he looked across at me, suddenly aware of what he had said, his face just a little red as a blush crept across his cheeks. He looked at the kitchen clock. "Well, must be off, Margaret will be waiting for me."

"Hope you don't mind my breaking and entering, Stewart?" Shelly chipped in.

"Not at all. Did I forget to lock up?"

"No, no. Your dad saw me looking through your windows after I tried knocking. He came and let me in and showed me how to use your cooker and where the microwave was and..." She smiled. "He seemed in a bit of a hurry to leave." The smile became a chuckle; it was pretty sexy and had me chuckling too.

I popped the white wine into the freezer for the few minutes it took me to shed my jacket and wash my hands. "Sorry I was late. Road work and bad traffic."

We ate the meal that Shelly had brought and drank the wine that I had provided. We smiled a lot, talked very little, and generally enjoyed the warm feeling that such occasions bring about. We took our drinks through to the lounge and sat close together on the couch, as though we had been doing this for years. No music, very little talking, and it was Shelly who finally stood up and led me upstairs.

It was quite a revelation. There had not been all that many occasions when I had made love to attractive women, fewer still to beautiful women, and Shelly was certainly one of the latter. There were very few words, though an amazing choice of tiny sounds. "No, no." She whispered at one point. "Not yet, not yet."

Fingers pressed along my spine, teeth bit gently at my earlobe. I learned that making love was a far more nuanced art than I had supposed and urgency came later, after an unbelievably long and languorous introduction. We had crossed the line beyond lovers. This was something I had never known before, addictive, compulsive: I could only hope that this lady felt the same way.

Later, I went downstairs and brewed Italian coffee. I found some cookies, put it all on a tray, and took it back upstairs. Still, there were few words, our breathing loud in the stillness.

That night was the most delightful few hours of my life.

Shelly stayed all of the following day, my good intentions of working entirely forgotten. We walked along the riverbank with Pip dashing from one bush to another. The weather was near-perfect, we met no one and although we spoke only occasionally, we did talk, sometimes frivolous, sometime serious. The silences were equally satisfying, proving that words were not always necessary. Just holding hands was enough.

It got to be quite late and I wondered if she wanted to stay a second night but eventually, she told me it was time for her to leave. Like me, she was at work on Monday and when she had started her car and driven off, the house seemed an oddly lonely place. It was then I remembered Connie Cleghorn and realized that I had only been playing at things.

William Weiss—formerly known as Leonard—went to a gent's outfitters in Wetherby where he purchased two sets of clothes, from outerwear to underwear. He asked for the tags to be removed from the garments and paid with cash before changing into one of the sets. He bundled his old clothes into one of the store's shopping bags, intending to get rid of them in a dumpster, along with his bicycle.

The figure leaving the shop bore little resemblance to the one who had entered. The white sportswear and sneakers were gone. In their place was a black suede jacket over a white collared shirt, a floral tie, black slacks, and black Oxford brogues: a young man about town. His new pockets held enough money to last him several months, even while staying at a quality hotel. He was not one to party and never had been, William's leisure hours were spent listening to music, reading and enjoying meals, hitherto, cooked by himself. For someone who could have almost whatever he wanted, he had asked for very little from life.

Joining the Six was an act of rebellion against a father who solved every problem by throwing a checkbook at it. The fact that Sheldon had talked about making large amounts of money was no special attraction; money flowed freely in the Weiss household and William had regularly liberated enough to deposit a substantial amount in a merchant bank, where neither his false name nor the absence of a credible background raised any eyebrows. They gave him a personal checkbook and a credit card in his assumed name and that was enough. He had also added surplus cash from his patio safe to this account.

He had never believed Sheldon's tale about making a film. It should have been obvious that the man was unscrupulous, with few morals. Still, liking the idea, William had decided to run with it. Sheldon's ideas had served to stretch his imagination, but his new ambitions were satisfied for the time being. Rather than the stylish hotel that had crossed his mind early in his transformation, William sought a comfortable bed and breakfast establishment with the intention of moving every few days. The little town was surrounded by some of the most beautiful countryside in Britain and he looked forward to exploring the area.

The future looked bright. He might never return to his home and overbearing parent again.

CHAPTER 12

The office was bedlam as I came in. I was going to call my sergeants together, but Barbara was already striding along the corridor when I opened the door. I held the door open and she stamped into my office...the sort of stamp that threatened something portentous.

"What's up?"

She stood with her weight on one foot, her hand on her hip. "I took a phone call meant for you earlier on. It was from Superintendent Bellamy, National Crime Agency. He said, near as I can recall, 'People, smugglers are busy, busier than usual and the NCA believes that they've found new places of entry into the country and Yorkshire is one of them.'" She paused and drew a breath.

"I see. Did he say anything more?"

"Wants you to tell the troops to be extra vigilant and look out for the smugglers so they can be taken down."

I took a breath but she forestalled me.

"He has reinforcements that you can call on at any time when—not if—you need them. Don't you think that was kind of him?"

Clearly, I was only getting the high spots in the conversation and clearly, Barbara had not liked the tone. "Okay Barbara, I get the message and I'll give it some thought. Thanks for fielding the call. More immediately, have we anything new on our friends from the bank, the bookies, and the fashion store, yet?"

Barbara was mollified, just a little. "The only thing I heard was that we have three of them on remand and identified. Their homes have been searched and sizeable chunks of cash recovered. Some of the cash is marked, part of that original bank job.

The guy they refer to as Leonard is one William Weiss, who seems to have done a runner very shortly before we got to his house, a kettle was boiling dry on the cooker. The Met have an APB out for him but no sign so far."

"Yes, and we will soon have the one caught in Lichfield, that makes four. How about the main man?"

"Ah! The totally invisible man. None of them have any idea who he is, only the color and make of his car. Leeds Met thinks they've found it or one like it at the airport. A police locksmith opened it but it's clean, like it was brand new. If he's gone somewhere by plane, Leeds and Bradford Airport reaches most of Europe."

"Hmm..."

"Paris, Berlin, Stockholm and all the others. Could be in Bali by now. Anywhere. But of course, that might be what he wants you to believe while he's actually a couple of miles away laughing at us."

I nodded gloomily. "I suppose we've got all the alerts out to airports and seaports?"

"We have but our description is vague. The Met's artist did his best to do a reconstruction from his little gang's descriptions but they don't seem able to agree on much: how big is his nose? What shape is his chin? Even his eye color varies from blue to gray. They agree he was blond and over six feet."

I snorted. "Sure, and did the blond come out of a bottle and did he have lifts in his shoes?"

Barbara summed it up. "Easy to disappear if you don't answer to a description." She continued, warming to her subject. "Pity we can't come up with DNA traces. Of course," she paused, thinking. "He may have been careful with his own stuff—his car and so on—but less so when he was visiting."

She was obviously thinking and I stayed silent, not wishing to disturb her train of thought. She snapped her fingers.

"Boss, he spent a fair amount of time at William Weiss's home. They held their war councils there. Perhaps he got careless and left prints, DNA."

"Barbara, you're on fire! In the bathroom, on towels, tiled surfaces. We've got those items from the others while they were under arrest at the Met. Now let's see how thorough they were at Weiss's place. Stuff that's not accounted for."

Barbara called the team office to get someone to check what had come over from the Met offices.

"This Sheldon, or whatever his real name is, might be number one by name and nature, but the old proverb is still true: you can't put an old head on young shoulders." She paused, thinking again. "But suppose he's not young?"

"The others all said early twenties, twenty-five at the most."

"Yeah. I remember a film with...who was it? Drew Barrymore. She played a twenty-five year-old copy editor who wants to be a reporter. She re-enrolls in high school to get a story scoop."

"The idea's sound. Suppose Sheldon is a baby face, much older than he looks—"

"More mature—"

"Had several jobs—"

"I wouldn't be surprised if he'd had those burglary jobs planned long before he got his gang together."

There was a tentative knock on the door. A tentative knock from Alec Bell—a first! I gestured to him to come in.

"I didn't expect you back yet."

"Nothing to do at home. Thought I'd be better helping out here."

"I'm sure we can find something for you to do. That right, Sergeant Patterson?"

"Certainly is. Shall I come back later?"

"That would be good. Sort out an order of precedence...oh, and he could liaise with Ranjit. There was some talk of organized people smuggling gangs, right in our bailiwick."

It was not Ranjit who came up with the goods.

The phone rang, echoing round my office and I couldn't locate it until I realized it was coming from my briefcase.

"Morning."

"Morning Mr. White. It's Leroy."

"Oh, yes. I know that, Leroy. These two phones—yours and mine—only connect to each other. No one else to listen in."

"That's good, Mr. White. Remember you told me to use my ears? Wondered if that included smuggling?"

"Smuggling? Almost certainly. What sort of smuggling?"

"Well, we need to meet up. I've a man you need to know about and it's kind of difficult over the phone."

CHAPTER 13

Sadik El Safari's family now occupied the entire seventh floor of the Hotel Mir in Beirut. The top floor was his headquarters, offices, and private depository. From here, he ran his empire of procurement and smuggling: girls, hashish and drugs, diamonds, high-end weaponry. None of these was worth a damn compared with people, though. From the dross of the world, as Sadik considered them, to the super-wealthy, Sadik moved flesh at enormous profit.

Syria was, of course, at war, and the source of much of his current trade. His richest pickings came as a result of Russia's support for Bashar al-Assad and their indiscriminate bombing of the Syrian rebels. When the Russians backed out for a time, Daish and other organizations filled the butchery gap.

He provided the refugees pouring out of the country with an escape route at a price which, though high, was tailored to be just within the reach of his customers. He was considering extending his activities to France, Belgium, and the Netherlands to take customers from there to the UK.

Sadik also circulated his own rumors. He was a cousin of the Ayatollah, his roots reached back as far as the wars with the Shah of Persia and the Iranian revolution. As time moved on, he carefully edited, then replaced the original tales, implying that he was the son of a river pirate, and that his father had died when the Americans had bombed Sadam Hussein's Iraq. Whatever the truth, there was little doubt of the man's shady past.

Anyone showing interest in his history was swiftly discouraged; tongues had a habit of being removed, throats slit. There was even a story, maybe a rumor, that Sadik sold "pork" to the Christian residents of the city, thus, they fed on his victims.

Sadik got richer. Unable to trust any bank, he kept petty cash—several million dollars in eight or ten currencies—behind sturdy doors on the hotel's top floor. The hotel had been built in the sixties, a time when the Syrian and other Middle Eastern royal families were the high spenders of the world and the Syrian oil fields surpassed the production of any other in the region. The Mir Hotel, across the border, had hosted feasts and celebrations that were whispered about but never reported in detail.

Marble was the material of choice throughout the building. The ground floor was colored in rose pink; the top floor in green and black. Sadik enjoyed the opulence of the marble and the natural colors of satin woods. His own bedroom suite had been appropriated from London's Grosvenor Hotel by the simple expedient of purchasing the premises for an unheard of amount of instant cash, removing everything—paneling, carpets, furniture, bathroom fixtures—and shipping it all to Beirut. His suite now rejoiced in English burr yew veneer throughout. He'd put the Grosvenor back on the market when he was done stripping out what he wanted.

Sadik liked to imagine he had liberated the suite's decorations from the clutches of Western decadence. The idea that he was pandering to his own self-indulgent decadence never crossed his mind.

Outside, in front of the main entrance, three glittering fountains reached for the sky and played programmed games with each other. There was a substantial area of carefully manicured grass by the fountain. Looking down, he smiled at the sight of his four wives sitting on the lawn, looking after his children.

Here, Sadik was *persona grata,* as he was with the majority of states across the Middle East and North Africa. He was not quite so welcome in those countries into which he pumped refugees, or where his armament trading put lives at risk. His sales to I.S. and rebel forces around the Mediterranean bought him protection in all these places, and the resources he provided ran the gamut of military transport, women, and slaves.

Lebanon and, in particular, Beirut, offered him a small haven from where he could manage his business. By most standards, el al Safari was an evil man without conscience or principles. In fact, he did have one single principle: turn the stuff of war and dispute into money.

Sadik's expected Skype call came and for the next hour, his office door was locked. The woman he spoke to was unusual in that she was the only female on his staff. Fizzah Hammad shipped the poor and the downtrodden, the near-penniless, the sick, and the fugitive. She made the business pay by transporting them often—and in large quantities. Fizzah had a natural talent in the business and had risen quickly in the hierarchy.

Why he had taken her on was a mystery to him. It had been a hunch, a gut feeling that had worked out. He made her responsible for coordinating the transfers, even to developing her own contacts in the high-end trade, the wealthy and career-criminal fraternity. Sadik would, as always, move in and take over after Fizz had coordinated the details.

Sadik grew richer, as did Fizzah.

***

I had been back in the office barely a week, eight working days that already felt like months. The events of my enforced exclusion were fading into memory.

I re-organized the team back into squads with each one responsible for designated crimes. Barbara Patterson was still my assistant; Alec Bell was still the man to listen to the others' successes or sob-stories and to bring me up-to-date. It was a scheme which seemed to work. While I had always maintained an open-door policy, it appeared that word had got around that leaving me alone was good: don't awaken the sleeping bear. Not a strategy I liked, but it did allow me to do some catching-up.

There had also been some reaction from the Leeds Met regarding the two missing members from the gang of six. It had taken some digging by my guys, a fact that surprised me. I had thought that Superintendent Holly, at least, would have been blowing his own trumpet.

The information came from an unexpected quarter. Just short of lunch, two familiar faces peered over the privacy panel in my office door. I welcomed in Sergeant Ranjit Patiala and his new boss—my old one—Superintendent Clive Bellamy.

"Come in, for goodness sake; don't stand on ceremony."

"We'll come in just for a moment," Bellamy said, "long enough to invite you to lunch."

This was something new. In all the time we had both worked in these offices, Clive Bellamy had never invited me to lunch. I was a little taken aback.

"As long as we can keep it to an hour, Clive, or thereabouts. I have a meeting with the Chief at two-thirty." I didn't like untruths but—a time and place for everything.

"Whitelock's sound okay?" asked Clive, all geniality and bonhomie. "We can manage that if we get off now."

Had they done away with the real Clive Bellamy and recruited a look-alike?

"Great. I'll just let Barbara know on the way out."

***

Whitelock's is a three-hundred-year-old ale-house with a wooden bar and stained-glass windows. They serve traditional English meals, heavy on the beef and mutton, and a stock of well-kept beers and lagers. It was originally called the Turk's Head and is still situated in the Turk's Head Yard.

Clive ordered and I opted for two Scotch Eggs, a welcome change from the usual cheese and crackers I ate at lunchtimes. I turned down the offer of a lager and asked for fresh orange juice. I wanted to keep a clear head for our lunch.

Bellamy started talking as soon as we chose a booth and sat down. "People smuggling, Stewart. It's going on wholesale in your area as well as conveniently placed coves along the northeast coast. Anywhere a boat can get in and disembark a load of people."

"I've heard a few tales." I wasn't going to bring up my approaching meeting with Leroy Richards on the same subject. "But why has it moved up here? Do we have any ideas?"

Clive shrugged. "The Channel Tunnel is getting harder for them to get through with us contributing towards the French customs costs and building more and higher fences, other places in the south are more watchful than they used to be."

I shook my head in disbelief. "I'm obviously out-of-date. I thought we'd resolved most of this a few months ago when we accepted thousands of refugees."

"The cheeky beggars are using rubber dinghy tactics across the English Channel now. What next I wonder?"

Ranjit laughed. "Those that are already here, and I include myself among them, are a beacon to the ones who still want to come. Africa, as well as the Middle East, is an inexhaustible source of such unfortunates; whatever it costs them, they think it is better than staying where they are. I also see how the UK is simply not large enough to provide homes and work for so many."

I frowned. "I'm not totally convinced, Ranjit, but surely this is a Border Control matter. Not ours?"

Clive smiled and raised his eyebrows. "You're right, Stewart. But they can't cope with the numbers of refugees. And it's not as if we're being asked to stop the influx. No, our problem is far worse. When they started coming, they were just content to get here, find work, or accept benefits. Those that are coming now have seen fighting and that is going to affect the way they think. They won't be satisfied with living in tents and existing on subsistence-level handouts. They're going to do what they're used to in Syria and Libya, in Iraq and so on; they're going to try and take it."

I looked at Clive with mouth open, incredulous. He sounded like he was quoting headlines from the tabloid press, the papers with the red mastheads.

"I can't believe this, Clive."

"All true, Stewart. There are gangs coming here and setting up operations anywhere and everywhere they can find premises. Last week, it was Norfolk and camps going up all around King's Lynn. Local police can't cope: sheep and cows stolen, butchered, and roasted over open fires. Not just meat is getting stolen, either; vegetables and stuff to feed livestock is going missing, too."

Clive took another deep breath and tapped the table in time to his words. "The Territorial Army have been posted but the problems are in rural areas. Our guys can't cope with people who just melt into the landscape."

"I guess it's the problems these people are fleeing from that need to be addressed."

Ranjit was grim-faced. "Those problems are too large, sir. It would take twenty years to make any difference. The Syrian President murdering his own people, the Russians making things worse. I'm afraid Daish killing is something we'll be seeing for the long haul. As the Super says, these incoming refugees may be bringing their own weapons and, if so, then they'll simply take what they want."

I said quite forcibly, "This is not a police matter. We're not a military force. What are we expected to do?"

Clive smiled and gently shook his head as though he was admonishing a child. It did nothing to improve my opinion of my former boss.

"You're right, of course, Stewart, but that doesn't alter the fact that they are still coming. Sure, it's a matter for government, but the crimes they'll be committing—that they have already committed—are a police matter. You are concerned with organized crime and believe me, we have organized crime."

His voice was a little firmer and I sensed he had got off his hobby horse and was now dealing with hard facts. "We've identified a group near Immingham. They have several transports available, both private and commercial, with annual passes for the Humber Bridge."

I considered what I knew. The Humber Bridge levied tolls. Vehicles with a pass did not need to make a stop, so a run from, say Immingham, north to Hull and back again was all but invisible unless the authorities had registration numbers. There was no way to tell what was being transported, no information as to where from or where to. Illegal immigrants, large trucks, containers…I was looking down a narrowing pathway; I needed to see the bigger picture. Drugs?

Ranjit interrupted my thoughts. "We have our men and women out in force but they are well-organized. Too well-organized. Someone is feeding them information and we need to find out who it is. Now, you have two teams working for you and all we ask you to do is get them to keep their ears open and their eyes...skinned? Is that the word?"

I nodded and said, "Information is the key—ours as well as theirs."

I spent an hour researching what Clive Bellamy had talked about and came up with news concerning forty-two illegal immigrants who had managed to enter the UK and stay here. Most had regular jobs. There was also the Government admission that perhaps forty thousand immigrants were in the UK—and no one knew where they were.

Even forty thousand and forty-two immigrants did not sound like the major law-and-order breakdown that Bellamy had forecast, but perhaps I was biased. I decided to talk with two senior uniform Police Inspectors I had known in the Midlands, who were now located in East Anglia.

"Cattle rustling? News to me," said one. "Roasting carcases on open fires in the fields? Ah, yes. *The Mirror* reported a couple of dozen chickens stolen from a frozen food factory and suggested it was connected with a campfire that had got out of hand."

My other call was to Norwich.

"Oh, hell. That holiday cruiser incident on the Broads? Three families larking about; they managed to capsize the bloody boat. Illegal immigrants? They were West Indian; the families had been here since 1965, where does your guy get his facts from?"

I suggested it might be a newspaper.

"Could have been. *The Norfolk Gazette* suggested they should have been deported."

CHAPTER 14

A week ago, Leroy had proposed a meeting between us and a third person unknown to me. I had been pretty busy, but finally I'd agreed to a lunch meeting at the Ferryboat Inn in Boothferry Bridge, not far from Goole.

The two of them were there well ahead of me. Leroy's companion turned out to be a homunculus of no more than five foot two, he was unshaven and seemed prematurely bald. Both had pint glasses and as I approached, they sank them in double quick time—hinting, no doubt, that a second would be welcome.

I was in the mood for something citrusy, so I walked up to the bar and ordered a pint of lager shandy for myself and refills for Leroy and his guest. As the drinks came, I looked at them and nodded across the room. "Shall we take a booth over there? Bit of privacy?" Once settled, my back to a wall, I smiled at them, took a sip. "I'll let you start."

Pointing to the other, Leroy introduced us, "Simon Crossland, I know him as the Hobbit. Simon, this is Mr. White."

"The Hobbit, I can guess why." I leaned across to shake hands.

"Sure you can. But Simon and I go back quite a ways. He was a miner before that strike in the eighties. Now he might not be tall but he makes up for that in many ways."

"Like?"

"Like he's one of the sharpest guys you'll ever meet."

"Astute."

"That too, probably. Very handy to have in your corner, carries a vicious left hook."

"So what do you do now, Simon? Mining's all done with now."

Simon was about to say something but Leroy carried on answering for him. "Put himself around a lot since those days..."

"You remember them well, Leroy?"

"Now, Mr. White, no need for that. Simon's earned himself a living in many ways. Mostly legal though I think he'll agree that there've been one or two jobs," he thought for a moment, "...a little on the edge, shall we say."

"Leroy, I'm not interested in Mr. Crossland's possible misdemeanors, I'm sure we all have a few. I want to know what this is all about. Can he speak?"

Crossland gave a huge grating laugh, a bit like emptying a sack of coal. "Yeah. It's just that I've never thought of speaking to a copper before, so Leroy thought he would smooth the way."

Crossland's mouth had tightened into a straight line of compressed lips. I did my best to defuse his anger. "I can see those days on the picket lines might influence your thinking, Simon, but they're long behind us and not every copper is proud of what happened. Let's just stay on course shall we? I've a load of jobs I need to take care of and, like Leroy, I'm not old enough to have stood against any picket lines." It was my turn to scowl. "What am I here for?"

"Tell him, Si."

Simon sighed, he relaxed a little. "Don't feel right, Leroy, but you talked me into this." He turned and looked straight at me. "I work as a truck driver, Inspector. Farmer's haulage. My job is to transport container freight from the docks all over the country. Now, two weeks past, I picked one up at Immingham for delivery out beyond Pickering."

"Pickering? Where..."

"A170, Kirbymoorside. Pickering, Thornton Dale..."

"Yes. Of course."

"Yeah, short run, usually gets me back for a pint at lunchtime. Well, 'bout twenty miles from the docks, there was this banging and clattering going on and it could only be coming from my load so I pulled into a lay-by to see what was wrong—something loose, maybe. I was a bit reluctant to open the container—you hear some of the damnedest tales—but there was a hell of a din going on, shouting." Crossland licked his lips. "So I did. Open it." He paused, almost reluctant to continue.

"Well?" I prompted.

"Well. All these men come boiling out. They was all foreign, no one spoke English. Seemed that the air vent on the roof was closed, jammed. They was running out of air inside."

Shades of Clive Bellamy. I'd almost misjudged the man. "What did you do?"

"Me. What could I do? There was a truck stop a mile or so up the road so I locked the cab and lit out like my pants was on fire."

"And that's it?"

Leroy leaned across and tapped my arm. "Let him finish, Mr. White. This is where it gets real interesting."

Crossland took a deep breath and calmed down. "Right. I got to the cafe and got myself a strong pot of tea and sugared it well. Sat by a window. Still didn't know what to do. I didn't want the blame for bringing them into the country."

"Well I can see that, it's understandable." I used a calm, reasonable tone. "Your story won't go any further than this table, promise."

"Right. Well. I was keeping a low profile and a smart Merc, a class E? Anyway, this Merc pulled up near the door and a man and a woman got out and came straight in and looked around. He, the man, pointed me out. The woman came across and sat down like we was old friends!"

Crossland was getting breathless, I patted his arm. "Remember, just between us, okay?"

He nodded. "She said, 'I understand that you have just done a really good deed. Those men you saved from asphyx...asphyx'—you know what I mean."

"Asphyxiation?" I asked.

"That's it!" he said. "She talked really posh, but just a little bit foreign. 'They aren't economic migrants, you know. They were refugees from a war zone. You did them a really good turn and I want to reward you,' she said." He paused to gulp at his beer. "You know what she did then?"

I shook my head.

"Dropped a bundle of tenners on the table in front of me. I reckoned there was a couple of hundred there—maybe two, three thousand pounds in all. Didn't know what to say. She told me that if I wanted, I could earn as much as that for each job she would arrange for me."

"Each job being to pick up a container of men?"

Crossland nodded. "I was a bit pissed off, to tell the truth. I told her I couldn't 'cos the truck wasn't mine."

Crossland put on a stylish accent. "Then she said, 'We'll buy you a truck. You use it for the jobs we want you to do, and between times you get to use it for yourself.'"

He grinned a little self-consciously. "Couldn't see my way to doing that. So I said I'd have to think about it. She said the next job would be in about four weeks so I'd have time to consider. I gave her my mobile number."

Crossland put on the phony accent again. "Then she says, 'May we give you a lift back to your truck? It's quite empty now.'"

Back to his own speech again. "I took the ride back. Then I got hold of my old mate Leroy for some advice."

Now it was Leroy's turn. "I told him I could okay this with you. All this was two weeks ago and she phoned him yesterday to go and inspect the truck she's got for him."

"Yes, sorry for the delay," I said. "There's been a lot going on, but I'll reply promptly from now on." Then, turning back to Crossland, I asked if he knew of any other people shipping refugees in.

"Not here. Not through Immingham. Heard a bit about it going on in other places, Hull like, but they been using the regular ferries. Walk-on, walk-off people."

"A lot? More than, say, half a dozen?"

"Been a few times at Hull over the past year. Ten or a dozen at one go, once," he laughed.

I told him to go and see the truck with this woman and to go along with what she says. "Leroy has a phone that's just for my ears, so he'll keep me up to date. You keep your eyes and ears open, and ask some questions."

"What like?"

"Like will it always be people they want to move? Where will you have to take them? Do they buy fuel, or do you?" I stood up to go and thought of something else. "Did this woman have a name?"

"Nickname, I reckon. The guy in the car called her Fizz."

Crossland got up to visit the gents; Leroy stood up too. "Thanks for seeing Simon," he said. "Glad you take him seriously. I'll wait outside for him."

We shook hands and I also headed for the restroom. I passed what I thought was Crossland, another small man, "Cheers then, glad to have met you." He walked on, his face carefully blank. *Mistaken identity,* I grinned.

The barman grinned too and waved an admonitory finger at me. "Talking to strangers, sir? Not a good idea." It made me grin again; at least it had lightened my mood.

———

Two weeks and two days had passed since Leonard had taken off and disappeared into the countryside. Sixteen days of biking, of walking and dining in small village cafes and sleeping at out-of-the-way bed-and-breakfast establishments. He worked out the cost of living like this and calculated that he could last for about four years on the money he had access to. There was always more available from his dad of course, through banks.

He enjoyed the life but was intelligent enough to realize that it wouldn't last. He would come to miss the accustomed comfort of his own home.

That wasn't the reason for his present discomfort however; he had caught someone looking at him a bit too intensely. Although he didn't think the police had tabs on him, he intended to cycle perhaps as far as Leyburn and buy a newspaper every day. He had been in a pub a day or so ago and had heard about there always being plenty of work to be had at the many horse stables. So rather than risk staying and always looking over his shoulder, he decided the prospect of putting in a few days' physical labor would make him feel both better and safer. The further off the beaten track he could get, the better he would feel.

The infamous group he had just left was something he missed not at all. He occasionally visited a village library to check the newspapers and always looked for mention of the group, but there was nothing new to catch his attention. Two or three days after the robbery at Harold Nicholson, it was all old news and forgotten, but it would only take one lead to start it all off again.

Would it be a good idea to carry a laptop and use it to check up? There were WiFi points in most pubs nowadays. But then again, a Smartphone would work too.

Sheldon...the more he thought about Sheldon, the more he realized how he had been taken in by a stranger at the rowing club. Sure, Sheldon had promised adventure, and he had certainly not needed the money—perhaps the other four had—but it was small change to himself. His father would pay for almost anything; drop him a fifty as though it was a packet of crisps.

"Oh, bugger," he said out loud. It had been a diverting few weeks of excitement, but if he was ever exposed and caught, his reward would be a criminal record and a jail term.

After he paid Mrs. Reilly for the bed and the breakfast and said goodbye, he wondered if he should throw himself on the mercy of the law and expose the others. As he wheeled his bike out of the gate, he grinned to himself: there was nothing to expose. He knew absolutely nothing about any of them.

He wondered how it was that Sheldon had never been caught, despite the other five being taken into custody. That meant that all of them really knew less than nothing about the guy. Despite the planning that had gone into the fashion store and film jobs they had undertaken together, there had been very little money actually shared out.

What had been Sheldon's take from the fashion store job? It had never been reported; it might have been a big round zero.

Alan strode purposefully into the foyer of the Caleta Palace Hotel in Gibraltar. He crossed the polished marble floor to the reception desk. "The key to room twenty-three, please."

Ignoring the elevator, he climbed the stairs to the first floor thinking back over the quick shopping foray he'd made along Main Street. On his visit to a ready-to-wear outfitter, he had acquired new slacks, two shirts and a pair of Italian shoes. Checking his watch, he reckoned on a half hour's grace before she arrived. He took another shower. It had scarcely been ninety minutes since his last one, but it was hot and humid and Alan liked things as near perfect as he could arrange them.

He pulled on his new clothes and checked his appearance in the mirror. The off-white pants worked well with the black, tooled leather shoes with snakeskin panels. The heels—somewhat Cuban—added an extra inch to his height. The pale blue faux-silk shirt completed his ensemble and after carefully combing his newly-colored hair, he felt ready.

Alan was on the balcony, just out of reach of the sun when he heard the clatter of heels on the stone floor of the room. He stepped back inside and lifted the ice-encrusted bottle of champagne and the tastefully discreet bottle of expensive merlot in the other. He smiled, eyebrows raised in query.

"The merlot, please, dear, it is so nice that you remember my tastes. Am I late?" She pulled the cuff back on his left wrist and looked at his watch. "No, I don't think so. Oh! A Patek Philipe now," she said, tapping the watch. "And I do like the trouble you have gone to with your outfit." She tapped the Champagne bottle as she passed the ice bucket. "That might be refreshing later." Her English was accented, but perfect.

Alan mentally tipped his hat to the designer of her ensemble; everything in a matching peach color. Fizz came slowly towards him as he poured the dark wine into glasses, he drank in the view. She embraced him and his hands, holding him in such a way that his hands and the glasses were effectively tied.

He used a trick he had learned to avoid bodily reactions at inappropriate times. He imagined himself back on the balcony watching the stream of passers-by. Thus his material body remained still and perfectly under control.

"Fizzah." He breathed the word into her ear and drawing a breath, smelt her perfume. "My God, woman. I have missed you. These separations are just too long."

Fizzah took her time in kissing his lips, his neck, and his chest then raised her face to breathe agreement into his ear. "I know. But we agreed on the rules long ago. Our objectives must come first; all else, later." She pressed herself against him and her musk grew thick about him. "Thank the Fates we agreed to this. I would have gone mad otherwise."

Alan knew she meant their occasional meetings. He nodded and eased himself far enough away to offer her one of the glasses. They sat on either side of the small dining table, neither wanting to spoil what was to come.

There were also matters to discuss.

Looking her straight in the eyes, he spoke carefully. "Well, Fizz, I've raised my half-million sterling, and there's enough to spare to make this little break from business a really memorable one."

White teeth and black eyes, Fizzah looked good enough to eat, but she remained forthright. "You and your body are quite enough for the moment. But I suppose you want to know how I did?"

She waited until Alan's lips curved into a smile.

"I raised my share, and with a bonus, too. I've deposited a million sterling in the HSBC here in Gibraltar less than half an hour ago."

"Great—"

She held her hand up. "It's in your name, in the numbered account you gave me, so you can do whatever it is you're planning. Tell me about it again so I understand, and then we can test the bed springs."

Later, when Alan had fallen asleep, Fizzah sat leaning against her pillow, watching the steady rise and fall of his chest. He was definitely an energetic lover, and the skills in which she chose to initiate him merely added sweetness to the banquet.

She sighed. At least, achieving her aims was a pleasure with Alan. Unlike the grasping and avaricious Sadik, the younger man mixed his ambitions and inclinations carefully.

Their first meeting had been organized by Sadik to finalize details of the agreements he had put in place with Alan's father. Those plans had largely stalled when the older man had been jailed by the British. Still, even in British jails, limited control of a prisoner's organizations could be continued once the right palms had been greased, but some sort of face-to-face negotiation between Sadik and Alan's father was still called for. Thus contact between Fizzah and Alan was arranged, and plans were made to break the prisoner out of jail.

Of course, money would be needed—and Sadik guarded his own money very carefully. A joint fund was a necessity for third party payments, equipment, and other, unforeseen expenses. They had agreed on a million, half of that sum from each party.

Fizzah had no qualms about investing in this venture from her own growing account; she stood to gain profits far exceeding that once the jailbreak had succeeded and the partnership between all four of the players was complete.

And, of course, there were other compensations to be enjoyed in the meanwhile. Fizz looked at the sleeping Alan and her thoughts turned once more to sex. She sighed again. That was one of her minor problems—once started, she could never get enough.

As for Sadik, so long as he had no inkling of her own ambitions, she was safe. She dismissed him from her thoughts.

CHAPTER 15

I still enjoyed checking my mail before the troops arrived in the morning. Much of it was petty officialdom but sometimes I could imagine that a brown paper envelope might contain something special. And this particular morning, my imagining was justified. I hadn't received an engraved invitation to a sumptuous dinner or a map showing the whereabouts of Captain Kidd's treasure, but the notice that my Chief Inspector rank had been confirmed. I was no longer an acting D.C.I. but a real, official one.

The confirmation had come through faster than usual. I wondered if my recent suspension and reinstatement had had a hand in this—perhaps an apology for my treatment. Possible, but something I might never know.

There was one other thing: an internal memo from the Chief Constable, and this meant a gathering of my teams. I summoned them to the conference room. There was much scratching of heads and quizzical glances from those tall enough to see over the privacy screen across the corridor window. I chuckled to myself; it was only to be expected. Once they were all settled, I started straight in.

"Don't expect me to make a practice of this; I know how much it interferes with your work, how you can never make the time up and all that sort of stuff. So, this is a one-off."

I waved Vance's memo in the air. "The Chief has ordered that we give help, as and when, to the Border Agency, Customs and Immigration, the Territorial Army..."

I heard someone say "For God's sake..."

"Well, yes, I tend to agree. But the Serious Organized Crime Agency...sorry, someone said something?"

"Um, we haven't been SOCA since last year," Barbara said and went red in the face.

"Is that what I said? You're right of course. The National Crime Agency—as of 2013—has always been known to give help to our less fortunate colleagues and this time it's about the unprecedented numbers of immigrants flooding into the country illegally. I know you're wondering, what's that got to do with us?

"It seems that the Euro Tunnel is no longer the path of choice into the UK. These unfortunates are coming in by ferry and by goods containers—again, not our immediate concern but what they get up to when they're here is."

I checked to see they were listening and continued. "I've been told that some are joining up with organized crime gangs and even forming new groups. So, no longer content with living off the public purse, they're getting involved in thievery and mayhem."

The expressions of utter amazement on my officer's faces made me really feel for them.

"Again, I'm told that carrying and using guns, indiscriminate killing and maiming are becoming second nature. This comes straight from the horse's mouth and it seems that our superiors are taking all this quite seriously. We have to prepare for the worst."

I took a drink of water and carefully replaced the glass.

"Now, I must emphasize, we cannot give up on our normal everyday work. What we can do is to keep our eyes peeled, listen to what your snouts tell you... where are these gangs, how big are they, what are they doing?"

A voice from the floor broke in with the first question. "Where are these people coming from, sir? If we knew that, it might help us concentrate our inquiries."

"Good question. Not a good answer though. Eastern Europe, Syria, Libya, Ethiopia, Som...I'm afraid I don't know."

"Check the red top newspapers," someone said. "They'll know."

Apart from raising my eyebrows, I ignored the remark. "Anything of interest that you hear, report it to your sergeants. This isn't just our area, it's country-wide. In fact, it's global."

"Who's concentrating on the docks?" This was from Barbara Patterson.

"That's not NCA business. Our job is to keep tabs on what's going on in our cities and countryside. I'd suggest calling on estate agencies handling commercial properties. New gangs are going to need new places to meet, new places to stock material."

A hand went up. "Heard that a guy opened a shop behind Welbourn Street in Bradford, last week. His stock is East European, they say. That the sort of thing?"

"Sounds pretty harmless but log it, all the same. But check whatever you can, passports, invoices and so on."

Ten minutes later, I wound it up.

"Who was that mentioning the red top papers?" I asked Barbara, afterwards.

"Bob Paxman. Thought the idea was a bit funny."

"I used to but I'm slowly—very slowly—being convinced. Not by the Daily Express but by bits and pieces I've been hearing.

Shelly rang just before I left the office. "Like to meet up this weekend?"

"Sounds nice, sounds very nice. How do you fancy a meal at Salvo's?"

"That's, um, where?"

"Headingley."

"How about the Aagrah in Garforth?"

"Okay. You like Kashmiri better than Italian?"

"Not necessarily, but it's nearer your place."

"Ah. Great." The future looked back over its shoulder and smiled at me.

Dad, bless him, had a meal cooking when Pip scampered through the hatch on my return. "I know what that is," I said as I opened the door.

"Well some of it you will," he replied.

"Steak and onions. Mum's favorite."

"Steak and onions with bacon if you don't mind. Mum would never let us eat it any other way. She used to say, 'Get it down you it'll put hairs on your chest.'"

I grunted.

"Had a good day?"

I grimaced then gave the old feller a hug before collapsing into the easy chair with dog on my lap. "One of those it's best to forget, I think. Too busy to think properly and too many worrying things going on."

Dad served the steak up, brought a baking tray of roast potato wedges to the table and two sides of veg. "There. King's food."

"So, how's Margaret? Haven't seen much of her lately."

His expression turned serious. "At her sister's place. She's not well—the sister, not Margaret. No doubt she'll ring when she's coming back."

We got seated at the table and an unusually long silence reigned, punctuated only by the sounds of mastication. Eventually, Dad swallowed and spoke. "I didn't want to mention it before, but you seem pretty detached since you went back to work?"

He had framed it as a question so I gave it some thought before I answered. "Things have changed just lately, since my suspension and other things. This week, even my day-to-day job has changed."

Dad frowned. "How do you mean?"

I drew a deep breath. "In the past, it's usually been a case of one or two bad guys and, by and large, it didn't take us all that long to find out who they were and then it was just leg work to catch them."

"Seems right, so what's changed?"

"Well, for starters, even after discovering most of the buggers who got me suspended—leaving my DNA at crime scenes, we still don't know why. I know I'm not in charge of that investigation but I can't think of any reason why anyone would want to do that."

Dad clattered the plates together. "Maybe someone paid them to do it. Maybe they got told to do it."

It was a thought and I was still considering it when he continued.

"Look, all I know is this: life's too bloody short to be unhappy in your job. If that's what it's doing to you, it's time to pack it in. We can find you something to do with a lot less stress."

I sighed and grinned at him. "You're a wise man, and I'll certainly take your ideas on board but actually, the main reason for unease is that the job itself is changing. We're under orders to search out immigrant gangs that Bellamy says are landing in Yorkshire."

"Bloody Bellamy. I remember that name, smarmy beggar."

"Maybe, but he tells me these people are coming by the hundred, by the thousand. They're coming here from war zones, fully armed, ready to create mayhem. If that's true, our armed units may not be able to cope. But whatever—it's not the job I want to do."

Dad sort of backed into his chair, hands shaking. I wondered if I should have told him as much as I had. "You know Bellamy better than I do," he said at last, "but from what you've said, it sounds as though he's doing his best to make a mountain out of a molehill. He's building his own way up the food chain."

An old man whose ideas of policing never got beyond "Dixon of Dock Green" perhaps, but his words made sense.

"You'll call in the bloody reinforcements at the first sign of that sort of trouble. Promise me?"

"Promise, Dad. And...and you've made me feel a lot better."

But I would follow it up and check.

———

Alan flew back into Luton with Easy Jet. To all intents and purposes, he had been on a holiday break—just another precaution. He dozed all the way back, thinking slow, disjointed thoughts about the last few days, about Fizzah. His dad hadn't raised stupid kids; asking him to plant White's DNA had needed no explanation. Likewise, he knew that Fizz was nobody's fool. Half the time he had pretended to be asleep he would catch her looking at him in the same thoughtful way he thought of her now. He knew that Sadik took up one half of her plans, the other half was pure Fizz. What those plans were was anybody's guess. Alan certainly could not fathom them; she gave little away even when she was scheming. And she was insatiable in bed; it would be a wonder if his genitalia didn't ache for a week.

All of it had been worthwhile, of course. That Fizzah should contribute a million to his working fund was pretty wonderful; now he could really begin to put his own plans into action. He had already sounded out the line foreman for the main rail tunnel and a little bribing went a long way. Drilling for the tunnel was running on time and the foreman would be keeping him up to date with progress. He'd need a small workforce of about six when he started his own drilling. He now had money to buy the diamond drill heads he required to cut his own path. He could have tried to hire them but that would mean form filling and leaving a paper trail, which he always tried to avoid.

The next thing on the agenda was a place to store them until the time was right. Once it was all in place, he could give Fizzah and her paymasters what they wanted and, hopefully, his father would be free and clear to join him somewhere British police would not be welcome. Sadik, Fizzah's boss in their present enterprise, intended to drastically expand his share in the world's drug trafficking, as drugs were easier and cheaper to move than people. Alan's father was key to a sizeable portion of the UK market. The profit margin for Alan's dad might drop a little, but the volumes would rise and he, safe in some off-shore base, would remain the main distributor, taking over the territory of lesser suppliers. One thing he did know about Sadik was that he had a huge workforce. If ten percent of them were as good as Fizzah, the future could be rosy.

Once he arrived back in the UK, he did something he had been putting off for a while. A feeling, a portent even, forced him to call his sister Mel.

"Hello, Mel dear." Al had a mental image of probably one of the rarest flowers on the planet, a sibling who had shared a womb with him, she being black and he white.

"Hello, Al. To what do I owe this pleasure?"

"Oh, I don't know. Suppose I just felt I should call. What's up?"

"Nothing bro' but summat must be up wit' you. You never call at this time." Mel had slipped into bro-sis speak.

"Yeah well I'm sorry about that but I thought I should tell you summat."

"What's that, then?"

"Just wanted you to know that I love you lots and that I am going to do something soon to help our dad. He might act all big and powerful, but little birds tell me he's having heart scans and I aim to do something to help him."

"I didn't know that. What you gonna do?"

"Can't tell you that, but if it goes pear-shaped I'll probably be goin' away for a while."

"Goin' where?"

"Inside, might even end up with Dad, ha, ha. So you'll only have to make one trip to see us both. But don't worry your sweet head—I'm not planning on that happening. Must go, much to do, places to go. Catch you later."

———

Fizzah was quite accustomed to visiting Sadik's home; she had been given a key to the private elevator, something possessed by very few.

She stopped on the seventh floor to visit the women's quarters. Most of Sadik's family, except for his number one wife and children, were accommodated on this level. Perhaps not unexpectedly, it was the hottest place for rumor and gossip, and thus well worth a visit. Within five minutes she was ensconced among soft cushions, sipping from a glass of tea and eating sweetmeats. Because she came from outside of the enclave, Fizzah was a popular source of fresh gossip. Within ten minutes, she had turned the conversation to Sadik's family, his workforce, and his visitors.

On earlier visits, Fizzah had learned that Sadik had a very low opinion of women except for childbearing and providing pleasure. The few who had worked for him never lasted more than six months. By then, Fizzah had been associated with him for almost nine months and, though she imagined that she was a cut above the others, better at her work than those she had met—including most of the men—she had become used to watching her back.

Fizzah opened her case and brought out box after box of sweets: Turkish Delight, flavored with cinnamon, pistachio nuts, and almonds. These were from high-end confectioners, in varieties that she knew the women liked and unobtainable in Beirut.

"Shall I save some for your husband?" she asked.

The woman she had asked made a face. "He is in a bad mood, my sister." Her voice sank to a whisper. "One of his biggest boats has been sunk. Two thousand passengers. I hear the captain had been hailed—is that the word?"

Fizzah nodded.

"The captain wouldn't stop for the British gunship that was looking for people smugglers."

Fizz opened her eyes wide, an invitation to confidences. "What happened then?"

Her informant's voice sank even lower. "He tried to run for Turkish waters, I hear. The ship fired its cannons and put a hole in my Lord's boat."

"Were many drowned?"

"None, as far as we heard but the boat now rests on the bottom of the sea with all those others."

Forewarned, Fizz took the elevator up to the top floor. Sadik met her as she crossed to his office. His face spoke volumes. "Faisal has just cost me hundreds of thousands of dollars—and that's not counting the income I'm going to lose without the Caliph."

Fizzah tutted loudly. "You have him here?"

"No. He ran away, wise man. If I ever get hold of him he's a dead one and he knows it."

"His brother keeps a tea-house in Istanbul. Perhaps he's gone there or, if not, his brother will probably know where he is. Then you can kill him."

Sadik's black eyes took on the color of a thunderstorm. "He is not there, I've checked already and his brother doesn't know where he is."

Fizzah did not ask what had caused the loss or why the Caliph was out of commission. Instead, she blinked her eyelashes at him and her lips half-smiled. "You want me to fix it? You know that I can."

It was as if Sadik had put on a new face. His manner changed on the spot and he gestured to his office. "Wait for me in there. Five minutes, no more."

Fizz spent the time looking out of the wide window at what her employer called his view. Immediately below was a busy street, the Rafiq El Harari Avenue. Directly across was a distant view of the sea with a long line of beach. Closer, the road ran thick with bumper-to-bumper traffic, horns blaring, exhaust fumes turning the air hazy. At least above, the sky was blue and covered in fluffy white clouds. The whole was like a picture in a tourist brochure; yet it left much to be desired. She compared it with her memory of the vista outside the Caleta Palace she had so recently left: the beautiful blue sea, the fine sandy beach. She knew which she preferred.

Sadik returned and closed the door carefully. He bustled across to his chair behind the long rosewood desk. "Bring him to me."

"Very well, as you wish—but you know he was only following your example by filling the carrier to its maximum to maximize your profits—as well as his own, of course."

"I know that; that is not what I blame him for. He decided to run from the British gunship rather than spending a year or two in prison. By choosing to do that, he sent my ship to the bottom. My property!"

Fizz shrugged.

"Not only that, but it could have cost two thousand lives and that would have cost me far more...my reputation. No one would have wanted to use my boats, and even more importantly, I would have lost face."

Again, the woman shrugged and made a moue.

"Go. Bring him back, whole or in pieces."

CHAPTER 16

The elevator was just moving out of sight as I walked in the door. I used the stairs, two at a time for the first two floors, more moderately for the third. I snuck quietly into my office and switched the kettle on. I filled the French press, counted to sixty and poured my first cup just as there was a knock on my door. I expected it to be Barbara or Alec at this time of day but no, it was Superintendent Holly.

"Come in, sir. A little unexpected but coffee's just made. Take a seat?" I pointed to the chair on the other side of the desk.

Holly nodded, walked to the chair by the window, and put a slim leather case on the windowsill. He spoke with his back to me. "Nice view you have, D.C.I. White, much better than mine. Still, your chief picked this location for himself, I heard."

"I wouldn't know about that, sir."

"No, I suppose not. Us Metropolitan bods—bodies—got told where and what we were going to get. That was it."

"Hmm. Before I arrived."

I didn't like his tone or where this seemed to be heading. I didn't care to have jealousy aimed at me. I tried to change the subject. "Finished the 'Gang of Six' investigations, sir?"

He stared back at me from eyes that seemed to have sunk back into his skull. "It's what I've come to see you about. Sort of a courtesy call, you might say."

I put a couple of sugar cubes in the saucer and carried his coffee over before I sat down myself.

"Thanks," Holly said. "As you know, we have four of the six in custody. They've all been charged with armed robbery and several lesser offencees for now." He waved his teaspoon, disparaging the "lesser" offences.

"Questioning has really only led us to the conclusion that they were all duped. The man they knew as Sheldon was responsible for everything, the choice of targets, the planning of the robberies. They're young and he convinced them all that they were shooting a film, some sort of 'Robin Hood' adventure with the bigger part of the profits being saved for charity."

I guess my mouth fell open at this point.

"True, Chief Inspector. They've all confirmed these facts independently."

The Super picked up the leather case and extracted a cardboard file with some pages inside. "Identikit pictures of Sheldon and Leonard, one of each of the offenders."

I leafed quickly through them. "But, these all..."

"You're going to tell me that all the images of the one we know as Sheldon are different."

I nodded.

"Well spotted. Quick. It's as if not one of them saw him in the same way. The written descriptions—also in there—depict him as long-chinned in one case, fat-cheeked in another, and high-cheeked and jowled in still another. Take your pick. They're even uncertain as to eye color: brown, piercing blue, or hazel. About all they could agree on was his height: about six feet."

"Weird."

"Unlike Leonard's details, which are all much the same."

"Did anyone know where he lived?"

"Absolutely. Roundhay, Horsforth, Meanwood and York Road. About as far apart as you can manage and still be within the city."

"Fingerprints?"

"See what you're thinking, D.C.I., but looks like he didn't have any."

"But..."

"But that's stupid. You hear of people burning them off with acid or domestic bleach. Not many people are prepared to do that, though. We found six sets of prints at that bank job, remember? One of them was yours."

"Well, I'll use sandpaper next time."

Holly grinned, just a little.

"Your prints were quite interesting, what you'd expect if someone had secured them and then transplanted them onto the window glass where they'd entered. And the DNA belonging to your friend Leroy Richards is most unusual."

"My friend?"

He leaned forward confidentially. "I know Richards is your snout."

"Ah!"

"Ah, indeed. We did get a half-hearted explanation from three of the four about why you two were targeted. Sheldon boasted to two of them that he was dropping you in deep shit. One of them suggested much the same about

Richards, although they didn't know who you two were, why you were being targeted, or what we had found."

"The buggers. There was DNA too. A smear of blood, I think," I said.

"There was...how did you know about that?"

"A little bird told me. But you were saying?"

"What do you think caused this clever chap to hate you and Richards in equal measure? Think of any connection you may have had with someone capable of this. Someone in your past, someone clever, someone who plans things meticulously."

Before I could answer Superintendent Holly got up. "Well, that's about it, D.C.I. You'll get a copy of my complete report in the fullness of time. I'll bid you good day." He finished the coffee in one gulp and left even faster than he had arrived.

———

I went along to the team office and poked my head around the door, looking for Barbara Patterson. She was not in evidence, but Alec Bell spotted me and followed me back to my office. He stood in the doorway and gave me a leaf from his notebook with a telephone number.

"Man called wanting to speak to you but you were busy, seemed important? Didn't want to speak to me at all but I convinced him that I was your right hand, and without me—well..."

I ignored the question mark dangling off the end of Alec's sentence and took the paper. "You are so right, Sergeant Bell. What did he say?"

"Said his name was Crossland and to tell you that the woman has been in touch about the rig, he's seen it, and it's all right. He's got a date for the first pickup. That's his cell number, but he won't be on it 'til after seven tonight."

"Got it. Thanks."

Chief Superintendent Flowers chose that moment to ease himself past Alec Bell and into the room. Everything all right?" he asked.

"Sure, can you give me just one minute?"

He nodded affably and sat in the chair in front of my desk, no silly chit-chat about the view. The office had once been his.

I turned to Alec. "Okay, Sergeant, I'll get in touch after seven as requested, not sure what to say to him yet. Where's Sergeant Patterson?"

"Checking a lead on one of those cash converters, off Meadow Lane, huge place, upper floors seem to have been let. Might be one of those we've been told to look out for, gangs and so on."

"Okay, Sergeant Bell, I'll catch you later."

I told Joe Flowers about Simon Crossland, his message, and Crossland's contact with the people smuggling organization. "Could be our first chance to nip this illegal immigrant smuggling in the bud."

Joe Flowers took the seat across from me. "Nip it in the bud, eh? If only it were that simple, Stewart. But Simon Crossland? Not Simon Loiner Crossland by any chance? Three feet tall and thinks he's about seven? "

"Could well be. You know him?"

"I might do if it's the same one. Ex-miner. Crossed paths with him back in the eighties at the 'Big K' pit, at Kellingly. Ye gods, I was a part of the thin blue line in those days, trying to get trucks into the pit." Flowers shook his head at the memories. "I was a weedy little sergeant, Stewart, and right next to me was a big special sergeant, a Geordie. Crossland was out in front and whipped a punch which must have started somewhere near his knees and connected with our chap's chin, way above the miner's head."

"Certainly sounds like the Crossland I know. Still bitter about those times.

"The boy was so surprised when his punch went home that I took advantage and slipped the cuffs on him." He leaned forward and said, "Think you might be getting a break with this new stuff, this refugee stuff?"

"Well, I'll know better tomorrow," I replied as I poured coffee for us both from my ever-ready press. "By the way, did you get a visit from Holly of the Met? He came to see me and I definitely got the impression that he disliked me."

"He doesn't like a lot of people, actually. In your case, though, I'd say it's not you but where you come from."

I must have looked a bit blank.

"Brummies. I think he had a run-in with some when he was in the Royal Air Force. I think his PTI was a Brummie and he hated Yorkies."

"But I'm not a Brummie; I don't come from Birmingham, not even from the same county."

"No, I know that, you know that. But people go by accents. Up here, they don't like Cockneys, to people from the North; anyone's a Cockney if they're from the South. You've got a similar twang to a home-grown, dyed-in-the-wool Brummie. Not as pronounced, but it's there"

"Hmm." I never tried to hide my roots, but neither did I brag about them.

"You're just being thin-skinned and he's not all bad. He did come to see me. Called you a bloody good copper."

Aldo considered visiting his dad, but then dismissed it; it put his plans at too much of a risk.

No, he told himself. *Better to call him as usual to tell him about the success that planting the DNA had brought about.*

His other plans to break his dad out of jail were best kept a secret until much closer to the date. He wondered whether to confide in his sister.

CHAPTER 17

I phoned Dad before I left the office and we agreed that I should bring an Indian carry-out meal home with me. It really wasn't fair that he prepare dinner every night.

I tapped the horn as I brought the car into the driveway. Dad came up from his bungalow as I was sharing out the pilau rice to go with the rogan-josh. I must say it was good that he'd started to like the same spicy food as I did. I'm sure Shelly's jerked chicken had helped.

"Better day today?" he asked after we'd started.

"Busy, but I think we're moving in the right direction. Police work's not like painting houses. Some days not much is achieved without a necessary lead. And that reminds me, too. Got to phone someone later."

"Aha. A snitch or a snout."

"Something like that. Remember Leroy Richards?"

"Remember you fuming about him."

"He's a reformed character. This one's a friend of his, started giving me information."

"Hope it's good stuff, then, after the way you've been feeling lately."

I was just finishing off the last bit of lime pickle on a poppadom when the front doorbell rang. It was a bit of a surprise to find Barbara Patterson on my doorstep. I went into the kitchen to tell Dad that I had a visitor from work.

Pip scrambled out of his basket to say hello and a moment later, Dad put his head round the door and followed suit. "I put some coffee on," he said.

"Bless you, kind sir," she said.

"I'm guessing this isn't a social call and that you've not had anything to eat yet. Will a biscuit or three help?"

"No, thanks. I don't eat before nine, most nights."

When the percolator had stopped bubbling I brought a tray in with the coffee jug and mugs and a plate of mixed cookies.

I sat back with a mug and watched as she selected a chocolate biscuit. When she ate that and took another, I knew my instincts had been correct.

"So, what is worth chugging all the way out here for, Barbara?"

She lifted her mug. "This, for starters. What is it?"

"Columbian. Fair Trade. No big deal."

She took a ginger biscuit and said, "I went to a building near Leeds Bridge but it was a dead end. The guys who owned it were extending their business into market trading. Needed more stock, which was why they'd gone for the big premises in the first place."

"Fair enough. Pity you wasted your time."

"Well, not quite. I didn't bother going back to the office, tell the truth. I was going to head home early but I thought I'd go have a look at Weiss's house on the reservoir. The one we know as Leonard, remember?"

I did and nodded.

"I thought I'd compare notes with the Met. They only managed to isolate five sets of prints so I started looking again. There was lot of powder left around, scattered, so I knew every place not to look."

"I know you're bursting to tell me, Barbara. What did you find?"

"No, you have to listen to me. The floor was mixed slate and natural wood planks. There were marks where the couch had been, before it had been moved in front of the TV. Now, the leather upholstery had been dusted but I wondered how the thing had been moved. No drag marks on the floor, must have been lifted."

"You're a damn sight more observant than those dickheads at the Met, aren't you?"

Barbara smiled sweetly at me. "I tipped it up and on the base, just where the leather ends and the fabric begins, there were three prints that I could see with the naked eye when I breathed on them. I called our new boy in—Eddie—and told him what I wanted."

"You wanted them done yesterday, I presume?"

"Absolutely, and he did better than that. Did us proud, in fact. Eddie estimated that the prints were relatively recent because of the lack of dust. There was WiFi signal at the house so he got through to our records department. They're not on our database, but of course we need to test the DNA and that's why I'm here."

Now that knocked me back. "Care to elucidate?"

"I don't have the clout to wake the lab and get the work done overnight."

"And nor do I, Barbara. However..."

Superintendent Holly was not pleased. In fact, I thought he was going to hang up on me. I pointed out that one of my dedicated officers had found fingerprints where the Met had failed to do so. I pointed out that only that morning, he was bewailing the fact that we had no lead on Sheldon.

He agreed, reluctantly. Yes, my Sergeant would drop it off at the Elland Road reception within forty-five minutes. And, yes, he would light a fire under the necessary backside.

I grinned at Barbara. "Now that was very satisfying. But remember, DNA grows only as fast as DNA grows. Think about results being ready in twenty-four hours."

"I'll be off then."

"Take as many biscuits as you want...and my God, what's the time?"

"Seven-forty."

"Got to make a phone call. See you tomorrow, don't hurry in, and—thanks."

I phoned Crossland and confirmed that I had got his message. "That's good work, Simon. Let me know the date, time, and the whereabouts as soon as you know. Use Leroy's phone if you want, it only connects with me. Oh, and where you're to drop the package, as it were? You'll get a suitable reward, when it's done. Very discreetly."

I went to bed, tired but happy.

Breakfast, office, lunch, mid-afternoon. A call came promising me an email which duly arrived. I called Barbara. As Eddie had said, the prints were recent or recent-ish. Like the prints themselves, the DNA was unlisted; it came back male, black.

Barbara was crushed. None of the five in custody mentioned him as being black.

"A let-down, but it's nearly home time, girl. Get off and meet your boyfriend, forget all this." I could see I'd said the wrong thing. Her face fell a mile, her cheeks turned pink.

"Haven't been seeing each other for a while, couple of weeks."

"Oh. Sorry to hear that, Barbara. Thought things were going along okay." I put my hands up. "Not prying, sorry."

"That's okay. You're going to get the story from someone sooner or later. You might as well have it firsthand."

"Only if you want to."

"Oh, well. I got into the squad room one morning and caught him bragging to two of the other men about the size of my boobies. I was right behind him and he didn't realize I was there. I reached between his legs and got hold of his package and squeezed. Hard. I asked him if he'd told them about his little failures."

I laughed. "Wow, that must have hurt. I mean the squeeze."

"I guess it dented his pride. It must be a man thing. It's all right to talk about *my* private parts but not me talking about his."

"Hey, can I give you a hug and say that you did really well?"

She nodded; I checked there was no one waiting at my door. I gave her a hug and said, "You did really well." I stepped back, checking the door again. "Really. I sympathize with you. But you will get over it, won't you?"

"I don't know. I *do* know that I shan't be apologizing."

"I should think not. Now, since you're here, can I change the subject?"

"Sure."

"I've been wondering why you haven't asked about putting in for your inspector's exams."

"Quite frankly, I don't want to. If I passed, there's probably a ninety percent chance they'd put me back in uniform, like Shelly Fearon, and I don't want that. I'm a detective and I'm happy as I am."

"Uniform might only be for a year or two then you'd be back in plain clothes."

"Thanks but no thanks. At the moment, I'm happy, don't want to change. And, actually," she blushed, "actually, I'm working for a man I respect and I know I can trust him."

It was a moment before I realized who she was talking about.

She continued, "I've got a long memory. I remember getting drunk when I had that trouble with my parents and you could easily have taken advantage and you didn't."

It was my turn to experience burning cheeks. I shooed her out of the office and took a deep breath. I remembered when she had dressed up as me and risked being killed by the raving psycho who was waiting outside for me.

She was a bloody good colleague, reliable, painstaking. A right hand and I missed her when she wasn't here, an invaluable part of my team.

Fizzah landed at Sabiha Gokeen, one of the two international airports serving Istanbul, this one on the Asian side of the Bosphorus and further from the New City. She considered Ataturk, over on the western side and closer, the riskier destination.

She remembered Faisal well and if she had gone to ground as he had done, she would have had the airports and the docks watched. It seemed unlikely that he would think that Sadik had sent her; they had known each other for quite some time, ever since she had recruited the Turk into Sadik's organization. It was even on her recommendation that he had been promoted from the smaller boats to the larger Caliph.

Faisal's problem was gambling. He gambled as though money simply floated down from heaven, and he gambled sums far bigger that he ever had in his wallet before he captained the Caliph. Taking chances had become a way of life, he filled the boat to maximum and stuck his tongue out at the gunships.

It was almost as much of a misfortune for Sadik and herself as it was for Faisal. His knowledge and navigation skills would be difficult to replace.

Fizzah passed a café where the odor of baking bread, fresh from the clay oven, made her mouth water. She almost sat down to join the other customers cutting or tearing the bread, spreading butter and honey. She checked her watch and knew there was no time to spare.

She stepped on to a bus going past Taksim Square, her destination. It would save only a few minutes but it would not do to reach the tea shop hot and perspiring. She jumped off just short of her objective and walked onward.

Fizz sat down at a small table in a corner and looked at her fellow patrons. She was surrounded by old men drinking noisily, sucking the black tea through sugar lumps clamped in discolored and broken teeth. They played dominoes or cards and discussed everything from football to the latest fashions. None of them so much as glanced at the tall, elegant woman who waited for a waiter to notice her.

At last, a waiter did stop and take her order. She also gave him a card to pass on to the owner—Faisal's brother. She could not remember the brother's name but it scarcely mattered; after today they would never see each other again.

Fizzah recognized the family likeness although he was older and fatter. For his part, the tea shop owner guessed who she was and would have preferred not to speak with her. Nevertheless, to ensure that there would be no incident on his premises, he sat and attempted to keep their conversation equable.

"Where is Faisal?" she asked. "No; don't shake your head, do not tell me you don't know. It is my life that is threatened here, you don't matter, your family does not matter. Tell me the truth and you and your business will not be affected. Lie and this place will go up in flames. Do I make this clear enough?"

The proprietor was out of his depth, shocked at being spoken to like this by a woman. Perhaps he knew that these were not ordinary circumstances and that every word she said was literal truth.

His eyebrows rose, startled. "You are the one who employed my brother; it was you who made him think he was more important than he was." A sly grin crossed his features. "I remember who you are; you are the daughter of Imran the shoemaker, who got pregnant. They pretended you had gone to college when you really went to have your unborn child taken from you, and then—"

Fizzah was beside herself with anger. Under cover of the table cloth, she reached across and seized the man's genitals, squeezing in such a way that the pain caused him to whimper rather than to scream in agony.

"Tell me where your brother is and you can still escape with your life and livelihood. Tell me lies and you and yours are lost."

In a low voice, punctuated by moans and gasps, he told her. "Where you played as children. The cave." She released him and he fell back against the chair's bamboo frame, which shattered. Those customers nearest watched in amazement as the slim young woman stood up, ignored the man's anguish and walked calmly from the shop.

The cave had been in a rock-strewn hillside some distance out of the city. But Istanbul had grown since then. The rocky hillside was now two rows of small houses which huddled against ancient walls, the half demolished memories of bygone ages. The city had known seven empires, each leaving its mark in the diverse buildings.

Fizzah could afford no delays, it was all too possible that a runner could reach Faisal before she did. She took a taxi, guiding the driver from childhood recollections to a crossroads at the foot of the small hill. At its center was the rock whose silhouette was shaped like a camel; the rock had been a part of the games they had played.

She took off her shoes and left them at the roadside, and took a LED flashlight from a pocket and a matte black .22 pistol from another. Many, if not most men, would laugh at the small weapon but there would be no laughter if they took a bullet in the head. No one she had aimed at had ever lived to laugh again. Fizzah was supremely confident of her own abilities, weekly unarmed combat training brought its own self-assurance.

Minutes later, she was at the narrow slit of the cave entrance. She moved to one side and stood, eyes closed, ears attuned while her vision adjusted. She moved straight forward, until a wall halted her. The cave was T-shaped and one arm was a dead end. Twenty-year-old memories came to the forefront and she turned left and continued on until, again, her way was blocked.

Fizz aimed the flashlight upwards and turned it on. Even knowing what to expect, she was afraid that she had it wrong. There was nothing visible. She put the flashlight and the gun away, reached upward, bent her knees and jumped. Her adult height made it considerably easier than she remembered. A ledge, invisible from below; her fingers hung onto the edge and she pulled herself over it and forward on her stomach.

There was someone here, she could feel the presence. Nevertheless, she crawled to the edge of a steep incline. With flashlight and gun in her hands, she shone the light upward so that a dim radiance filled the shadowed chamber below.

Faisal lay sprawled on a thin mattress on the floor below her. Although he seemed asleep, it was the off-putting sleep of a cobra.

"Well, Captain Faisal..."

His reaction caught her off-guard and she fell sideways, which might have saved her life. She heard what seemed like one continuous explosion but must have been some sort of automatic weapon being fired. There were ricochets and rock chips showering around her, any one of which could kill her very dead. She used the .22, firing all seven shells at where she could see Faisal in the flashes from his gun.

———

On the plane back to Beirut, she checked the photos again. This time her hands weren't shaking. She had taken shots on her phone of the dead and bloody body for Sadik's reassurance and satisfaction. Considering the pressure she had been under in those final moments, she had been remarkably consistent; Faisal's only injuries were centered on his face, now a bloody mess best hidden by darkness.

CHAPTER 18

The day had been fairly quiet and I left the office on time. I was home by five-twenty, but no sign of Pip or my dad. *What should I do about tea,* I wondered. Then I noticed the letter propped up against the coffee pot, a piece of writing paper folded in half. I switched the coffee on and sat down while I read Dad's note.

Margaret's sister was back home but her prognosis, it seemed, was not good. The doctors had told her—I didn't know whether that was Margaret or the sister—that the cancer was terminal with somewhere between two and six months to live. Margaret was understandably upset and had asked Dad if they should get married as soon as possible, her sister might appreciate it. Dad had agreed and would be over at Margaret's discussing the arrangements. Pip had gone with him because he didn't know how long he or I would be.

The note ended, "And don't forget, you're best man."

It was all a bit depressing and I was not in the mood for fancy cooking. I opened a tin of soup, put it in the microwave, and popped a baguette under the grill on low. Then, with a mug of coffee, I sat back to watch a detective series, just to see how the TV cops did it.

I was tempting fate, as soon as I tried to relax, things always happened. The phone rang, it was the special phone in my briefcase.

"Leroy here." His accent—part Jamaican, part Birmingham, part something else entirely—told me that immediately.

"And this is Stewart White, Leroy."

"Simon's been told to pick his truck up from an old factory in Hull. He has to take it to the container freight section at Immingham docks. He doesn't know the container ID. Someone's meetin' him and he has to follow the guy to the pick-up."

"Okay. And where's he going after that?"

"Don't know that either, Mr. White. He has to follow the guy again, destination unknown. A green Audi."

That was the car he had to follow, I assumed. "They're playing things very cagey, but no more than you'd expect I guess. How soon?"

"Eight o'clock. Mr. White."

"Very well, do we have a day?"

"Saturday, four days from now."

"I'll make a note of it."

"You want some more news?"

"Always welcome."

"There's a gang of East Europeans taking over most of the area around Bull Street, that's the east side of Goole."

"You mean they're buying up premises?"

"No, no. Not that at all. These places are pretty shady, you know, pretty rough. They're like some of the areas in Hull. No questions asked, no one want' to know. No one want' to end up with broken bones." Leroy paused.

"Go on," I said.

"This gang, so I hear, waltzed in an' took about twenty men away, jus' like that. Never seen again. There was friends, they come an' asked what happen. They were lucky they only ended up in Goole hospital and they wasn't there for fist or boot bruises—catch my drift?"

"I do catch your drift, Leroy," I said seriously. "Believe me, I do."

"Every street that join' Bull Street, I hear, is empty now. Even barricades here an' there. There are people what don't speak English on street corners, people you got to ask if you need to go there."

"Could do with knowing how many there are. Are they armed, and, if so, what with?"

"Hey man, you don' want much, do you? Mr. White, I done my best." Leroy's voice had risen in pitch. "I should just suppose the worst. There's lots, tooled up like they was goin' to war. That's it, Mr. White. End o' message."

I didn't want Leroy getting angry with me and I attempted some damage limitation.

"Hey, I'm sorry, Leroy. I'm grateful for what you told me. This whole thing is getting bigger than I'd bargained for, bigger than I'd imagined. I can't give anything away but this is not just Yorkshire, this is national. I don't want to put you in danger but if you do hear of crimes being committed, just let me know. You and Simon are doing a great job. Oh, and speaking of Simon, tell him to do exactly as they ask him to, keep his eyes open, say nothing. I've got his back, okay? There might be armed response types getting involved but they'll know both your names and mine. If that does happen, just let them know who you are. Right?"

I could almost see his head nodding. "Pleased you said that, Mr. White. I was kind of havin' second thoughts."

"Second th...What about?"

"About...Well, truth is, the people I sort of call friends are mainly after my money, so they ain't really friends. An' me an'...we was thinkin' of getting married, y'know? Was wond'rin' if you'd be like to be ma best man."

Leroy's grammar was going to Hell. I didn't blame him, my own speech was a bit strained. Twice in one day! "Do I know the lady?"

"Not sure, Mr. White. Maybe yes, maybe no. But don't you worry, she's nice, she's bloody beautiful. Call her Evangeline."

Oh, yes, I remembered Evangeline: the voodoo girl who played with my mind at Leroy's fake memorial ceremony.

"That's a date, Leroy. But make sure the wedding doesn't clash with my dad's. He's getting married, too."

We hung up. All this after I had arrested him and he'd been jailed on my evidence and I was still better than the friends he had! I was touched. I was almost bloody weeping.

Later, I called the contact number I had for Clive Bellamy, no reason he should be able to watch TV uninterrupted. I passed on the information that Leroy had given me. I made sure he wrote down the names of my two informants so that they would be in the orders sent to our C19 division.

"That's well done, Stewart," he said. "We'll get the buggers, eh?"

"We'd better." And I chuckled.

"Don't worry. Get back to the TV now, it's one of those cop shows, where everything always works out right."

"Ah." I said to myself as I poured the cold coffee away and started a new batch. I called Joe Flowers to give him the same information.

Alan took the tube to Euston, where the contractor's yard for Beavers Group was situated. Having phoned beforehand, he was met by the underground contracts manager: Evelyn Grant, red-nosed and in his fifties.

He came straight to the point. "I know you're a driller, your resumé is excellent but we're really not up to that point yet. However, there are a lot of materials being moved in and out and we can use you. Turn your hand to shoveling, bucket loading—manual labor I guess—and using excavation equipment until the drilling starts. Same rate of pay as you'll get when you're drilling. That suit you?"

"Absolutely." It suited Alan fine. The work would keep his body and mind active. There would be plenty of private work too: observing and measuring, pencil and paperwork at his digs until he knew the workings inside out. London's underground system was a vast array of spaces with which he would need to explore and become familiar. There would be storage spaces he could use for his own tools and materials, to be brought in when shifts were changing.

Alan had already arranged to share a room with another Beavers Group worker in Camden Town. That was short-term since the man was working another line. Some of his free time went into recording what he saw on the new tunnel. From this, he learned in advance of the strata and what each layer consisted of. It gave him warning of the clay and when he would need to start mixing his own drillings with those from the main tunnel. It all saved him days of work. He also spent a considerable amount of time on the phone to his sister and in short bursts, to his father, assuring them of his good health. Calls to his sister tended to be about what he hoped to do while, to his father, he told encouraging things but not that he was planning to get him out yet. He trusted his dad, but not enough to hope he could keep such a secret for weeks.

The money that Fizzah Hammad had placed in his bank account was earmarked, along with his own dubious earnings, for the material and equipment he needed.

"There's no date yet," he told her. "I'm waiting on some of the main workings to reach a point where I can begin my own preparations. I can give you approximate dates but you must realize that just because we're making good progress at the moment, problems may crop up, and we need to be ready at any time."

It was close, he could feel it in the atmosphere at work. Progress was good and each target passed was just a little ahead of schedule. A few days after he had started the job, his colleagues coaxed him into joining them at their local club of choice. Alan did not like the idea, he did not want to make friends with the others, he did not want them taking too much interest in him. He had practiced a mild stand-offish attitude to encourage them to keep a distance but, ironically, it may have backfired and had the opposite effect. In the event, he complained of a migraine and left early, returning to his room and intending to be in bed when his flat-mate came back.

There was a knock at the door. Reluctantly, Alan went to open it and was pleasantly surprised. Fizzah stood there, smelling of something ravishing and entered, unasked. She said little until after sex was over and he took out the plans he had drafted and outlined the problems still to resolve. His manner was positive, however; nothing outside his capabilities, nothing to cause concern. Over the past few months of knowing the woman, he had realized that Fizz admired such an attitude in a man.

"So how long do you think? We have product coming into our warehouses. We need to be able to move it on very soon."

Alan topped up her glass and nodded understandingly. He admired the woman, desired her even, but that was as far as it went. He was single-minded when it came to his own task and it certainly was his—he had never thought of it in any other way since he'd conceived the idea months and months ago. His task, his job, his responsibility.

"I can say with some certainty that it will be between two and four weeks from now, I cannot be more accurate than that." He held up a finger. "I need a drilling rig and until it's brought underground and made ready, I can't start to use it. I'm sorry, Fizzah..." He smiled. "I can move mountains but not without the drilling rig."

"Can we buy another?"

Alan's eyebrows shot up towards his hairline. "We're talking of a multi-million-pound beast, my love. Even then, it comes in pieces and has to be assembled. All we want to do is to borrow it when it's ready and the bosses are saying around the end of the month."

Fizzah twisted her mouth. "It has got to be this drill thing? Not air hammers, or something like that?"

"Pneumatic drills? Well, yes, actually. We shall be using those once the off-shoot is cut from the main tunnel. Just here, see?" Alan pointed to the hatched lines which indicated the additional tunnel. "Ten feet for storing electrical kit. I need to take it further, another thirty feet, ten meters. We'll put in a false wall to hide that extra space, which is where I begin. Straight up—well, nearly."

"No other holdups?"

Alan laughed, the tension had been building. "What's this, twenty questions? I want this job doing more than you do, there won't be a moment's delay without good reason."

Fizzah backpedaled. She realized her pushing was triggering alarms. "Sorry, my darling. My boss is chasing me, if we have to find more storage space—discreet storage space—if we have to, he will just have to face up to spending a little more money." She was not being entirely truthful. Sadik was unaware of the money she was putting into the project, as well as the extra consignments of cocaine that she was funding from all parts of the globe. Her employer might be planning to become the richest man in the world; Fizzah's plans were for her to be the richest woman.

Fizzah knew to the nearest Syrian pound how much Sadik was making from the refugees she handled, ninety percent of that money went to him, ten percent to herself. But alongside the human traffic was drug movement which paid Fizzah one hundred percent—money which Sadik had no inkling of.

She dragged Alan back to bed for the purpose of making him forget his problems. Let both men think that they were the movers and shakers. After all, that's what Sadik was best at thinking. Alan's thought processes were more obscure; she had a feeling that where her English lover was concerned, there was more than sex occupying his mind.

Chapter 19

Sunday, and I had to go into the office. My promotion had brought with it what I most feared: paperwork. The only way to cope was to spend several hours of my own time clearing the mountain that daily grew taller and taller. Everyone—my bosses, the Home Office, everyone in between—wanted to know, in triplicate, what my teams were spending the taxpayer's money on. There were also literally hundreds of copies of finalized case files to prepare, and the biggest waste of my time: progress reports.

It was fortunate that I was alone in my office. Anyone listening would have been shocked at my language. It didn't do any good, it didn't even relieve my exasperation. After three hours of effort, I was seriously considering requesting a demotion. At that point I got the shock of my life. I wasn't alone.

I nearly hit the roof when an instantly-recognizable voice interrupted my thoughts, "Hello, never expected you in today."

Palpitations had nothing on the quake that took the breath out of my lungs. "My God, Barbara..." I got my breathing under control and perched my rear on the desk. "You nearly had to call an ambulance then. I thought it was your day off, too."

"It was, but I wasn't going anywhere so I thought I'd clear some paperwork."

I remembered she had finished with Sergeant Levy and understood. "Well, same with me. Three hours and I think I've shifted the top inch off the pile."

"You could do with a secretary."

I don't know why, but her remark struck me as the funniest thing I had heard in weeks. I laughed uncontrollably. "I'm sure you're right, Barbara. But it would only add to work. Every quarter, I'd have to explain how I could afford to pay for a secretary out of my budget."

Barbara laughed. "It was only the other day I was telling you why I didn't want a promotion. That's just added another reason."

"Know exactly how you feel...my God!"

"You already said that," Barbara said.

I nodded to my open door. "Don't tell me, you've come in to catch up on paperwork too."

"Not exactly," Alec Bell said, leaning against the door frame. "D.C. Foyle gave me a call. He has a lead on William Weiss and wanted to know how much we wanted to catch him."

"That's very considerate of him."

"It would involve overtime."

"Okay. Where is he?"

"Heard of a place called Leyburn? Up in the Dales? He's been spotted mucking out at some racing stables."

"Leyburn? Doesn't ring a bell." I did some quick mental calculation. "Is Foyle handy or do we have to send someone out there?"

"He's standing outside the stables now, the horses—and Weiss—are out on a gallop. Foyle knows a bit about horses, says it helps him pick winners."

"Occasionally pick winners." Barbara broke in. "Very occasionally."

"Tell him to pick up a local P.C. and go and get Weiss soon as he's back from his exercise. Bring him back here. Tell him I'll be waiting to welcome him in."

Alec pulled out his phone to ring Foyle back and pass on my orders. After that, my paperwork efforts hit a new low. Both Barbara and Alec were hanging on to check the outcome. They were more excited than I was about the unexpected break, I think. I looked round the interview rooms, switched the extractor fans on and off, checked the lights.

Half an hour short of lunch time, I gave Alec thirty pounds and told him to get us both take-outs for lunch and bring something for Foyle and Weiss.

"And the Police Constable too, I assume. A couple of rolls, ham or cheese or something?"

"And him." I gave Alec another fiver; he was going to have me feeding the biblical five thousand at this rate. But I had no idea how long the interview would take, and I had no intention of doing it hungry. When Sergeant Bell returned, I surmised he must like Chinese fare as he brought back duck in plum sauce, sweet and sour chicken, fried rice, a bag of spring rolls, and finally, three bacon baguettes from a café.

"Well done, Alec." I used commanding officer's prerogative to choose the duck and was pleasantly surprised. I made a note of the name and address of the take-out so I could add it to my short list.

We had finished eating when Foyle and a uniformed officer came upstairs with a dejected Weiss in tow. Barbara handed out the sandwiches while Alec made tea for us all. While that was going on, I tapped Foyle's shoulder.

"Give you any problems?"

Foyle shook his head. "Not at all, might almost have been expecting it. He kept telling me bits and pieces, I discovered his dad is the boss of a big merchant bank too, there was more but I told him to save it for you. Did I do right?"

I chuckled. "Absolutely. And great work."

"Well, thanks. Wouldn't have been out there if I hadn't been one for the horses. Well, that and the fact that we had his picture pinned up on the case wall next to my desk. Doesn't seem a bad guy, though."

"Barbara, you sit in with me, will you. Feminine touches and so on, in case I miss something."

We herded the young man into interview room number two and the others went on into the observation room.

On first impressions, William Weiss seemed a pleasant-looking young man; neat and tidy as befits the son of the CEO of a large merchant bank. Weiss and robberies seemed poles apart; money would hardly be an issue. The only conclusion I could jump to was the excitement, the kicks.

"So, Mr. Weiss, enjoy robbery?"

He was a handsome youth and would probably turn a few heads if he'd not been facing several years in prison; that sort of career did little for the appearance.

Weiss frowned. "Well…it wasn't really my intention. I have to admit, though, that's how it turned out."

"You never planned to rob that bank at Horsforth?"

"Frankly, it was the furthest thing from my mind. Sheldon, our number one, asked me to take a camera and record the proceedings. My phone was pretty well top of the range, I used that."

"What sort of proceedings?"

"The action in the main office. We were in and out in six minutes, I recorded what went on and that's all I did. Nothing else."

I looked at Barbara but she was watching Weiss's face. "For goodness sake, why?"

"I—we—thought it was a rehearsal for a movie. That's what he'd told me. When I found out that the customers and staff were real, not actors, I was stunned. I confronted him, he said I was now complicit in the crime and used all that to blackmail me into participating in another job: recording the action again, nothing else. I was under strict orders not to mention it to the others."

Barbara's eyes met mine, her eyebrows rose fractionally.

"You really expect us to believe that?"

"I've no reason to lie. I have proof; I can prove what I say." He took in my skepticism and continued. "Look, your desk sergeant has my phone. I told you it was a pretty good one, it'll record thirty minutes of HD digital. Both jobs are there in their entirety. It also records sound quite well. Both those conversations that Sheldon had with me are there, including the threat of blackmail if I didn't go along with it all and shoot the video. He had no idea I had the audio on after I'd finished shooting, of course."

I nodded and cleared my throat as other queries came to mind. "This Sheldon character, what did you make of him?"

"Character is the right word. Obviously, he's very driven by something, not that he ever let slip anything about reasons for doing what he was doing. He liked to be in charge. And he liked planning things—and went into meticulous detail."

Barbara interrupted him. "Did you know where he lived?"

"I know where he told me he lived but he lied about it. Didn't really trust him, I followed him one day after a planning meeting. Parked my car a little way away and went into a news agent's and watched. He has an Alpha Romeo, he parked it outside this place he was supposed to live at and in less than sixty seconds—the time it took me to pay for a tube of mints, he was gone."

"A bit extraordinary," I said.

"I knocked at the door of the place he supposedly lived at. I asked the woman if the man with the sports car lived there and she looked at me as if I was stark raving. Didn't know anyone like I described, had never seen an Alpha Romeo in her life. I asked if there was anywhere else he might be living in this block? She told me to piss off and closed the door."

I glanced across at Barbara to see if she wanted to ask anything more. She held up her hand and finished the note she was writing.

"What color was this Alpha Romeo?"

"Red, A really dark red. It's a Guilietta."

"Get the number?"

"YG66...that's all I can recall."

"What about the girls on the team?" Weiss seemed surprised; perhaps he hadn't realized how much we knew. "Did this Sheldon have anything to do with them? Did he have a girlfriend?"

"He had nothing to do with any of the others, except as necessary for the jobs he planned. None of us knew him outside of the meetings at my home when he went through the plans he'd made.

"Hang on...there was one night, we had champagne in and I'd guess he was just short of being drunk. What did he say?" Weiss fell silent for a few moments. "Said something like, my bird likes fizz. No, not quite right. My bird Fizz likes this. I asked him about her and all he said was that she lived a long way away, a hell of a long way away."

Again, I looked at Barbara but she was still writing. "Last question for now, then. There are, or were, six members of this team. Any of them black?"

"Like, skin color?"

I nodded.

"One of the girls is pretty dark but I wouldn't describe her as black."

"The males?"

Weiss shook his head. "Sheldon's blond with blue eyes; Howard is pretty light-colored, he's got reddish brown hair."

"OK."

Simon Crossland collected the rig as he'd been told to and loaded the container without a second glance. The only words said—or shouted—were: "Bit more, again, okay, stop."

There were a few creaks as the ties were winched tight, and he was off. As he pulled away from the dock, he saw the green Audi, not only because it flashed its lights but it was unmistakable as it drew out ahead of him. He flashed his own lights in acknowledgment.

The Audi led him out towards the Humber estuary and onto the toll bridge. The driver must have paid for him because he was waved through. A little later, the lead car drew into a rest area and made it plain that Crossland should do the same. A moment later, six rough-looking and silent males climbed up into the cab and made shift to sit, virtually on top of each other, in the passenger space. Nothing was said between them or to Crossland as they set off once more. The Audi took the next left and led the way through Goole to, by the look of it, an empty factory site.

Huge roller shutter doors opened ponderously into a poorly lit interior that suggested the gateway to Hell. He followed the Audi inside and the doors rolled down.

Crossland felt vague stirrings of concern as the possibility of escape was closed off. He had felt confident up to this point because Leroy had promised that his Mr. White had his back. However, waiting with his six silent companions and whoever was in the car unsettled him.

Through his rearview mirrors, he expected to see a stream of passengers jumping down from the container doors at the rear but there was nothing. His cab passengers climbed down, Crossland opened his own door, jumped out, and stood huddled with his back to the rig's warm radiator. Everyone ignored him. He got curious, and walked around to look in the container's doors.

The long container was filled with wooden boxes, stacked one above the other with a central walkway disappearing forward into the darkness. What had he got himself involved in? Drugs were the first thing that came to mind, drugs worth millions of pounds. The boxes were removed in remarkably quick time and set on the concrete floor. One by one, the tops were pried off so the contents could be inspected. Eventually those nearer Crossland were opened. Inside, gleaming in the low light were dozens, scores, hundreds of rifles, smeared with protective grease.

His blood chilled. Not drugs, enough weapons to start a war, and the six men who had come with him were handling and gazing at them with something he could only describe as rapture on their faces.

Every single person in the building jumped convulsively. The sound of hammering on the roller shutters was deafening. Someone was trying, unsuccessfully, to get in. For a few long seconds, Crossland considered his options: he was locked in with a bunch of heavily armed men. No doubt, those outside would break through the doors, would he still be alive?

His companions were shouting to each other in a language he couldn't understand and one or two—at second glance, three or four—were giving him menacing glances. Thirty yards to the doors, ten seconds...he grasped a door handle, the shutter was immoveable and there was movement behind him. Turning, he ducked as one of the men tried to bend a rifle over his head, but the greased metal slithered through the other's fingers.

Crossland had been raised in one of the most violent parts of Leeds, punch-ups were a regular Saturday night's entertainment and people often underestimated him because of his lack of height. He locked his hands together, stiffened his arms and brought his fist thudding home into the man's stomach; simultaneously, Crossland's knee jerked upward into his would-be killer's genitals.

His assailant lost all interest and Crossland, confident in his abilities, set about the others who had seen their companion's failure. He used his own natural weapons: head, arms, fists, legs and boots. Two fell in the first few seconds, a third traded punches but failed to land any. The remaining two who were confronting him went looking for something to keep him at bay. It gave him the few seconds he needed to find the bolt on the bottom of the door and release it.

D.I. White slid under the door as soon as there was room, he was first to see Crossland standing with the six or seven bodies strewn around him. He hugged the little fellow. "Bloody hell, Simon, looks like you've earned your bonus. Let the professionals take care of the rest, it'll give them something to do."

Twenty or more police operatives from various response teams, Clive Bellamy and Ranjit among them, crawled in as the door opened, and began a search of the building. It took, perhaps, fifteen minutes to declare the place secure, Crossland had already subdued all but two men.

"Thank you, everyone." Bellamy looked around. "Simon too, needs to be thanked for the information he provided and for handling most of the opposition. I'd like to keep him on our team, I truly would."

There were cheers and shouts of appreciation. Bellamy turned to Stewart, "We have eight men in custody; all of them foreign nationals, and they should provide us with quite a few tidbits of information, but today's big bonus has got to be these weapons." He spread his arms and turned a full circle like a circus ring master. "Worth millions of pounds I'd guess, but think of the mayhem that might have been caused if they'd reached the streets."

Simon was driven back to Selby in a NCA BMW. His five-feet-two would feel six-feet-two with bragging rights for a life time after this.

————

When I arrived home, I found Shelly Fearon asleep on the couch in my living room. It wasn't until then that I remembered I had a date with the lady. Great detective that I was; I noticed there was a wine bottle on the floor. It was almost empty but there was no sign of the missing alcohol on the carpet. I knew where it must be. I sat back in the recliner and watched her breathe. The air was heavy with her perfume, she looked...well...I got up and poured myself a single malt that had come all the way from Glen Morangie.

I must have dropped off too. Around two a.m. I woke up to feel something nibbling my ear. I remembered this happening before and I thought, perhaps, Dad had let Pip in but then, it didn't feel like Pip. It didn't sound like Pip when a voice whispered "Thanks for letting me sleep on. I think I only had four hours but they were the best four hours I can remember for a long time."

She gave my ear another nibble. "I guess you must have been pulled in on a job."

I smiled and opened my eyes fully. Shelly was there, her eyes looking at me, her fingers brushing my hair back. This was the best thing about a relationship with another officer, we all understood the job's ramifications. We could get a call-out at a moment's notice without knowing where you were going or how long you were going to be.

I pulled her closer, smiled. "Don't suppose you fancy sleeping in a bed for a few hours?"

"I did think of that, but only if you have the strength to make mad passionate love to me first." She nuzzled my neck.

I laughed. "I can certainly try, but what happens if I like it? I'm told it can be very addictive."

"You really must try. We've broken the ice, don't you think we should follow that up?"

"My God, the patience of this woman! Does it matter if I start now or does it have to be upstairs?"

There were a string of giggles and squeals accompanied by a filthy laugh, the like of which no young gentleman of my breeding should be privy to. I guess, knowing Dad was not at home just across the yard, helped me shed some inhibitions.

Fizzah fumed when she got news of the lost weaponry. Then there was also word of the loss of the factory and the men, in that order.

The man who had led the rig to Bull Street had watched in horror from his green Audi, parked at the other end of the street, as the rapid response units in their night uniforms arrived. He left once all eyes were on the factory, and called Fizzah on the car phone as he disappeared into the distance.

She was angry, first, at her caller, wondering for a brief moment, if he had engineered the whole thing in order to fence the weapons. Secondly, her anger turned upon herself. There was no way she had been double-crossed, no way. Somehow, her network had been infiltrated and she had lost not just the weapons which had taken the profits from two years of people trafficking to set up the various deals but also the contacts she had cultivated.

A second thought occurred to her. Could she do it again, without Sadik getting to know about it? The guy was overbearing, convinced that most women had only one use, but he was not stupid. He had been very pleased at her resolving the matter of Faisal with enough violence to deter others from getting inflated ideas of their own competence. On her return from Syria,

Fizzah had purchased a fleet of fast, rubber-hulled landing craft to replace the sunken Caliph. Perhaps, then, he would not be looking at her affairs too closely for some time.

She snapped out of her mood of exasperation and prepared to begin the process of reviewing the rush of would-be captains for her new fleet of landing craft. As a precaution, Fizzah had temporarily moved her business premises to a small office above a tourist shop in the Izmir suburb of Basmane. The town sprawled along the coastline of a bay which was full of little coves suitable for loading small craft with refugees being trafficked to Kos or Samos, only two or three miles across the Aegean.

There was a clatter of sandals on the staircase and Samir burst into the room too breathless to speak. He gave the two fingers and fist sign for trouble and collapsed into a chair. In the few seconds before she heard more feet on the stairs, Fizzah moved her desk chair, pulled a drawer partly open and checked her waistline and right ankle. Her preparations for trouble were instinctive, made without thought. Other women might have checked hair and lipstick, hoping a good looking woman's attributes would keep her from harm.

The bead curtain across the doorway was swept aside, two men burst in. They were fit; professional trouble makers, killers, she assumed. Their eyes swept the space, seeing nothing but a youth and a woman there.

One said something in Turkish although it was obviously not his native language. "If there is anything in your desk, I suggest you leave it there. You understand me?

Fizzah nodded. "There is a 9mm automatic in my right-hand bottom drawer. It is there for my personal protection."

The questioner moved across the room, he reached down and removed the weapon. Fizzah's legs were crossed, her short, western style skirt had slid some distance above her knees. The man looked at the bare flesh and licked his lips, his brain concentrating on all the wrong things for a moment. He nodded to his companion who still stood at the doorway.

The second man spoke to someone unseen. "You can come up now, sir."

Fizzah had already guessed at the third man's identity, it was only a guess though; she would not have been surprised if she had been wrong. Sadik entered the small room and it was suddenly crowded.

For some reason, she recalled an expression that Alan used occasionally and she had had to ask what it meant. It never rains but it pours. *Well, well,* she thought. *First the guns are taken and now this. Related?*

"Good morning, Sadik. Rather far from your hotel, aren't you? What has brought you out into the sunshine?"

Sadik smiled a very thin smile; his teeth, as white as his dentist could make them, gleamed, just a little. "I just wondered what activities you were engaged in, Fizzah, my dear. I've brought your bonus."

"That's a lot of trouble, sir. You really needn't have bothered, there's no hurry. As a matter of fact, I'm getting ready to interview the men who are expecting to captain our pontoons. It's hardly seamanship, of course; a few miles across some of the safest seas in the world, instructions on a cell phone with GPS. However, if you have something you would like to say to them, I could get them to come back tomorrow."

"Where are they, these intrepid mariners? I didn't see a queue of eager men as I came in."

"They're in the café across the street. The shop below handles tourists; the owner wouldn't want a crowd of ruffians putting them off their lunches."

Sadik hooked a chair with his foot and dragged it across. He sat down directly opposite her. "How many are you interviewing?"

"Perhaps two hundred but I'm only seeing around thirty at a time. Any more and people will get curious."

"All very interesting, Fizzah. I don't know how you pack so much into your day. Boat trips, job interviews, killing off bungling sea captains.... am I paying you enough?"

Fizzah all but closed her eyes, regarding the three men from beneath her eyelids without their realizing it. The sense of danger was strengthening. The talent had grown in her during the days she smuggled weapons through tunnels from Gaza into the Lebanon, into Gaza and Israel and between Gaza and Egypt. She waited for the signal or the word that her employer would give to his strong-arm men. Should she wait or act first?

After a long pause, he said: "Of course, you must consider that I don't since you've chosen to arrange gun-running into the UK."

"Sorry, I've lost the thread. What do I consider you don't?"

Sadik shook his head, made just a little uncertain by the non-sequitur.

"You don't think I pay you enough."

"Ah, perhaps you don't. What do you think, Samir?"

Samir, appearing to be asleep on the settee, stirred. He stood up, scratching, stretching; drawing all eyes so no one saw Fizzah slide the .22 from its ankle holster. No one saw the long thin blade sprout from between Samir's fingers.

Samir, despite his apparent youth, had been with Fizzah for many years. Unlike Sadik and his kind, he did not under-estimate the ability of this or any other woman. The first man, he who had taken the gun from the desk drawer had his own gun out, too late, the knife was driven up under his chin and through the soft palate into his brain.

Simultaneously, Fizzah's gun puffed twice, taking out the second muscleman. Her eyes came to rest on Sadik's face as both henchmen thudded to the floor. There was fear there, and fumbling, clumsy with shock, he tried to take his own weapon out of its shoulder holster.

"Sorry, Sadik. You never did learn to give women the benefit of the doubt, did you?" She shot him twice through the forehead, the two tiny bullet holes so close that they touched each other.

Samir dragged the bodies of Sadik's two bodyguards into a back room for later disposal. Fizzah stripped Sadik to his underwear and went through his pockets. She stacked everything on her desk, mentally checking everything she found: comb, a tin of throat pastilles, credit cards, wallet, keys, and money clip with a thick wad of notes in it.

She frowned. *So where was it?* The only thing still to check were his very ordinary looking sandals. Even on examination, there were no hidden flaps or pockets. There were insoles, she noted, something grabbed her attention though she could not figure out what for a minute, perhaps longer. Insoles might be worn with hard leather shoes, but with thick, rubber-soled sandals?

She used Samir's knife to prize it away from the interior. Underneath, there was a slit in the surface and inside the slit, was a small sheet of paper folded in two. The paper carried a short list of numbers written in Syriac symbols.

The keys would open doors and drawers, would turn the locks on safes but those notes might be the cryptic keys to open the way to Sadik's hidden billions. Fizzah had no idea of the where or even the how as yet, but somewhere in the hotel Mir, which doubled as office and home in Beirut...

An hour ago, she had had little more than her trafficking business and a few thousand dollars. She potentially now had access to money beyond her wildest dreams, if she could find it and remove it to a safer place. She need never break laws or even do anything dishonest ever again, if she could find it.

Actually, she might have thought of Sadik's wives and children, but she didn't. She had had to fight her way out of the hell-hole that was Gaza, why would she think of Sadik's family, who were still comparatively wealthy? Fizz up-ended a shopping bag. Fruit, a bottle of water, and a couple of bread rolls fell to the floor. She gave Sadik's money clip to Samir, whose eyes bulged as he counted the notes with trembling fingers. Fizzah dropped everything she had taken from her assailants' bodies, everything from her desk, including the accounts and a small amount of money and two cell phones, into the shopping bag.

"You have a passport, Samir?"

He shook his head.

"Get a passport, use some of that money. Go see Ali, he has them in his shop drawer, tell him I want him to do it for you now. Okay? Let's go. You go down through the shop so everyone knows you weren't here. Tell the boat men across the road to come in half an hour. Okay?"

"Okay." Samir said doubtfully.

"Wait for me in your pickup." He went downstairs.

Alone, Fizzah pulled all the drawers out of the desk, dropping two of them onto the floor noisily. With even more noise, she pulled the heavy drawers from the filing cabinet and dropped those, too, onto the floor. Finally, she found a floor brush and banged it down the back stairs to simulate, as far as she could, one or two men hurrying away.

Three minutes later, Fizzah was out in the street, thirty minutes later Samir had his passport and they were driving to the airport at Izmir. They would not be returning.

CHAPTER 20

The last few months had been a bit on the rough side. My suspension, of course, was on top of my list, but the way our office working practices had changed—despite Joe Flowers' assurances that they wouldn't—had taken a lot of the satisfaction out of my job. Despite all of that, I had to admit that that particular Monday morning ranked highly, recalling what had occurred between Shelly and me.

My dad was back in his home, his kitchen light was on, and it must have been late because otherwise he would have let the dog come across my house. I could have been a bit teed off about that. Pip was my dog yet he spent more time with Dad than he did with me. It was something that occurred to me every now and then but, usually, I remembered to ask myself, what sort of life Pip would have without his being around? A dog's life, I guess.

I had almost finished my second cup of coffee when I heard the dog-flap and Pip took a running jump onto my lap, as pleased to see me as always. I discouraged his attempt to lick my ears, as I now had a lady to do that, and then the old feller came in.

"You okay? Coffee topped up?" he asked as he drained the coffee pot into his own mug, and then came in to join me. "Your lights were all out when I got back so I thought I wouldn't disturb you."

"I was pretty well bushed from the night before so I made an early night of it."

"She's a fit and healthy one and no mistake if she's tiring you out like that," Dad grinned. Or, maybe, it was a leer.

"Hey! What have...how do you come to that conclusion?"

"Scent, son. Or perfume, if you like. It lingers and she's the only one I know who wears that particular kind."

"Well, I suppose you're right but just remember, it's me that's the detective round here. Actually, I was out on a job." And I told him about my adventures with Simon Crossland in Goole. "Those weapons are worth a fortune."

He sniffed and took a sip of coffee. "So who gets the credit for all that?"

"I don't know, to be honest. But it really doesn't bother me all that much, either."

"Don't you think it ought to bother you? Just think; if you'd had a few successes like that on your record you might not have had that suspension to put up with."

I sighed. "You're probably right. Anyway, I have to get going. Bad form to be late on a Monday morning."

———

I reached the office, parked my car, and locked up. I felt a presence behind me and turned to find Chief Constable Vance standing there, smiling at me.

"Morning, sir."

"Morning, Stewart. That was quite a haul you brought in on Saturday. We're not very keen on blowing our own trumpet of course but, in this case Superintendent Bellamy has been very effusive. His department had been getting nowhere trying to get information but you seem to have come up with the goods as soon as they made you aware of the situation."

"Well, part of all that is down to you, sir. Remember you were able to keep Leroy Richards from having to return to prison? This was one of the ways we're getting repaid for that."

"My, my." The C.C. was positively glowing with bonhomie as the elevator brought us to the office level. Once in my office, I shuffled paperwork until nine o'clock and then went through to the squad room where I told my crew about the bust. "Keep this up 'til payday and the beers will be on me."

Barbara Patterson walked back to my office with me. "William Weiss? Remember him?"

"Certainly do. Still one of our guests, I presume?"

"Certainly is. He was telling the truth. We've been through his cell phone. The two jobs are on his camera so we have total coverage of the two robberies exactly as they happened. Obviously, there's no image of him, as he was on the other side of the lens."

I chuckled. "That has to be a first in the history of policing. I wonder what our friend Sheldon wanted the recordings for."

"You'll want this, too." She handed me a USB flash memory. "Copy of Weiss' sound record of his arguments with Sheldon. Like the videos, it backs up what he said in the interview."

"Okay, thanks."

After all that, I was feeling quite pleased with myself and I thought Dad would be interested in Leroy Richard's sudden reappearance. I called him, he sounded surprised because it was not something I did very often.

"Thought I'd got rid of you for the day and here you are again, turning up like a bad penny. What's up?"

A bit churlish for my dad. "Remember Leroy Richards?"

"Course I do…"

"Remind me to tell you about him when I get home. Bye, now."

When I did get home, the kitchen was full of odors. "What's cooking, Dad?"

"Tuna. Tuna casserole with garden peas, blackberry and apple pie for afters."

"That sounds pretty good. Smells that way too."

"You told me to remind you about…"

"Leroy Richards. Yes, I did. My head's been so full of stuff today; I thought I might lose that bit."

"Leroy Richards. You jumped in the river to fish him out, same feller as robbed Mad Charlie's warehouse."

"Wow. So you do listen to me once in a while."

"Yeah, yeah, yeah. If memory doesn't fail me, he was supposed to have drowned up here, in the Wharfe."

"Not a lot wrong with your memory, old'un, but I may have failed to mention that he recently became my snout."

"No, you didn't forget. You told me that and about his truck-driving mate. Short-ass."

"Okay. Well, you might like to know that he's getting married. Leroy, that is, not Short-ass. Asked me to be his best man."

"Why on earth would he do that? Doesn't he have any friends, or what?"

"You've hit the nail on the head, Dad. None that he can trust, anyway. And since he's still hiding from Charlie Morgan, even while Morgan's in jail, he wanted someone who wasn't going to stitch him up."

"Sounds daft to me. Now, what's so important that you had to call me from work?"

I nearly choked. "What so important, Dad; is that I told him I'd be his best man so long as it didn't clash with your wedding. So get on and get a date fixed. Dinner ready yet?"

Alan aligned the drilling rig carefully; the laser beam from the theodolite centered the proposed tunnel entrance. The rig would follow it like a dog would a rabbit. He had already marked all other points of reference on the walls in blue waxed crayon: easy to see, much harder to rub off. These could again be used by the laser beam to check he was drilling straight. And by carrying the portable theodolite down to the twenty-five-foot depth below the new tunnel, the same could be done for all the remainder of the dig. That, however, was when manpower took over. Not even Al could drop the rig down the hole.

This was what he had been waiting for, the moment he could start his own drilling in the only tunnel that mattered to him. Once that small but essential part was completed, the pick and shovel guys would start.

He looked at his watch. It was four-thirty in the morning; 90 minutes before he was due to start work for Beaver's, the contractors. Normally, there were no supervisors, nor anyone above the rank of foreman, before eight o'clock. Before then, he would start the drill cutting and still have time enough to shutter the wall before anyone who mattered came through.

A shuttering joiner arrived to build the false wall in front of the cut and nodded to Alan, who had already paid him half of the promised sum for the work and would complete the payment as soon as it was in place and he had shown Alan how to open and close it.

The brand new diamond drill bits, purchased recently out of Fizzah's contribution, cut through the sandstone like a knife through butter; twenty-six feet in the allotted hour, sixteen-feet for the company, and ten feet for him. The bona fide part was for the storage: electrical gear for the underground track; Alan's ten feet was a place to dig a four-foot-square hole with enough room to hide the tools for his main job.

That main job was to be a five-foot high tunnel several hundred yards in length to a precise point beneath Brixham Prison. The work would have to be carried out by hand since the strata would vary in height and thickness, and the water-bearing layers had to be avoided as they showed up. There might also be unknown underground workings—sewers, concrete pilings and so on—to be bypassed.

Alan was employing three teams of four men, working around the clock. The covert work went ahead, though it seemed it went slowly. Finally, his day complete, he went back to the bed and breakfast place and showered before calling Fizzah. It was not something he did daily; the woman had an important job, after all. She could pay million pound sums into his bank account, not something the average girl Friday did.

"Hello, lover," she answered, recognizing the number. "How's it all going?"

Alan never fully trusted phone calls so he answered carefully. "Pretty well. The targeted material has been removed and now we play with buckets and spades."

Fizzah, knowing the general plan, grasped what he was saying. Even in Gaza, there had been beaches where children played. "That's good, then. I am pleased that it progresses well."

He smiled, even though they couldn't see each other, he could sense her presence, hear her breathing. "I'm smiling here; I can feel you're close, somehow. When can we meet again?"

Fizzah's face didn't change. "Not for a while, big fellow. I have much to do here, a lot of special arrangements to make. But don't let me bore you with that. Let's plan something. Will you be staying in London once the job there is finished, or will you be heading away?"

"Can't say which at the moment, things are not certain. Let's plan the what instead of the when."

Ideas were suggested about venues but with nothing really fitting the bill. At the other end of the Mediterranean, Fizzah suddenly realized the time was almost eight o'clock. "Alan, I am sorry but I must go. I have things to arrange, including a surprise job for a work colleague. Goodbye for now. Call me again in a couple of days, all right?"

Alan wondered who she meant but stopped wondering as soon as he sat back and closed his eyes. Hard physical labor put the body into automatic mode. "Five minutes," he promised himself. "Right," his body responded, sarcastically, and woke him up several hours later.

Fizzah's call went to voicemail. She tried again after ten minutes—and again and again. On the fifth attempt, it was answered.

"What?"

"Samir?"

"Mmm."

"Samir, this is Fizzah Hammad. I need to see you, can you come to the hotel? My office? And can you look smart?"

Samir acceded with little enthusiasm. It took him an hour to reach the Mir, during which time, Fizzah alerted the reception desk and returned to her office. When the clerk called her, she took the elevator, put it on "hold" until she had signed in a Samir dressed like no one she had ever seen before.

"Wow, Samir." She touched the jacket, medium blue cord over white jeans and sneakers.

She had an idea that he had just come from an outfitters. Fizzah felt the knot on the tie, tightened it infinitesimally. "Now, that is smart."

The lift reached the eighth floor and stopped. She took him to her office and locked the door. She pointed to the chair across the desk from hers.

"How's your English?"

"Not good."

"Ask me how to get to Baker Street, in English."

"Um, Baker Street...how must I go?"

"Actually, that's not bad, Samir. I want you to go to Leeds in England. There's an airport there. I want you to find a particular address, use a cab, and warn this man. Offer him money, or if not, suggest what the alternative might be." She handed him a photo. "He brought down an operation there where I had a lot of money tied up. Cost me a fortune. Can you do that?"

"I guess so, boss."

"I'll pay you well, you know that. I don't want him killed; just teach the bastard a lesson he won't forget and tell him to keep his fingers out of other people's business—especially the import-export business. "

"That's a lot to say."

"Well, practice 'til you have it right. If you can make him see some sense, he'll leave us alone in future."

CHAPTER 21

A number of jobs had come in during the course of the afternoon and they all needed dealing with right away. I didn't get down to my car until dusk. I pressed the remote and bent to pull the door handle just as I saw a shape materializing above my left shoulder. I sensed rather than saw the weapon coming towards my head.

I threw up an arm as a matter of reflex and deflected the metal tube before it brained me completely. I didn't feel the blow at the time; I just stepped in close and gave my attacker a short right to the solar plexus. I heard the breath whoosh from his lungs and took a step back. My fist was already low, somewhere down near the floor, and I brought it up in a vicious arc to the underside of his chin.

The man fell between my car and the next and, for a few seconds, I was confused, uncertain what to do. I heard voices shouting as I fell back against the car and wondered at the hurting in my head. Then I felt the blood coursing down my neck.

Voices again, someone saying, "Look after the D.C.I., I'll get the shit that did it."

And that was it until I woke up in the Emergency Room at the Leeds General. It was quiet and I thought I was alone until I heard Barbara Patterson's voice, and one or two others that I didn't recognize. More time passed. I probably dozed off until I heard Barbara's contralto again, closer than before. She was pretty excited about something.

"When the hell is someone going to tell us how he is? Doesn't the doctor know this is a Detective Chief Inspector and not the dog's breath who nearly killed him?"

Wow! She's giving somebody the best of her temper. I was well pleased it wasn't me. More silence, then, "Look, this isn't some bugger that's been picked up out of his own sick in the gutter..."

"Barbara!" I called although it might have been nearer a whisper. "I'm okay. Really. Did they catch the bugger?"

There was a rustle. A gap appeared in the curtains and a head of red hair poked through. "Good God! Hello Guv. Yes, they caught him—he was half rolled under a car. We haven't started questioning him yet because we need to get an interpreter. We're not even sure what nationality he is."

"Good. Hold him until I get out of here. I want him!" I got up; actually, I tried to get up. "Give us a hand, will you. Barbara? Please?"

Then, after getting two lungfuls of air, I fell back onto the bed.

"DOCTOR!" It was Barbara's voice. "Don't worry, you can probably tell there are a lot of concerned coppers out here. Even the Chief's leaving that police charity event to come in and see you."

Her voice changed as she released the curtain. I heard her say: "You touch me again young man and I'll arrest you. Yes, yes, I know he needs rest, don't we all?"

The curtain was drawn aside again and a woman with a clipboard in a smart suit appeared. She turned to me, and then took a look at her clipboard. As she pulled the curtain closed behind her, I saw Shelly out there, in uniform.

"Good evening, sir. Are you a celebrity? Nobody has told me anything about you. I am Doctor Papali."

"I'm just a police officer. Sorry about the trouble this seems to be causing, all I want is to get out of your way. As you can see, I'm fine."

She checked her clipboard, picked up my wrist and frowned at it. At last she spoke. "The blow to your head could have fractured your skull but you're a lucky man, the x-rays are clear. However, your pulse is too high to let you go tonight. We'll have to find a bed for you until tomorrow."

She had let go of my wrist and I put my hand to the lump on my head. It was like a tennis ball covered in bandages and I had a feeling they'd shaved my scalp around the wound. I also noticed how my other arm was strapped up. I still felt that I should be free to go. I said, "But we've got the guy that did this in custody. I need to question him."

The doctor turned large, black, understanding eyes on me. "It will have to wait until tomorrow, Mr. White. I can assure you that the world will not come to an end before then. Now, you may have one visitor only for five minutes. Who do you want it to be?"

I wanted it to be Shelly but despite the wishful thinking, it had to be Barbara. "Sergeant Patterson, please."

Barbara came in immediately, her face filled with concern. "Are you okay? You look okay, more or less. Anything life-threatening?"

"No, it's all rules and regulations. You're the only one I can see tonight. Will you tell everyone thank-you for coming and it'll be all right to come tomorrow?

Oh, and if anyone knows how to stop the Chief, please do it. No point in his coming anyway if they won't let him in."

"I'll tell him you're at death's door and the shock of seeing him might kill you."

"If we don't have it already, there's a metal pipe down in the parking area that he tried to brain me with—fingerprints, okay? I actually hit him a couple of times before I started to lose it."

"Ha, ha. Before you passed out, you broke his jaw and we've got the pipe. When you see it, you'll realize what a lucky man you are. And you've always said that you couldn't fight."

"Me? No, no. I meant I didn't like to fight; I can stick up for myself if I need to, I just don't get any pleasure from it. The pipe...fingerprints. I want to know who he is, what he is and why he is. Was he just trying to rob me? And if not, what and for who?"

"Whom, Guv. For whom. We have the prints, we have his DNA. By the time I get back, we'll have checked every database we have access to and we'll know the little shit's every last detail. I have a feeling he's Turkish."

"What do you mean, for whom?"

"Who is bad grammar."

"Barbara, you're asking for a fast slap, you know that, don't you?"

"You want me to say anything to Inspector Fearon?"

The doctor was back before I could think of what to say. "That's it for tonight, sir. Time to go."

Barbara stood up. "Inspector Fearon?"

"Tell her I'm being kept in for observation, will you please. That should cover the situation."

A big male nurse arrived and easily lifted me on to a gurney. "Off we go, say bye-bye."

I snagged Barbara's sleeve on the way out. "And phone Dad for me please?"

Barbara nodded. She winked. At that moment, I had no idea what I would do without her.

Fizzah still stayed at the small, nondescript hotel on the outskirts of Beirut where she felt rather safer than at her own home. The following morning, she entered the building without her customary gifts for the wives. Despite Sadik's absence, there were reports to read, work to do. She arranged for pilots to run her small boats from Kusadasi to Kos and other Greek islands. Until she could find qualified help, the show must go on. Leaving the elevator, she took out the keys she had appropriated from Sadik's pockets, and stepping out onto the eighth floor, she noticed it was unusually quiet. There were housekeepers here and there, dusting and polishing, but none of the usual hustle and bustle.

Presumably, it was known that the boss was not in residence. Would the news of his death have reached Beirut so soon? It was possible that when inquiries from the seamen looking for work had had no answer, the door to the office above the tourist shop might have been broken open. Indeed, it was only to be expected sooner or later. Fizzah put those thoughts aside, went to her own office, and placed the contents of her shopping bag into her own safe. Next, she walked briskly along the corridor to Sadik's office suite, passing it by for the moment, returning when the passageway was empty. One bunch of keys let her in, another unlocked the truly massive safe where there was a collection of items best left for later investigation. What she needed was a list or a floor plan of Sadik's rooms, telling her what purpose each of the rooms served.

A wad of photocopy paper marked with black lines caught her interest. However, except for page numbers in the corner of each sheet and an occasional cryptic note, all added by hand in Syriac characters, the pages were enigmatic. A reference on the first page: 1.00 in Syriac characters, meant nothing. Similar notations followed: 1.04, 1.02, followed by what seemed like a dollar sign. She took the thick pad across to Sadik's desk and wondered where there might be explanations of the codes; then she remembered the doubled over paper from her boss's sandal, still in her handbag. There were, she counted, seven numbers in the list, each with an inscrutable symbol before it. The third line was crossed out.

Fizzah was concentrating so much on the codes that she hardly noticed the door open. She looked up, surprised. The woman who had entered was wearing a burka, but when she realized that only another woman was present, she removed it. Fizzah recognized Fatima, Sadik's senior wife.

"Fizzah! I'm pleased that you are here, what can you tell me about my husband? I want to know how he died. Was he killed by someone or did he die naturally?"

So soon? Her eyebrows rose. "Dead? Sadik? How did you hear this, Fatima?"

"Yesterday there was a phone call from the manager of a shop in Basmane. He said that they had broken down the door of the upstairs office and found my husband there; dead. There were two other dead men there too. They had heard a commotion and when they went up, this is what they found."

"Basmane?" She feigned surprise and confusion. "That's where the Syrian refugees go, no, I mean leave, from. We have an immigrant business there. What was he doing there?"

Sadik's wife shook her head. "Something to do with the business, I suppose. But why are you here? This is my husband's work place."

"It is mine too; surely you know I work as his secretary? When he is away, there are often things that need to be seen to. I was just about to arrange interviews for pilots for the boats we purchased to replace the Caliph, you know about that?"

Fatima nodded.

"Now I'd better organize storage for the boats until we know what to do." Fizzah arranged and re-arranged stuff on the desk, a perfect picture of a woman unsure of herself. "Oh, Fatima, what do I do next?"

What she did next was to cry and put arms around Fatima.

"You can imagine that I conduct all sorts of business for your husband and now—oh, my head is such a mess." She wiped her nose, and patted Fatima's hand. "Thank you my friend, what a terrible shock for you yesterday. I do feel more composed now. I've just had a thought, we have a policeman in our pay in that place. Let me get hold of him and find out what really happened and, secondly, I must speak to the bank and make certain that you have access to money and so forth."

She pulled open the desk drawer. "I do think there should be something here, yes." She took out a leather-covered box. "Your husband always kept his petty cash in here. Look."

Inside the case, there were notes, mostly Lebanese pounds with a few other denominations, and a large pocket filled with jewelry, single stones, a few finger rings.

Fatima would have made a good gambler. Her expression, her demeanor never faltered, she gave nothing away. "The bank, yes that would be very wise, Fizzah."

"I'll be along to see you as soon as I know what is happening. And, if I didn't say it before, I am so sorry for your loss, so very sorry."

Fatima spat on the floor. "Do you really believe that I don't see right through you?"

Fizzah stepped back, genuine surprise on her face.

"You stalk in here as though you own the place; you bring us cheap candies and twist the thinking of the younger wives. That doesn't work with me.

You're here to pick the bones of the dead but you are a failure, a has-been, of no more account."

Fizzah perched on the edge of the desk, shaking her head, looking sorrowful.

"You, talk to the bank?" She gave a twisted little smile and pointed to herself. "I know where his money is, I watched him hide it behind these walls and I shall protect it until my sons are of age and can..."

Fizzah cut her off with a gesture, wondering how much of this tirade was true. Did Fatima really know what Fizzah had in mind? She played what she hoped was her trump card.

"Maybe you do know, Fatima. Maybe you do but without me, you will never be able to move it. Wait until the Finance Ministry's tax collectors come calling. They don't care how Sadik made his money, they'll want his share and the tax man's share will be far bigger than mine."

"And what will you do with it?" Fatima was literally dribbling with fury, spittle running down her chin. "You'll put it in your wretched boats and spirit it out of the country. Oh no; my family comes from the desert and that is where it will go to, where my blood has meaning and power." She picked up Sadik's little hoard of money and jewels and closed it.

She left the room.

Fizzah Hammad took a deep breath. She crossed the room and closed the door, locked it and went back to the desk for what she felt was the real treasure, the list of numbers from Sadik's sandal and the photocopies.

She spread the sheets of tracing paper out on the desktop and gazed at them. The boxes drawn on the paper were mostly square and oblong, some were also odd shapes, some had letters from the Syriac alphabet marked in them, most were empty; they suggested...rooms, perhaps? Perhaps copied from a building plan? There were eight sheets, which also suggested...eight floors!

Fizzah looked at each one. The first one was obviously the ground floor with its big reception area and, there was the top floor, the eighth, a few yards from the elevator was her office, here was Sadik's, where she was sitting. Sadik's office was a part of a cluster of rooms, she looked at the doors into the other parts of the suite which corresponded with the gaps in the lines on the trace. The office where she sat had the number 1.0 in the corner; three of the other four rooms opening off the office had no number while the fourth was number 1.4.

She looked closely: Syriac notation, followed by the emblem that looked curiously like an American dollar sign. There seemed no sense to it. Fizzah had thoughts whirling through her head, even though she dismissed them and started all over again. What they meant was just too stupefying to work out. She would need more time to work on it.

She returned to the hotel she was using; her associates and Fatima knew about her apartment. At length, giving up on the enigma of the number system, she went to bed wondering whether to order another attack on White or to put it down to experience.

White, she had learned earlier, had raided her warehouse and stolen her guns. A guarded conversation with Alan had informed her that White was also a thorn in the sides of Alan and his father. Vengeance would be sweet, of course, especially so if...

She slept fitfully.

CHAPTER 22

My bed linen had been tucked in, breakfast had been served, and I had been allowed to change into proper pajamas when Dad came in at eight o'clock. He was obviously concerned about my injuries but was doing his best to hide it.

He squeezed my shoulder. "Hello, Son. Margaret brought me in her car; couldn't leave Pip by himself so she's walking him round the car park."

"Nice to see you, pull a chair up and sit down. They won't let me out of here before I've been seen by a doctor, but there shouldn't be a problem. A nurse says my readings are good, I had a quiet night."

Dad looked a bit relieved. "What happened to you?"

I shook my head in puzzlement. "Some guy was waiting in the car park outside the offices and tried to bounce a heavy metal bar off my head." Unconsciously, I touched the dressings on my head.

"Looks like he succeeded."

"Not really. I stopped most of the blow and don't remember feeling a thing until after the scuffle."

Dad eased himself down into one of the uncomfortable hospital chairs, I saw him grimace a bit. He leaned forward, something confidential was coming. "Took a phone call last night, from a Mr. Richards. Asked me if I was your dad and when I said I was, he asked when I was getting married. Said he was getting married as well but didn't want to clash with mine. Well, I knew who he was 'cos you told me. I said we hadn't actually set a date yet but probably in the next two or three weeks."

"Right, now I know too."

"Sarky...one of these days...Anyhow, he was fine with that and damn me, he started on about what a great feller you were and ended up inviting me to his wedding."

I was going to say something else but, having been warned, I kept my mouth shut.

Dad continued. "I thanked him and told him that most of my weekends were spent visiting at a hospital—Margaret's sister."

"Hmm, yes, I know."

"Mr. Richards said that was okay because his soon-to-be wife's church opened every day. He'd arrange things for a weekday. Wasn't that nice?"

"Really nice. I guess that's Leroy for you."

"Leroy. Aha, thought it might be him. Said he'd been a bad boy for some time, but he'd put all that behind him."

I chuckled. "Told me much the same: going straight and that's how he was going to stay. Mind you, I reckon a lot of that is down to the lady he's marrying. Very powerful, very persuasive lady."

"Hmm. Big woman?"

That made me laugh. "Just the opposite, but I've learned that size isn't everything."

It was Dad's turn to laugh. "Know what you mean, your mother was no bigger than five-foot-four but her left hook was awesome."

Did he really mean that? I wondered and decided to take it under consideration. "Believe me, this woman does not need hands or feet to make her point, just mouth and brains."

Dad harumphed, "Guess I can see that. Certainly brains could persuade some people."

"Wait 'til you meet her. She's a Voodoo Priestess."

"You mean that black magic mumbo jumbo?"

"That's how it may seem to us, chum, but to someone who believes, she can stop a man with a look. In fact, I heard how she spat a mouthful of rum over one guy. He was virtually catatonic for three days..."

A female voice interrupted, "You're scaring your dad to bits!"

My enthusiastic tale was cut short by Shelly Fearon, my favorite Police Inspector. Dad looked at me, then at her, smiled, and levered himself out of the chair's grip. I think he could see how I felt about her.

"Well, time for me to go. Margaret will be wondering what's been happening. Nice to see you, Shelly. Be seeing you tonight, son."

"I think so. I'll call you if I can't get home."

Shelly waited until Dad had moved out of sight then moved in close and gave me a kiss. "Don't know if that's allowed but I thought I'd take the chance before someone makes it illegal." She ran fingers through my hair, which must have some grey hairs in after last night, tutting and making reassuring noises.

I held up my hand with the little clip on the finger. "If this shows my pulse going off the top, don't blame me."

Other than that, we just sat there, smiling at each other until visitors started forming a line. It was one of the nicest ten minutes I could recall spending for a long time.

There was Barbara and three more of my sergeants, including Alec, and they got chased off by Joe Flowers and the Chief.

I held up my good hand. "Put the cuffs on then, Gentlemen. Although, if you'd waited, I'll be back in tomorrow."

Although I was joking about the cuffs, I wasn't joking about intending to be back in the office the next day, but they just laughed uproariously. Vance asked if there was anything he could do for me. Ordinarily, I'd have laughed the idea off but overnight, while I was feigning sleep for the nurse's sake, I had been thinking about the job, this particular job.

"Actually, sir, there is. Could, um, could..."

"Go on then Chief Inspector, spit it out."

"Well, would you mind asking the Chief at the Leeds Met if I could interview the gang of six? Well what they have of it, I mean. I know it's treading on toes but I have various bits of information that I'd like to follow up. For instance, why a young eastern Mediterranean man should want to beat my brains out."

Vance chuckled, he turned to Joe Flowers. "Now that's what I meant before, when I said nothing could keep White down for long, he just keeps getting up again." He turned back to me. "Give me twenty-four hours, I'll fix something up."

CHAPTER 23

It was a nice day to meet outside. I had already experienced the blank, bare walls of the drab meeting room downstairs, today I was trying something different. At my suggestion, the prison Governor had kindly had a table and chairs set out on the flat roof of the office block. There were glasses, a few bottles of Coke and a plate of biscuits on the table. From this vantage point, if you kept your gaze on the green fields, the high security fence with its ugly concertina rolls of barbed wire was almost out of sight.

Her eyes were drawn immediately to the North Yorkshire countryside and I watched her reactions to the view as she was escorted by the Governor in his smart, green, worsted suit, fortunately a shade which didn't clash with the surrounding countryside.

He gave me a look expressing his impatience as his charge dawdled along and I gestured to him to just let her look a while. I did not wish to rush her. Her friend Penny had not really been able to help much, so I was pinning all of my hopes on this girl. She must have seen me, obviously, and after two or three minutes, I spoke. "Come and sit over here, would you? You can still see the hills and woodlands while we talk."

The girl—I only knew her as Bernadette—although her bio was being prepared back in the office as I left, turned, came toward me, and sat down. I had explained to Phelps, the Governor, earlier that we were not dealing with hardened criminals but rather, young people who had been talked into wrong doing by someone older and manipulative.

"Want me to call you Bernadette?"

She grinned a little and spoke quietly. "No. I prefer Becca. And you are?"

"Sorry Becca, should have told you straight away. I'm D.C.I. White, from the NCA in Leeds. I'm not going to tell you that you've been led astray; it makes you sound like a stupid teenager and I know you aren't one of those either. Let's say that you were—made use of. I'm hoping we can be of use to one another."

She didn't say anything for a time, so I watched her. She had brunette hair with red highlights; her sleeves were rolled up and I could see she had the arms of an athlete. She should have been running or rowing perhaps instead of being locked up. She could be here for years.

Becca pursed her lips and looked at me from the corner of her eyes. "What sort of help's that, then? It's too late now. I've just been stupid, but I'm not stupid enough to fall for your line too."

The inference was clear. "Becca, I'm out to get the one you call Sheldon. It seems to me that he left you to take the blame while he took a runner. I can't promise but I might be able to talk to the C.P.S.—that's the Crown Prosecution Service—and do something about that. Help me, and that's not sexual innuendo, and it will help your case."

"Can't promise and help my case doesn't sound very likely to help."

"Becca. I can understand you being pissed off with your situation, you could have exercised better judgement, but this is probably your best chance. Do I make myself clear? Get real."

She glowered, wavered and eventually, eyes brimming, tears rolling down her cheeks, she nodded. "Sorry, Mr. White, I'm just feeling sorry for myself."

"Okay. Forget it. Tell me about Sheldon."

"He's a self-important prick; thought he was God's gift. Never happier than when he was giving orders, shouting the odds. Know what I mean?"

I nodded. "I know the type. Did he have any friends besides you five? Women, perhaps?"

"Talked quite a lot to his girlfriend—at least, that's what it sounded like. Her and, oh yes, he spoke to his sister occasionally."

My ears pricked up. "When did he speak to them?"

"Any time. Spent hours on his mobile when we were up at Leonard's place near the reservoir." Becca closed her eyes for a moment. "Wow, it was good food. Leonard had it delivered in. I reckoned it was prepared by a Cordon-Bleu chef."

I was storing this away. We knew about Leonard's residence of course, but nothing about phone conversations..."Did you catch any names?"

She laughed. "Called his girlfriend Fizzer, like the fireworks."

She fell silent but I could almost hear her mind ticking over. There was more to come.

"One time when he called her his beautiful brown sugar. Another time he called her his Arabian Princess and asked if they could meet up in Switzerland."

Black? No, Middle Eastern, I thought.

"He was nuts about her. If he was on his mobile to her, he would look right through you as though you weren't right there in front of him. Spooky! She must have been looking after him very well because he never bothered either of us girls."

"I see."

"It was this Fizzer that reminded him about things. The night before we were doing the modelling job, we were at Leonard's. Sheldon had his smartphone out and he talked and talked. I stopped and offered him the cheeseboard. Might as well have been on another planet, there was this dark-haired girl on the screen, really pretty. They were making plans to meet at a hotel, the 'Cally Etta Palace', something like that. 'On the Rock', he said. I thought it was somewhere like the Cow and Calf Rocks at Ilkley."

She paused. "Can I have one of those Cokes? I'm dry as dust."

I took the top off a bottle and passed it to her.

She took a long drink. "But I think I was way off. They weren't meeting around here. Next thing I knew he was calling this black girl. She looked pretty on the screen, and he called her 'Sis', which I assumed meant she was his sister. Do black girls get called Sis, do you know? Like black guys call each other Bro?"

"I don't think so. My girlfriend's black, I'll ask her."

"You got a black girlfriend, Mr. White? Now that's epic. A Detective Inspector with a black girlfriend."

I think that really broke the ice, even if I was too polite to correct her by telling her I was a Chief Inspector. "Tell me this, Becca. Did the other police ask about this? These telephone calls, I mean."

Becca shook her head. "No. They wanted to know what Sheldon looked like. You know: how tall was he, the color of his hair and so on. His hair was blond but that wasn't him, any girl would tell you, his roots were black or maybe dark brown. And he always wore flat shoes, like what a really tall guy would wear. That was funny. I could have understood if he'd been six foot six but really, he was no more than six foot two. How's that for noticing stuff? By the way, what've you done to your head?"

I touched the bandages and winced, "What, my head? Oh that's a long story. But that's good, Becca, what you told me. Really, and I promise I'll do my best for you. I'll let you know whatever happens, good or not. Okay?"

"Okay."

And when she went back with Phelps, I heard her say: "That Inspector, he's got a black girlfriend." Then she turned and asked me, "What's her name? Your girlfriend?"

"Shelly," I said and grinned.

She waved and turned, giving the countryside one final look before she was taken downstairs.

———————

The hole in the floor was large enough to take a generator and pneumatic drills. Alan climbed down a metal ladder to where, in four days, Barney's work force had driven the horizontal tunnel a bit more than a hundred feet.

Five feet in height and illuminated by a single battery powered LED, the passage was the minimum space possible to move and work in. The stratum of blue clay they were cutting through was comparatively easy to work with sharp spades, and softwood beams were sufficient to support the roof.

Two men worked side by side, cutting and pushing the clay back for two others to clear and bag the diggings. The smell of sweat was heavy in the enclosed air as they counted, low-voiced. Every ten bags, they stopped, took a breather, then hoisted the bags up into the storage area hidden behind the false shuttering. Later, they would be taken out and emptied into dumpsters along with similar material from the legitimate workings.

It was almost the end of the shift when Alan arrived and tapped Barney's shoulder. "Good job, Barney. It's going well."

"Better than we planned for, but don't get too enthusiastic. These things can change in an instant."

"Still, looks good, though. We aren't likely to hit concrete or granite at this depth, are we?"

"Probably not, but water's the main enemy. If this seepage gets any worse than this, the clay will become a quagmire, we'd need pumps and somewhere to pump it to."

"Where's the seepage coming from?"

Barney shook his head. "Don't know. I'd say we're way too far from the Thames. Could be an old Victorian sewer with perished mortar in the joints. We're going to have to dig sumps at regular intervals and if that doesn't work—well, it'll be pumps."

"Any point in asking how much further?"

"You can ask but I can't tell you with any accuracy. We'll let you know when we get there. Now cheer up and put your hand in your pocket. These lads of mine want paying and they damn well deserve a drink."

"Can't argue with that."

Once the men had been paid and had trooped out of the workings, Alan checked the time and rang his father. He had only spelled out to his father what he was planning a day or so ago. The older man wanted to know everything. He had decided to tell him just so much but not everything, now he would tell him a little more.

His dad had several cell phones hidden here and there in case of searches finding one or more of them. Alan always called after mealtimes. The older man listened avidly but rarely spoke more than a grunt or two in case he was overheard.

"The tunnel's well on now and going smoothly so far. No point in giving you a date in case we have problems, but it won't be long. Promise. Just be ready to move when I say so. You'll have to do that trick of yours to get put in the infirmary."

It was now twenty past five and he decided to eat with his workers at the pub. A bit of fraternization would go down well after such favorable progress.

There was no hint of dawn when Fizzah suddenly woke. The single sheet which had covered her was twisted like an old rope, testimony to her uncomfortable night. However, what had been going on in her brain had borne fruit. Answers to her questions sat there in the forefront of her mind as clearly as if they had been written down.

The photocopies she had been looking at in Sadik's office were, as she had guessed, the layout to each floor of the hotel. She had identified Sadik's office and, seeing the arrangement in her imagination, those rooms which had an annotation were those rooms where her boss had stored money or valuables. Sadik's office was in a corner of the top floor. The marked rooms were, for the most part, along the outer wall of the building; the symbols which accompanied the numbers denoted the nationality of the currency. Thus, the symbol next to Sadik's office, the one that looked rather like a dollar sign, was a dollar sign.

Fizzah got up and switched on the overhead light. She pulled a robe over her shoulders and took the eight sheets of paper from her bag. Looking at the layout with clear sight, she saw that the two rooms next to the office were unmarked; the next carried a Turkish Lira symbol and—somewhat unlikely since its loss of value—a Syrian pound marker. Now, the little slip of paper from Sadik's sandal was merely a note of the amount of money of each nationality. The same symbols appeared in front of each numeric value: an *aide-memoire* should he have needed to negotiate the purchase of goods or services.

Satisfied that she had solved the puzzle, Fizzah smoothed out the bed-linen and returned to a deep and dreamless sleep until her alarm call woke her in time for breakfast. Afterwards, she took a taxi to the hotel, stepping out at the back near the staff entrance.

It was still early and she took the small elevator up to the floor below the office level. She walked up the stairs along the silent corridor to Sadik's office. There was no sign of any of Sadik's wives or family. Taking care not to rattle the keys, she let herself in and locked the door behind her. Apart from the huge safe and a bar cupboard used solely for visitors, there was only one other door. This led through to a small anteroom with three more doors.

One, she understood, led to a bedroom with en-suite facilities; she was unfamiliar with it, and so avoided it for obvious reasons. Like many men, Sadik looked at her as though she was a ripe fruit, ready for plucking. Fizzah worked for him because she was competent at her job, including the unsavory parts, but sex was not on the agenda.

The second room was a lounge with comfortable furniture and low tables, a television, and a music center with a radio. The fourth was a storage area with bed linen, again, she had had no cause to see inside. She checked the bedroom: a door opposite her and left of center. One was large, with a double and a single antique-style wardrobe and heavy drapes to keep it cool during the day. The other two doors were opposite and to the right. The lounge was as she had last seen it, curtains drawn. The fourth was a surprise: narrow to the point of being claustrophobic and no window.

Curious, she checked the other rooms along the corridor from the office and then went back to look at the photocopied plans. She nodded. Those with inked-in references did not have the double windows that the others had. Locking and leaving the office, Fizzah went outside and looked at the outer wall from across the narrow street. All those rooms she had noted had had half the windows bricked up.

Back inside, she went to what she had assumed was a linen cupboard. The light fixture was not central, being far closer to the outer wall than to the inner wall. Unlike the rest of the room, it was papered with a heavy flocked wall-covering. A heavy paper knife from the office made short work of the covering. It came away in long strips to expose a plasterboard surface. A paperweight and the knife made a hole big enough to look through, then to step through. A plain wall light screwed to the wall illuminated the contents.

There was just sufficient room to walk around the outside of the open shelving which occupied the center. From floor to well above Fizzah's head, there was money, stacks of dollar bills in denominations of one thousand and five thousand dollars. These were the proceeds of people smuggling, the cost of travel out of the hell-hole built by Assad and harvested by Sadik. If his small, almost casual, record was anything to go by, there were millions of dollars here and other nationalities in the other rooms close by.

Fizzah had found paradise. She reached up to pull some of the bundles from the top when a small noise disturbed her. She turned to find Fatima, her eyes narrowed and gleaming, looking at her.

"You look surprised, Fizzah. Did you think you were the only one with keys? The only one with brains enough to figure out where the money was?" She shook her head. "Wrong, my dear. You got so many things wrong. Surely you had learned that my husband liked his girls young? Even at sixteen you would have been too old. The only thing that kept you here was your ruthless efficiency."

Fatima shook her head again.

"Who do you suppose moved his 'helpers' on when he was done with them? That's what he called them, helpers—including you. If he had had his way, of course, he would have had a harem. But that's not legal, and so I moved them on."

Fizzah listened, she even looked as though she was listening, fascinated. She was also looking for a way out. Could she strike a bargain? It seemed unlikely, but: "There's more than enough here…"

Again, a shake of the head. "No, there isn't, Fizzah. There's barely enough for what I want."

Fizzah backed up a little, pretending compliance. "Well, take it, Fatima." A little further, she was almost at the corner of the racks, now. "Take it all." A few more inches. "I'll go now, leave it with you."

But Fatima stayed where she was, blocking the main door.

"How did you find out about—?" Fizzah waved her hand.

"I watched the workmen sealing off the rooms: one, two, and then one untouched, three, four—"

"So you know about the others? Just let me out, Fatima."

"Of course I know. Sadik told me. He shared much with me in bed. We still slept in the same bed, you know. He would not share the money with my family."

"Your desert family? Have you considered how to get it there? How many days it will take to pack all this? And find transport? I've a ready labor force, men you can trust with your life."

Fizzah rushed her as she spoke the last few words, pushed and tried to circle around the woman but Fatima had a knife, held close to her gown. She brought it up, cutting through several layers of clothing into Fizzah's arm and chest. She could feel the blood running, warm and tickling across her skin, disgusted that she had not known the knife was coming. She held her other arm across the wounds while Fatima gloated.

Fatima waved the glittering knife. "I've cut up scrawnier chickens than you." And she came again, knife raised—until Fizzah lifted her .22.

"Fatima stopped. "You won't shoot here; it will bring a crowd of servants."

"This?" said Fizzah. "You wouldn't hear a thing." She shot Fatima in the eye. "Would you?"

As Fatima fell, Fizzah went to the drinks cupboard, which perhaps contrary to most expectations, held medications and first aid items, field dressings and anticoagulants, all because gunshot wounds were a daily possibility in parts of Beirut. Removing her top garments, Fizzah cleaned the knife cuts and bandaged the wounds to her arms. There were adhesive dressings in the cupboard, too. She cut them to a butterfly shape and brought the edges of the chest wounds together. After inspecting the injuries, she decided that they looked worse than they were and would heal if she put no strain on them.

That was easier said than done, as Fatima's body had to be concealed. Back in the bedroom, she opened the double wardrobe and found it filled with bed linen, but the other side turned out to be a dumb-waiter some four feet wide and of a similar depth, having been recessed into the wall behind. Had it not been for the cuts she had suffered, Fizzah could have hidden Fatima's body there and moved it down between floors, but the exercise was too dangerous. After some thought, she took a blanket with her and rolled the body on to it. With a combination of tugging and rolling, she moved it slowly into the bedroom and beyond the bed. A little more pushing with her feet rolled Fatima's remains in the blanket and under the edge of the bed.

Finally, it was time to do what she had originally hoped to do. In the smaller wardrobe, she found a set of matching wheeled suitcases. Taking the largest of these into the room which had concealed the money, she filled it with the highest denomination dollar notes. Then she placed a phone call to the travel agent she always used. Finally, she tried Samir's phone for the umpteenth time. She was quite astounded to hear a female voice answer using English words with an accent like Alan's.

"Hello, can I speak with Samir, please?"

"Who is this?"

"Just a friend."

"I'll put you through to someone who can help."

There were clicks and then a male voice spoke. "Detective Chief Inspector White. How can I help you?"

Detective Chief Inspector White. How can you help me? By keeping your interfering fingers out of my business!

She turned the phone off.

———

Fizzah made a quick trip to the family floor to leave a message with one of the other wives that she and Fatima were travelling across to Basmane for Sadik's funeral after the police autopsy. The body, she explained, would be brought back in a week or so.

There seemed to be very little in the way of grief.

An hour later, a taxi picked her and the suitcase up at the staff entrance and shortly thereafter, she was on a plane to London.

CHAPTER 24

I called a team meeting for nine-thirty in my office; I thought we could all squeeze in. The new squad leading the Gang of Six investigations had been put together from A Team because I knew them. Not that I doubted the abilities of B Team, but it seemed better to do things this way until I had spent more time with the men in B Team.

I'd chosen D.S. Beatty to be the new A Team leader. I would have preferred to have put Barbara Patterson in charge but she was far too valuable as a maverick—she would have loved to hear me use that word—but Beatty had impressed me and I'd given him the job on merit. B Team already had a highly competent O.I.C. in Detective Sergeant O'Grady and although this team mainly concentrated on other crimes, I thought well of them all.

The team could just fit into my office, even with Alec Bell joining us. I teetered back on my chair's back legs—not advisable—and told them about the interviews with Leonard and Bernadette and how their information would likely help us if we followed the pointers.

"D.S. Beatty is the new O.I.C. for this squad. I want to concentrate on finding Sheldon from our Gang of Six. I'll run through what we have from Leonard, whom D.C. Foyle fingered for us, and some new stuff that I got from Bernadette, one of the two girls in custody. First—"

There was a tap on my door and Sergeant Patterson looked through the glass. I waved her through and we all squeezed together to let her in.

"First, let's forget what we think we know about Sheldon's appearance. He's not blond; in reality, his hair is either dark brown or black and he bleaches it. He's also not as tall as we thought because he wears lifts in his shoes, or he's taller than we thought because he wears flat shoes with low heels. This suggests he's been trying to keep his identity a secret from his gang."

I looked around; everyone was nodding.

"Any shade of hair and six feet or six four, depending, then," Barbara said, rather wickedly.

I ignored her and went on. "He's also a whiz at manipulation. Leonard is no dunce and neither is Bernadette, who I've had words with. Both thought at first they were rehearsing scenes for a film, that the other people were actors, that they didn't know each other because it was *cinema verite.*

"William Weiss figured out that they were doing something shady early on, while Becca—Bernadette's real name—finally realized it at the end. Oh, and Sheldon has a black sister, real or adopted, I'm not sure. He also has a girlfriend he calls Fizz or Fizzy, and they had a meet up a day or so before the Harold Nicholson's robbery. These two met at a hotel called the 'Cally Etta Palace on the Rock.' I've run searches without much success; nearest seems to be a place on the Costa Brava."

Beatty stuck a finger in the air. "Only rocks I know of are Alcatraz or Gibraltar and I doubt its Alcatraz."

Barbara broke in. "It's Gibraltar. My cousin had her wedding reception there." She looked at me, all steely-eyed and business. *Had I upset her?*

"Okay, let's check the name."

"Caleta Palace Hotel. C-a-l-e-t-a. That's what it's called."

"Great. We'll agree on who is doing what and then get back to our own desks, okay?" I laughed. "I don't think this office is big enough for so many people."

Beatty and his squad departed with a scraping of chairs on the floor. Alec and Barbara sat tight.

"Okay." Alec said, Glasgow accent prominent. "What about me?"

"You, Alec? You know what you're best at. Keep on top of the squads and see that they miss nothing. Any ideas, let me know; any news, let me know. And Barbara..."

"That's me."

"Don't know if this is up your street. Do you know if a black woman could have a white brother? I mean a biological brother, not a bro."

"Well, of course. Different set of parents, mixed colors, remarriage, or just plain infidelity."

"Straight-forward, but in this case...suppose a white child from black parents? Natural, not with makeup or skin problems."

"That's stretching things. I remember a news report where a couple actually had twins with one white and one black. The parents were both black and moreover, there had been two or three black children previously."

"Was there an explanation given?"

"This was years ago so I'm really not certain. Perhaps there was a white grandparent and the white twin was a throwback. That would mean they weren't identical twins of course, fraternal twins, two eggs involved."

"Hmm. Possible, I suppose."

"You'd better ask a doctor."

Alec butted in. "Has this got something to do with that DNA from the lake house?"

I nodded. "Something that Becca mentioned. Could be that Sheldon is white, or passes for white, but with black DNA?"

"You need an expert."

"Absolutely, but I didn't want to ask stupid questions. And I have to ask myself if finding out these things really matter in the scheme of things."

I turned to Alec. "So, that business aside, anything to tell me?"

"Well, yes and no. I don't know that we want to go down this road but I've been following up on that gang bust you made for Bellamy. I heard from our old mate, Ranjit, that they were going to start questioning these types at six o'clock this morning. He invited me to sit in the observation room."

"Must be a Bellamy thing. Catch them while they're sleepy."

"Don't know about that but they had them there for three hours. Thought I'd better get back and report, only just made it with your call for nine-thirty."

"Well, don't just sit there, report."

"Just to keep you in the picture. These blokes they brought in were all from the old Soviet Republics."

"My God." Barbara said.

"Seven men, three different languages and four of them never said a word. I think they were all ex-forces personnel and they were under the impression that they were coming here to do a job, get paid well, and then go home."

"What about forming gangs to work over here?"

"The question was asked but they denied the idea. They'd been told that they were being transported in a container because none of them had a visa. Two of them said they'd been employed by someone called Fizzy Ahmed."

"Fizzy?" Barbara said. "Like you mentioned earlier?"

I nodded, several times. "Could just be Fizzah, not Fizzy. And the surname... perhaps not Ahmed. I know that mostly as a man's first name. Maybe Hammad with one 'm' or two?"

"Is that a lead?"

"It's a glimmer of an idea. Bernadette mentioned Sheldon having a girlfriend, said her name was Fizz or Fizzy—Fizzah. It's too much of a coincidence; it has to be the same woman. Tell Sergeant Beatty to mention the name when he calls the Caleta Palace."

I made some coffee when they'd gone and thought things through. I hadn't got to the end when Beatty came back with a list of dates that he slapped down on my desk.

"That was quick."

"Well, they're up two hours before us, Guv. I didn't need to read his notes; he recited them while I poured him a coffee. Fizzah Hammad and Aldo Morgan, that's according to his passport, he prefers Al or Alan. They stayed at the Caleta Palace in Gibraltar from the sixteenth to the eighteenth of this month."

The names meant nothing to me at that moment, but I had no doubt that eventually, they would.

In the meanwhile, I went back to my glimmer of an idea. That meant a meeting with my new friend, Leroy Richards.

I met up with him at the Selby Fork Hotel, a place I had used for this sort of thing before. This time, it was lunch and Leroy tucked into a huge Carpetbagger steak while I settled for a filet mignon—one that helped to make up for the one I'd left uneaten in the pub in Vicar Lane. That went with new potatoes, garden peas, and broccoli.

We live high on the vine in the NCA.

The food was good but I didn't stop talking to savor it. I started in immediately. "I want to talk about Charlie Morgan, Leroy."

Leroy nearly choked on his second mouthful. "Mad Charlie? Why, you heard something? Hey man, he doesn't know where I am, does he?"

"No. Calm down. Nothing like that. I want to test your knowledge, because you and he were mates inside, weren't you? Winson Green Prison, if I remember."

He brandished his steak knife. "You remember well enough, Mr., er, Stewart. But not mates, not exactly. I kept in with him 'cos it was safer that way, being one of his boys. He controlled that place, you know. There was rumors he had all the guards on his payroll."

I nodded, cutting a forkful of meat. "And family?

"Family?"

"Family. Did he ever mention them?"

Leroy screwed his face up, sorting out memories. "He did. Had pictures on his cell wall."

"Anything strike you about them?"

Leroy's mouth opened in a big grin, all perfect white teeth. "You want to know about that son of his?"

"Just curious."

"He had more'n a touch of white about him. Three photographs. His mother, she was black. His daughter, she was black. His son, he was white—old Charlie musta played away that time."

"Or it was Mrs. Morgan who played around. How old is he, do you think?"

"Then? Those pictures were years old. The kids, I'd reckon—" Again the facial contortions to force those little gray cells into working. "I'd reckon they was 'bout ten or eleven. Now that's a guess an' it's been a few years since I was in that place."

"Names? Remember their names?"

"Not really, not that interested, but..." He pointed his knife at me. "I remember the boy's name because of something that happened. One of the other inmates said to Mad Charlie, 'How's your boy Adolf, then?' Now Charlie went mad, you know the size of those fists. Broke bones in the guy's face. 'My son's name is Aldo,' he said. 'Aldo, you little prick.' I can see him now."

Again, I nodded. "Aldo."

"Yeah. When it was all over, he told me he'd named his boy after an actor who'd been a war hero. The Green Berets? John Wayne? Or was it Aldo Ray? I don' know. Before my time."

"Before mine as well."

"All that of any use, Stewart?"

"Could be. Remember what brought us together?"

"You not talking 'bout that goddamn time in the river?" Leroy almost snarled at me.

"Good Lord, man. What are you talking about? I mean that time when our DNA was found on that job. A break-in at a bookies."

Leroy was back to smiles again. "Right on."

"I have an idea that Charlie Morgan's son is behind our recent troubles. He seems to have grown up into a really devious young man."

"Well, I'd like to get my hands on him, then."

"You and me both. Ever heard of a woman called Fizzah Hammad?"

Leroy shook his head and ploughed on through his steak. "Never heard of her. Sounds foreign. Wait—didn't Simon say that woman who gave him all the money had a name like that?"

I shrugged but didn't go any further; I'd said more than I should have already. We finished our meal while discussing inconsequentials and left the restaurant. I told him I'd be there for his wedding and we left. Since I was near my home, I paid a visit there before going back to the office. Dad was cutting a bread pudding into slices like Mum used to do.

"Want a slice?"

"No thanks, Dad. I've just finished a heavy lunch with Leroy Richards, who you will be familiar with. Or as my Sergeant would undoubtedly tell me, I should say: 'with whom you will be familiar.' Our lunch could prove very useful. Is that Mum's recipe?"

My dad grinned from ear to ear. "Remember what she used to say to people that asked her for a bite?"

"Over my dead body," we said in unison.

I pinched a mouthful and chewed. Dad gave me one of his enigmatic looks. "Look at this." He crossed to the table and picked up a polished wooden box, I could recall Mother keeping it in her kitchen. On the top, burned into the wood were the words *My Dead Buddy.* I lifted the lid and saw several books inside. I let the lid close and looked quizzically at my dad.

"An American air crewman, billeted with your mum's family. She was just a youngster. Never came back from his last mission and he'd been working on that box but never finished it. So she kept it and kept her recipe books in it. Now when she said over my dead body, she was joking, but I reckon she was thinking of that feller."

It's funny how these stories come up out of the blue like that. I gave him a big hug and because the dog was looking put out, I gave him a good fussing too. "Keep yourself well, Dad."

Alan took Fizzah's call half an hour before she landed at Heathrow. He had just risen from his bed after working through the night. Her message alarmed him; he dressed at speed and reached the airport in time to arrange a private ambulance with a medical team on standby at a Harley Street clinic. He met her at the entrance to the arrivals lounge as she cleared customs.

She was pale and drawn, walking awkwardly, favoring her right-hand side. He barged forward with the British Airways-sponsored wheelchair and she eased herself into it. He pushed the chair with one hand and dragged her suitcase with the other. Once they were out of the crowd, he left it to the experts to get her into the ambulance.

Her only words were, "Take care of my suitcase."

He followed behind the ambulance back to the clinic. While she was being examined, Alan paced the deep pile carpet in the clinic's foyer. He was on edge and incapable of responding to the offers of coffee or tea during the two hours that Fizzah was out of sight. Finally, a doctor approached him. "Mr. Morgan?" The doctor spoke with a South African accent, he was also extraordinarily tall and had to bend a little to face Alan.

"Yes, I'm Ms. Hammad's friend."

"Well, she's lost a lot of blood. We've treated her wounds—what a plucky lady—and there's no sign of infection. She obviously used sterile dressings and good antiseptic preparations. Even her handiwork with the butterfly dressings worked well; I've stitched the wound before it became too ugly."

Alan was nodding in time to the phrases and suddenly became aware that the doctor had paused, awaiting a response. "An accident, I hear, with something sharp. I've not had a chance to speak with her." The words were only just beginning to sink in: cuts, butterfly dressings, stitches.

"She's lucky to have had you here to help her. Very lucky. Now, you are the Mister Morgan who booked the ambulance and our services?"

"Yes, indeed."

"And we can present you with our account?"

"Of course. I can do that now if it helps."

"In that case, it is exactly as you said, sir. An accident but she may need blood transfusions and of course, she must remain in our care for a few days. Give your details to the receptionist, your home address and so on, and medical insurance, or will you be paying cash?"

"Absolutely."

"Then everything is fine." The doctor gave Alan a knowing look which he would have been unlikely to have received at a National Health hospital, and he walked off.

He spoke to the receptionist, paid the required fees, and was guided to the private room made ready for her. She was surrounded by stands with bottles of blood and others with plasmas and antibiotics. Alan kissed her gently on the cheek and sat down.

"They say you'll have to stay here a few days, you've lost a lot of blood."

Fizz smiled wearily. "They're going to get a bit of a shock when they clean that toilet on the plane; I think half my four and a half liters must be there."

"What happened?"

"Sadik's principal wife happened. She found me examining his money stash and—where's my suitcase?"

"In my trunk, on the private lot round the back."

"Oh, what a relief. She cut me with a paring knife. Just a single slash, right across my arm and my chest. I should have seen it coming, but I didn't. She was like a bloody cobra, just as dangerous and just as fast. Anyway, that's over with. What kind of place are you staying at?" she inquired.

"A bed and breakfast, kind of a little hotel. Why?"

The injection she had been given had left her pain-free but woozy. "Get us a better place. A double room, one with security on the front door. Don't worry about what it will cost, I can take care of that now. And your tunnel, how's that going?"

"Very well. We had a holdup when we had to detour around some sheet pilings—"

Fizzah was asleep but roused as he stood up. "It's going okay?"

"We're back on track."

"You forget I'm a tunnel rat myself. I've dug more holes through Gaza mud than you can imagine. Most of them under the noses of Israelis—" And she was unconscious again.

Alan kissed the sleeping woman and left.

A little later, she roused and panicking for a moment, wondered where she was. Then it came back to her and she realized how grateful she felt to have someone to turn to. She had not planned to develop feelings for him; he was not even the sort of man she would normally go for.

He was not an expert in her chosen lifestyle; barely a keen amateur, really. She had only stayed that first night with him because of the wine, but she was starting to like him more and more as time went by.

Could she get rid of him if she had to?

Fizzah snorted and closed her eyes.

CHAPTER 25

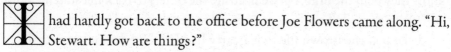had hardly got back to the office before Joe Flowers came along. "Hi, Stewart. How are things?"

"Can't grumble, Joe. How's your wife?"

Perhaps I shouldn't have said it, his face changed. "I don't know whether I told you that the radiation therapy didn't work. The latest specialist wants to perform a biopsy with a view to operating. That's if she can stand the anesthetic."

"Isn't that a good thing?"

"It could be, Stewart, but she's not happy. She doesn't like the idea of being unconscious—in case she doesn't wake up."

"Well, I don't know all the facts, Joe, obviously. But there aren't a lot of alternatives. Isn't having something done better than nothing?"

"You're right, of course, No doubt she knows that too, but...human nature, it's a funny thing." Joe sighed heavily. "Anyway, what's happening? Last I heard, you had just helped Bellamy's lot out of a spot of bother."

I looked across my desk top at a file that Sergeant Beatty had dropped there before I came back. "You're right; put that way, it sounds more flattering than it deserved. But right now, I'm wondering about the missing leader from the Leeds six."

Joe looked puzzled. "Thought the Met had that one."

I chuckled, "They did, but things have moved on."

"Go on."

"We know now that Sheldon is Aldo Morgan, son of Mad Charlie Morgan, who blames me for his imprisonment. Remember the DNA evidence that had me suspended?"

Joe nodded. "All connected?"

"You can say that again. I can't prove it yet, but I'm damn sure young Aldo planted the DNA that incriminated me and Leroy Richards."

"Motive?"

"His father wants to get even. Blames the two of us for him having to do fourteen years."

"Any evidence?"

"I have a witness who is prepared to swear that Aldo Morgan ordered the DNA collecting and the planting. But I need to question her some more to see if it really supports the suggestion."

"Who is that?"

"The one we know as Penny. She's playing ball now—they all are, since they know they're in the mire. All we need are the others to back her statement up."

"Okay, then. Tell me how you intend to get them to do that?"

I slapped the brown file that Beatty had left. "By devious innuendo, of course. And I've got a squad working on it. Young Morgan's also involved with a female gun-runner who's been trafficking people into the U.K. That's all provable and I have a snout who will swear to it."

I stopped abruptly. "Damn!"

"Problem?"

"I took a call that came in on the cell phone owned by the punk who clobbered me. The call was transferred to me—a woman's voice, asking for a Samir. She hung up when I got on the line."

"If it happens again, get it traced," Joe said, shaking his head. "This is starting to sound like one of those TV thrillers with a weekly cliff-hanger ending. What are you planning to do next?"

I tapped the file. "This is Aldo Morgan's life history. Did you know he's a well-paid civil engineer who doesn't really need to be involved in criminal activities? He's making more money than most of us and legitimately, I might add. He's a trained drilling operator, if that's the right terminology, the sort of skill they used for the Channel Tunnel. What does he need to steal this much cash for?"

Joe was silent for a while. I could see the little wheels turning in his head. "Do you think he's trying to break his father out of jail?"

I was a bit startled that Joe had picked up on my thoughts. "It's crossed my mind, but Birmingham is slap-bang in the middle of the country."

"Birmingham? You sure Morgan's in Birmingham?" he asked.

"Last I heard."

"Check again—or I will. The Prison Service has a habit of moving its inmates around without telling us." He thought for a moment. "If he's a channel-tunnel type driller, maybe Mad Charlie is at The Verne, on the Isle of Portland?"

"The Verne's been 're-purposed' as they say, sir. Immigration detainees are there now."

Barbara Patterson joined me as soon as the Super had left. I looked at her until she spoke. "Guv, you're looking at me as though you expect me to pull a rabbit out of a hat."

"Barbara, you're my best rabbit-puller. In fact, you're a star when it comes to stuff like that." I meant it, too, although she probably wouldn't have believed it.

"It doesn't always go your way, does it?" she asked.

"It doesn't but—"

Quite suddenly, without warning, I sneezed. And then I grinned, tapping my nose. "This nose of mine tells me that Aldo Morgan and his gun-running girlfriend are up to something very bad. I don't know what yet, but if we don't find out soon, it'll be too late. I suspect the man who jumped me has something to do with it, but he won't say a word. He could prove to be a dead end with a false passport. According to European records, he does not exist."

"And I've just got a rabbit by the ears...maybe. You know how when we go outside the EU, whatever hotel we stay at takes our passports and registers the details with their police?"

"I do. Happened to me several times: Turkey, Denmark, Isle of Man."

"Get away."

"I'm joking. Sorry, pull your rabbit out."

"How about Gibraltar? If they do that, then we could at least check out this woman, Hammad, find what her nationality is. And if they scanned the passport, that will tell us about her travels. Unless her name and everything else is a scam."

"Get onto it, Barbara. It's only a small lead, but any lead's good at the moment."

"And about your pipe-wielding attacker—"

"Ah, yes?"

"Had a passport stuck down his underwear. He's Lebanese and his name is Samir Batuk."

"Samir! Yes!"

She looked at me with an unreadable expression. "Sir?"

"The name is significant," I said

"He admits to battering you. 'A private matter,' he says, and clams up. But that's it, he has a smattering of English, but we got him an interpreter. His counsel says he will say nothing. Personally, I think his English is better than he pretends."

I took a moussaka home from the Greek Twilight restaurant off the Headrow just up from our offices. Dad hadn't started cooking because I was home early.

"A bit of plonk to go with that, do you think?" he asked.

"Sounds good. We've got some red on that wine rack that needs testing. The label on the bottle said it was from Chile, but how would I know?"

It was one of those evenings when there was nothing planned, no work files to catch up on, no library books waiting to be finished. Dad too, seemed in no hurry to get back to his little pad, so we sat in the lounge and watched the sun set across the river.

"You know," he started after a while, "had a word with Margaret and she suggested the Saturday after next, for the ceremony. Now, I was thinking, if you wanted to give that Mr. Richards a date, sometime before or after would work well. What do you think?"

I thought about it. I had a case that I would have liked to put to bed, but thinking again, that was always likely to be the situation. "Bit late now but I'll call Leroy and fix something," I said. "At least, it'll give me time to get my best suit cleaned."

"Ah, yes. Weddings, funerals, and christenings."

Ishmael Mustafa was in a thoughtful mood. He had been Sadik's fixer since they were boys, and the sinking of the Caliph had been a salutary lesson. While he was keeping a jaundiced eye on repairs to the ferry he was considering as a replacement, he thought about alternate business plans. Was it not a better solution to hire other men's boats—or women's, remembering Fizzah Hammad—than to spend so much money on acquiring them?

His deliberations were cut short by a short phone call.

The call was from Beirut, from one of Sadik's wives and at first, he could not understand what she was saying.

"Slow down, tell me again."

"Our husband is dead, Ishmael. Dead, murdered. You are needed here. The Hammad woman has gone to Basmane, to bring his body back here."

Ishmael's mind was in a whirl. He concentrated on the news, then spoke slowly. "There will have to be an autopsy," he said. "And probably a funeral there. I will return immediately."

Ishmael landed at Beirut-Rafic Hariri within hours. He had time on the flight to adjust to the new situation, decide what needed to be done—and what it could mean for himself. He called Sadik's home from the airport. Brahmin, the second wife, answered.

"Are there any visitors I should avoid?" Ishmael asked.

"None," she replied, "It is chaos here. Fatima went with Fizzah Hammad to Sadik's funeral and took all the keys with her! We need supplies, even fresh food is low, and we have no money."

Ishmael doubted the truth about the money. However, what did it matter? He would take charge in minutes, be in control. "I will be there as soon as I can," he said to Brahmin. "I will see you in the family area."

Later, he listened as the story was repeated several times and made calming gestures and reassuring responses. At length, a sort of order was established.

"Now, keys to the office?" he asked, "No one has them? Brahmin, you come with me."

Outside Sadik's office, watched by Brahmin, a handful of cleaners and other staff, Ishmael took out his handgun and asked everyone to stand back. The lock was pulverized, the door swung open. Inside, on the desk, was an assortment of first-aid items; on the floor was a scattering of large denomination dollar bills but no petty cash, as he had hoped.

He and Brahmin went to the bedroom, where there might be some money. They opened drawers and cupboards—and then Brahmin nearly tripped on an ankle protruding from under the bed. She screamed and tore the covers back from the edge to find Fatima staring back at her, one-eyed.

"Come away," he said, tugging her shoulder.

She nodded, stunned and stony faced, beyond tears.

Ishmael checked the other rooms and came to the smallest, where years before he and Sadik had had a false wall built, one of several throughout the top floor. He saw the hole smashed into the surface, the remaining money still stacked behind the broken wall.

"Bring me one of the security men," he ordered. And when the head of security arrived, he pointed to the door. "This door is to remain closed until I get a locksmith to repair it. When he comes, your man will watch him at all times until he is finished and the door is locked. Bring all the keys to me. I will be in the family area."

The other nodded. "As you order, sir."

The "sir" almost made him smile.

"The rest of you return to your places." He turned to Brahmin, "We shall go to the family area, I will speak to you and to your sisters."

During the discussion with the women, it was assumed Fizzah had been responsible for Fatima's death and the missing money. Apart from Sadik, she had been the only other person with a set of keys to virtually everywhere.

After the women had left, Ishmael hugged himself. It was all he could do to stop himself from breaking into laughter. All these years, since they had skipped stones across the river, he and Sadik had been friends. As Sadik prospered, he had remained the favored friend, the trusted one.

Until Fizzah Hammad had appeared.

She had knowledge and contacts far beyond the close community in which Ishmael lived. She expanded horizons, brought new ideas: drug trafficking, perhaps arms transportation. Ishmael was out of his depth.

He would track the woman down, he would wreak revenge—for the wives—revenge for Fatima's death. He had no doubt Fizzah had been involved with Sadik's death, too. How else could she have been there before him?

But she was dangerous. She came from Palestinian stock, a tunnel rat in Gaza. Ishmael thought of Fatima downstairs with one eye missing. She had been good with a knife. But Fizzah was also good—too good—with guns, with blades, even with her bare hands. He would not underestimate this woman. He sat and thought, gave more instructions, and the building returned to a semblance of order.

Information soon came back to him. He had informants: cousins throughout the city. It was a matter of hours before he had reports of Fizzah's arrival at the airport, a woman dragging a suitcase, pale and favoring her right arm. She had flown to London; he assumed she had used a fake passport.

CHAPTER 26

Dad and I met Evangeline and Leroy outside the temple where she practiced.

"This is a Voodoo Temple?" Dad asked, looking at the building. It seemed like all the others in the area.

"*Vodou*," Evangeline said as we followed them into a small room.

It was very different from the meeting room where Leroy's counterfeit memorial service had been held. The room was completely lined with black and white timbers. I'm no expert, but I wondered if the black was ebony. The white seemed to be light-colored wood limed or treated in some way. There were black leather sofas and an old man led us, creakily, to a pair of these. Another man stood at a lectern, reading from a book.

He lifted his head as we finished getting seated: Dad, next to Evangeline, then Leroy and I. He started to speak, perhaps in a language only Evangeline might have understood. He droned on, almost hypnotically, and I began to wonder what I had expected: cockerels decapitated, seven-foot-tall black men in top hats?

The priest, or whatever he was, changed his manner. He began to speak in heavily-accented English.

"We respect our visitors today by conducting this joining in English. The Priestess, Evangeline, has ordered that it be so and has also asked for no live sacrifices. Our drink will be mulled wine infused with a few drops of blood. Those wishing to be joined will now step forward, barefoot. Evangeline and Leroy, please."

Evangeline smiled at me as she stood, a black angel in black shimmering robes. She strode forward looking at least a foot taller than her actual five-foot-two.

Leroy likewise smiled at me as he, also, stood. I smiled back, thinking of his background and life and how lucky he was to have found this black rose in a field full of thistles.

The priest began to speak once more. I was surreptitiously watching my dad, who was obviously fascinated by it all. Not just fascinated, I'd say he was gobsmacked. His mouth was half open, his features slack, and eyes glazed—or perhaps, that was my imagination.

As ceremonies go, it came and went. I wondered when the live sacrifice would have happened if my dad and I weren't present. The only thing of note was the couple sealing their vows by having their forefingers pierced by a silver needle and then licking the blood from each other's fingers. It reminded me of the "blood brother" ceremonies I'd seen in movies.

They exchanged rings and bracelets and hugged and kissed, though whether that was a part of the ceremony or not, I didn't know. Once at an end, the two led us through to an anteroom furnished with comfortable chairs with a table filled with delicious-looking delicacies. Evangeline talked with Dad while Leroy came to me and offered his hand. "Thank you Stewart," he said. "I know this was not in our Po-lice agreement, but I'm really grateful to you. Now, tuck in, there's jerk chicken, if you like hot stuff, you'll love that. The hot sauce is a family secret, so no questions."

I did like hot stuff; I tried it and came back for seconds. As hot as an Indian Madras curry but a sweeter, fruitier flavour. I tried other things, too, and it was all good. In fact, I tried something which until now had been just a word in a song my mother used to sing, jambalaya. I knew Creole jambalaya originated in the French Quarter of New Orleans. Evangeline told me both New Orleans and Haiti traditions inherited customs from the French-speaking Africans.

We began our goodbyes, Dad wanted to speak to Margaret and he was worrying about Pip. But he got the couple both together and invited them to his own wedding.

Evangeline gave me a hug and a peck on the cheek. "Not as flashy as the last time you were here?" she said to me.

"Not by any means. But a whole lot nicer."

Barney took Alan to the end of the tunnel, where it swelled by a few feet on each side. He pointed to the darkness twenty-five feet above them. "We've done it, Al. That's right under the bloody showers in the ground floor medical center."

"That's great, Barney." Al shook the other's hand.

"All your Dad has to do now is to get there and phone us when he does."

Alan grinned, then laughed with relief. *He'd done it!* "I'll call him from above ground and don't worry about him getting there. Cast iron modus operandi—nutmeg's the secret."

"You're kidding me!"

"Ground nutmeg in some sort of powder, a teaspoonful will send his blood pressure though the roof. He lies down and calls for help."

"Fantastic, but he needs to be somewhere adjoining the showers."

"That's what friends are for, the sort of friends who like tobacco, lots of it."
Barney was puzzled.

"No money in prison, is there? Nothing to spend it on. Tobacco, that's the real money up there." He stabbed a hand towards the target above. "Until they ban smoking in prison, anyway."

"I'd not like to be the man who bans your dad from doing anything. One punch from him was like a stallion's kick."

"He's mentioned you, said you were the only one he'd fought who might have managed to knock him down. Mind you, I think that was a few years past."

"Too damn right. I was middleweight and landed quite a few in that last fight but I might just as well have been punching granite. You know the old saying: a good little'un can't beat a good big'un."

"Sure you're right. Now you and the lads knock off early. I think I did say that the best time to get the old bugger is on a weekend, around breakfast time. That's after the night shift are getting ready to go home. I'll talk to him and let you know for certain."

"No worries. We'll need an hour to clear the last foot or so and another hour to break through the floor. Although..." Barney considered. "What I'll do is drill a hole up through the floor first and poke a camera through to make certain everything's okay."

"Great. Tell the lads there's a bonus coming when we're done."

Alan checked his watch. There were three hours or so before his own night shift started; he decided to go to the Balmoral and see how Fizzah was doing. Everything seemed to be going well but as with the prison break-in, there was still a little way to go.

At reception, a letter awaited him. Worried, he tore the envelope open and read what Fizzah had written:

> Alan,
> I've not been able to catch you on your cell. I have to go away
> for a few days on business but expect to be back before you
> have to be there for your father.
> Love, Fizz.

He shook his head in disgust. What could possibly be as important as springing his dad? It pushed his determination up another notch. Coming for you, Dad!

After Leroy's wedding, I had politely refused any more drink after the first celebratory glass so I could be clear-headed and drive Dad up to Margaret's. Going back to my house, there was a call on the car-phone from Alec Bell.

"Alec, I'm on the road so keep it brief, would you?"

"Sure, boss. Just to let you know what we've discovered."

"Hit me with it."

"Right, Charlie Morgan. He's been in Brixton for the past six months and his son, Alan 'Aldo' Morgan is registered under his own name with the civil engineering firm that's extending the new line out to the Croydon area."

"And—don't tell me—the line is not a million miles from Brixton. Hold on a minute, I'm parking."

Two minutes later, I was stationary. "Okay, carry on."

"Yes, young Morgan. He's actually number two driller operator working the night shift."

"Hmm. Do you know if the Chief Constable is in his office at the moment?"

"He is, but he's in a meeting."

"Right. I'm going to try to call him but if he won't take my call, I'll get back to you and I shall order you to go and hammer on his door."

"That'll be interesting. I take it we think alike? Young Aldo's planning to break his dad out?"

"Plain as the nose on your face. I don't know how, I don't know where or when, but we can't afford to wait."

"Shouldn't we let Scotland Yard handle it?"

"Absolutely, and that's why we need to speak to Vance. It's our case, our suspect. We can handle it the same way they would if one of their villains was on our patch. Offer them assistance but let them run with it."

I rang off, called the Chief, and he took my call. I apologized for interrupting his meeting and I heard him say to whoever was there: "Give me a minute, will you, please?" Presumably, he was taking the call elsewhere. He came back on the phone. "Sorry about that, I'm quite pleased to get away from the meeting—budgets send me to sleep. Now, I guess this must be important Stewart, you wouldn't be interrupting me otherwise."

"Absolutely, sir." I gave him facts.

"Pack a bag, Stewart, and get ready to travel. I'll need to get in touch with the Commissioner himself. Shouldn't be a problem, know him well. Hmm, the Railway Police would be better, I'll let you know. What about warning Brixton?"

"I'd like to say don't, sir. The first thing they'll do is move Morgan Senior somewhere else. That'll fix their problem but make ours worse. Charlie will probably have a mobile phone and access to a runner to warn his son. We'll have little or nothing to charge him with and they'll be free to do the same again."

"Just what are you thinking, Stewart? The wall round Brixton is pretty high and I can't see how a helicopter could be landed in the yard."

It dawned on me that I hadn't mentioned Aldo's profession. "Aldo's a driller, sir. He's working on the new underground line in that part of London. Seems to me that the only logical way would be to cut a tunnel."

"But we don't know where the tunnel is or where they're planning to surface?"

"No, we don't—and of course, it would be better if we could catch them red-handed. If I do go down to London, I'd rather like to take Sergeant Patterson with me. Her strong suit is in thinking outside the box."

It was ten o'clock when we caught our train from Leeds to King's Cross. It had taken a few hours for the Chief to clear everything, even down to having one of the bosses from the tunnelling company present to travel with us across London Underground. It was just past eleven when C.C. Vance rang me back, telling me my thinking was correct.

Charlie Morgan had been moved into the prison hospital, on the ground floor. Seemed like all systems were go.

Fizzah got back to the Beirut office after midnight. With the exception of one light outside the door, the place was in darkness. She ran up the stairs rather than make noise by using the elevator. In her own office, she retrieved the small handgun she had left there before going to the airport. Her objective, now that her cuts were healing was to move the body left in Sadik's bedroom and to check on the money.

Everything was as she had left it; the hole in the wall: and the money still there. "Damn!" Somehow, her hand had become wrapped in a piece of cord. She pulled at it, felt something give and she was free. She went into the bedroom, to where she had left Fatima's body. It was still there of course, wrapped in sheets. She dragged the dead weight across the floor and slowly into the lounge.

Fizzah struggled a little but gradually managed to lift it into the unused dumb-waiter and moved the cage down to hide Fatima's corpse out of sight between floors. Taking another of Sadik's suitcases, she returned to the money stash; another case of high denomination bills wouldn't go amiss. They helped a person deal with the day-to-day problems of life.

She had almost filled the case when there was a sound. The door opened slowly and the wrong end of an automatic assault rifle pointed at her.

"Hello, Fizzah. How lovely to see you, my dear. Thank you for using the alarm we installed."

Exactly how could she talk her way out of this? There was no way she could survive a shootout with her .22.

As if thinking her thoughts, Ishmael said "Forget that ridiculous little pop gun of yours. You'd be dead before you could lift it. You wanted Sadik's money, now you can have what's left in here. It's all yours." Ishmael kicked the door open; he grinned and left-handedly fished a cheroot out of his shirt pocket. He took out his lighter and lit up.

It was a stupid act of bravado. He lost concentration and never noticed Fizzah's boot coming up like a missile until it smashed him under the jaw. Cherootless, gunless, he fell back as she slammed the door in his face. A single rifle shot through the door discouraged Ishmael from trying to re-enter. Wisely, he turned the key in the lock and moved out of range. Just in case, Fizzah sent half a dozen rounds through the door, hoping that Ishmael would take her point and move right away.

What should she do? Fizzah paced and stepped on something hard and bright. Ishmael's lighter: a large gold Zippo, his initials engraved on the front. She flicked it open, pressed the action and was rewarded with a steady yellow flame.

Something to burn.

She turned around and around, but there was nothing but money. A small pile to the left of the door, close against the far wall, was ideal, it even started the carpet smouldering. But the fire alarm didn't sound.

The lit Zippo, held as near to the fire detector as she could reach, did nothing. Eventually, she tried a burning bank note next to the fire detector and the smoke set off the alarm system. She fed more bank notes on to the fire, started several more, then turned off the light, and retreated to the right of the door where it would hide her, should it be opened.

More time passed, running feet pounded along the outer corridor past the office; a few minutes later they returned. The outer door opened, someone entered, paused. Fizz pictured them looking about, sniffing, crossing to the office, opening the door to the suite of rooms. The lock turned in the door to her prison, it opened and two people with fire extinguishers came in, glanced briefly around the room and rushed to the cozy fire she had set.

Fizzah slipped out behind them, unnoticed, she hoped. She didn't slow down to find out until she was at the top of the stairs to the ground floor level. Fire alarms were ringing throughout the building, people were hurrying down the corridors. She shrank into a corner behind the marble statue of a well-muscled athlete and waited for the exodus to thin out.

It must have been fifteen minutes before all the staff, the family and the few guests had reached the front of the building to huddle, waiting for someone to tell them what to do. The alarm was switched off, which Fizz thought was a pity.

She returned to Sadik's office suite, packed her suitcase with cash and used a smouldering fifty dollar bill to reactivate the alarm. She wheeled her suitcase along to the small staff elevator. Of course; in a fire emergency, no one used the elevators, and the staff elevator would take her straight down to the street.

The elevator came up from the ground floor, stopped in front of her. The doors opened—it was already in use. Ishmael had guessed at why the fire alarm was going off and had come up to investigate. Fizzah stepped back, and as Ishmael exited, she fired. The two little pellets took him in the forehead with less than a finger's breadth between the two wounds.

Fizzah's signature shot.

Fizzah left the Hotel Mir and would not return.

Ever.

CHAPTER 27

At five-forty-five in the morning Alan climbed off the seat of his rig, and although this was probably going to be his last shift, he was disappointed he had only managed three feet of drilling. He had known from experience that one or more of the diamond cutters had broken because it sounded like a screaming banshee. It took the engineers four hours to strip the cutters down and replace them with new diamond-tipped ones.

He was still thinking about it when he made his way back out of the main tunnel and headed toward the shuttered storage area. The joiner had made a masterly job of concealing what lay behind it. Even Barney, who had seen more miles of shuttering than most men still breathing, had not spotted how to open it.

One of the four-by-six horizontal support members had a wooden dowel drilled and secured at high level, too high for a man to see unless he knew it was there. But once the dowel had been removed, the boards moved sideways and back to the wall inside. In an emergency, perhaps someone becoming trapped inside, there was a pry bar to snap the dowel.

Alan opened the shuttering, stepped through over the false baseboard, and closed the shuttering behind him. He trusted that this would be the last time, so he switched on his flash light helmet and strode purposely to the hole in the floor's center. The tunnel beyond caused him to stoop so as not to bang his head, but the passage floor was flat and rock solid. He took his time since he was early and was pleased he had done so. Shortly the floor grew decidedly muddy. It hadn't been as bad as this yesterday and he wondered what had happened. As he progressed the mud turned sloppier and soon covered the tops of his boots, but he pressed onward until he reached a spot where the passage widened and men were doing their best to bag mud.

"What's gone wrong?" he asked.

One of the men said, "It was fine until we reached six feet up then suddenly it was as if we had hit an underground stream. It started coming down and flooding everywhere and we don't have any way of stopping it."

"Where's Barney?"

"He's up there, under the concrete. He's drilled a tiny hole and has had the camera through, He gave me the signal and I've passed him the shaped charges."

"Sounds like you're ready to blow your way through."

"We are, it's the best way to do it. Less noise than a pneumatic drill and all over in a split second. As long as your dad is ready to react it will be perfect. You'll be able to talk to Barney about it anyway. There's no way he'll stop up there when he sets them off. Not unless he wants a ton or more concrete falling on his head."

It was after three o'clock in the morning when we met up with inspector Ohoru of the London Railway Police Force. He had been well-briefed and would be our guide to the tunnelling operation. He took us to Blenheim Gardens where a temporary structure in the car park housed the main entrance to the workings.

"Tradesman's entrance," he announced. "Trucks pulling in and out of the ramp here all day normally. Can be a problem."

Barbara said what I was thinking. "I hope there's something more unobtrusive than this?"

I nodded. "Foot traffic only?"

The Inspector chuckled. "Of course, this way."

Beyond the door, the walls were lined with ceramic tiles of a color that had gone out of style more than a half-century ago. "Both this and the ramp go down to where they are building the southern extension," he said. "I've been down here a few times, and if you can tell me what you're looking for, I might be of more help."

I pondered for a few seconds before saying, "We're looking for one Aldo Morgan, a driller. We have reason to believe he may be exploring ways to enter Brixton prison."

Ohoru smiled. "God, man, are you serious? I just can't believe anyone could be stupid enough. That place has more alarms fitted to its walls, floors and ceilings than anywhere in the UK. Not even a mouse could get in there without being photographed and x-rayed."

I grinned back at the Inspector. "Sounds funny, I know. But if you recall it's not so long ago that a few men broke into a safety deposit vault in Hatton Garden by drilling through a twenty-inch reinforced concrete wall. My experience tells me that the harder the obstacles you put in the way of a crook, the more he wants to overcome them. Shall we head down?"

The passageway descended until we ran out of tiling and the tunnel opened out to an area resembling a subway platform under construction.

"What the hell's this place?" I asked and stopped us just short of entering the area.

"Brixton's the southern terminus of the Victoria line. There've always been plans and applications to develop the sub-surface assets; but the developers ran out of money more often than not. This area was excavated to link up foot traffic to the nearby surface line."

"And now?"

"Now, they're planning to extend the underground to the leafy suburbs of Croydon and beyond. The existing tunnels go as far as the South Circular but were never used."

I stood back in the shadows and checked my watch. It was approaching five-thirty. "What time do the shifts change?" I asked. Both of the officers confirmed what I already knew: six o'clock.

"Let's make ourselves comfortable then. If my thinking is right, I'm sure the procedure will be to take Charlie out before the doctors do their rounds, in case they check him and find his blood pressure's gone back to normal. And they will want to move him when there are plenty of people about, such as shift change."

Barbara nodded. "And Aldo working the night shift means it has to be on a morning? Now I see it, must admit I didn't before. Thought you must have a crystal ball."

An occasional person walked across the area ahead but no one that fitted my memory of Aldo Morgan's picture. It was five forty-five when an individual exited the shaft and walked across to the blocked off part of the tunnel.

Barbara could see more of his actions from where she was standing. "He's just disappeared, boss. There's a doorway of sorts in that shuttering and he's just gone through it."

"Could he be Morgan, do you think?"

Barbara shrugged. "He could. He's wearing work boots but I guess he's as tall as me."

"Right. Give him a ten minutes start then we'll go in after him. Inspector, would you mind manning that false wooden wall and stop anyone trying to come through it?"

Ohoru nodded, looking pleased. "London area heavyweight boxing champ for the past two years. It'll give me a bit of practice." Ohoru took his mobile out. "No connection here, won't be a moment." He walked fifty yards back towards the station and made his call. Returning, he told us: "My lads'll be here any minute."

At five-fifty-five Barbara and I pushed through the newly opened door and I nodded soberly at sight of the hole beyond. I pointed my flashlight down and inspected knotted climbing ropes attached to the stone walls. Barbara never even hesitated; she sat on the floor, found the rope with her fingers; and dropped. I was only a few seconds behind. Here was a newly cut tunnel and, as we started along it, we learned quickly to bend our heads and knees.

Barney climbed back down the last three meters below the shower room. He winked at Alan. "The charges are in position; there'll be an explosion when I set them off, obviously. Not a deafening one, in fact, them upstairs," he hooked a thumb towards the prison above, "they might not even hear it and if they do they'll probably think it's a backfire. If I've done my job right, the concrete will fall down the hole in one piece and your dad will be following it. Does he know what to do?"

Alan nodded. "He'll be ready, I've called him so he knows. He's waited over a year for something like this and now that it's on he's raring to go."

"Right, well. Let's give it a go. I suggest we all move a little ways up the tunnel."

Alan nodded. "Let's go." And seconds later there was a noise, very much like a car exhaust blowing back. He didn't see the concrete but he saw the dust and watched it settle on the water now covering the tunnel floor.

Charlie Morgan heard the sound outside the closed door to the shower room; he threw the sheets off him, rose with the makeshift sheet rope in hand. Inside the shower room, he saw the hole, moved two quick steps forward, and dropped the weighted end of his improvised rope into the hole before slithering down its length. It must have been near the bottom when his grip failed, but he still fell some distance. He lay there, regaining his breath, pretty certain he'd cracked a rib.

Alan seized his dad and pulled him erect. He knew once the guards discovered Charlie gone they would be following. He muttered encouraging words as he pulled his dad along the tunnel, but with having to stoop and Charlie saying that he'd hurt his chest, they were not making fast progress.

Coupled with that was the cloying mud which seemed to have grown worse in the last hour. Alan had not known that a thick bed of blue clay had been holding back the water, probably for decades. Barney and the lads had broken through part of it while digging the vertical shaft but the lump of concrete from the top of the shaft had demolished the barrier, opening the vein further and speeding up the flow of water.

They had passed no more than fifty yards down the tunnel when a light shone in their eyes and a voice said.

"I'm Chief Inspector White of the National Crime Agency. Looking at you, Mr. Morgan, I suggest you come along more slowly. There's no point in rushing, I have been waiting for you for some time."

Charlie had been struggling, but when he heard those words, like most villains, his first thought was of escape. Seeing a tunnel offshoot to his right, he dove through it.

The offshoot was one of the sumps Barney's men had dug to collect water and it was full. One second Charlie was standing in mud up to the ankles, the next he was in very cold water and it was over his head.

"Dad!" Al shouted and went after him without a second thought, into the water which was easily six feet deep and more in length.

———

Stewart, who had kept his head down in the tunnel as the workers ran past, saw where Charlie and Alan had disappeared, did what he did best. He went in, too.

They—Stewart and Barbara—managed to get an unconscious Charlie out first and laid him on his back above the floor. Stewart then clambered out and offered Alan a lift.

Alan, all six feet plus of him, was crying uncontrollably as he looked down at his father. Stewart watched, trying to get his breath as Barbara attempted CPR. When the paramedics arrived, they discovered her efforts had been in vain. Mad Charlie Morgan had died from a heart attack. The police who had accompanied the medics led Alan away.

Stewart and Barbara followed behind.

Inspector Ohoru met them as they exited the escape tunnel. He was holding his truncheon in one hand and a stun gun in the other. Seven men sat or lay on the floor against the wooden shuttering.

"You never said anything about men coming in, D.I. White—and five of them together. I asked them nicely to behave, but it seems like they fancied their chances with this," he said, waving his truncheon. "The other three came out of the shaft and gave themselves up."

"They probably saw what you'd done to their mates, Inspector, and didn't fancy getting more of the same," White said. "Well done. It has been a pleasure working with you, and that will be reflected in my report. Don't suppose you know where they've taken the young tall one?"

Later that day they travelled back first class and Stewart treated Barbara and himself to a three course dinner in the dining car. It was lemon sole, rather nice.

As briefly as he could, he brought the Leeds teams up to date, thanked them effusively for their work on the case, and then headed home for a hot bath and an early bed.

CHAPTER 28

Alec, Barbara, and Shelly had been invited to the wedding. Dad had raved on and on about the marvellous colleagues of mine that had rushed to my side when I was in trouble, and Margaret had insisted they all come. There was no further discussion.

Alec Bell had more connections than a fuse box. He overheard me looking for a car to transport us all to the wedding and—obviously—he knew a man with a white stretch limo.

The limo had two bench seats facing one another inside with an extra two seats next to the driver. We all chose to sit in the back, Dad and Margaret, Barbara and Alec on one seat, Shelly and I on the other. I don't know why that was but there was so much nodding and winking going on among those opposite that I felt pretty certain that it had been a set-up but I was happy with the way things stood.

Dad and Margaret were getting married at a church in Middleton on the Wolds, it was where Margaret had been born and where her sister, who had cancer, still lived. The driver, a Pakistani gentleman with an ever-smiling mouth full of white teeth, said he knew the area well.

Had it been my wedding I would have probably considered inviting more of my colleagues: Clive Bellamy, Joe Flowers, Chief Constable Vance, and Ranjit Patiela. In fact I was surprised by the number of my colleagues who had wanted to come. Dad had even invited Leroy and Evangeline but they had not turned up.

Someone once told me when I first came to Yorkshire that the Wolds were the elder brothers and sisters of the Dales. Here there were no mountains left, just rolling hills worn down by time and weather. Today, the usual green hills were mostly white and Dad had said the cold didn't matter because the frost had given them a white wedding.

My two lady police officers looked simply great, even though we were bundled up against the cold. Shelly was dressed in a dark plum-colored dress topped by a velvet black half jacket and looked more demure than I had ever seen her. Barbara's emerald green dress and matching shoes were a little more striking than her usual work attire. Margaret, in a long lilac dress, gave our driver directions interspersed with commentary on the places of note we passed on the way. The driver nodded and smiled as though it was all brand-new territory.

When we arrived at the church, everyone got out except for Margaret. She remained seated and asked to be conducted around the town once more on her own. My father confided, "She's going round the place first so her relatives and friends will see her arrive on her own, rather than arriving with all of us."

Whatever rocks her boat, I thought and grinned, while we all stood outside and waited.

A gleaming black Jaguar turned the corner, pulled up just past the church gates, and you could have knocked me down with a feather when Leroy and Evangeline stepped out.

They were both smiling at me and I had no problem smiling back. It had only been a few days since I has been best man at their wedding, after all.

"Morning Stewart, or should I call you Mr. White?"

"Stewart is fine. I thought something had come up and you weren't able to come."

"Never break a promise. Besides, you and your colleagues have removed Mad Charlie, my nemesis, my reason for hiding away out of sight all these long months. My precious here has been garaged all that time so I decided to treat her to a spin."

I winked at Evangeline and said, "I didn't know he referred to you as his precious, but I can see why he might call you that."

Leroy said "Eh," and smacked me on the back, at which moment the vicar came out, just as Margaret pulled up.

She had not been merely touring 'round the village; she had been to pick up her sister, a fold-up wheel chair was tucked nicely in the trunk of the limo.

We entered the church and found Margaret's friends and visitors already there. The ceremony was not a long one, no different to a million others I suppose. But to us, of course, it was pretty special.

The reception was held in the back room of the Black Bull. It was a lovely room—all waxed beams and horse brasses with a large open fire ablaze with huge logs. The fare was fit for royalty. Alec Bell found that the landlord had a collection of twenty or more single malt scotches, I think Alec's intention was to sample every one of them.

After the meal, we gave the mandatory speeches. Of course, as best man I had to give one, it was met with much whistling, clapping and more noise than one could have thought six people could make. Then we went back to Margaret's family home, where her sister still lived.

"There's enough food in the larder and drink in the cellar to last a month and we've no shortage of rooms for anyone wishing to stay," Margaret said. "I'm told we have home-prepared hams, salmon, bread and deserts; my sister and her friends have been busy all week. So I hope—"

A loud voice which I would have known anywhere interrupted the proceedings. I looked across to the front door to see the enormous shape of John Merrick filling the doorway. The Sheriff of Highlands County, Florida, was saying in a voice loud enough for everyone in the village to hear, "Only got permission to get the time off last night. I flew into Manchester, got into an argument with one of your customs guys because he found I was carrying my hog's leg. Held me up for an hour or so."

"His what?" Shelly whispered.

"He brought a ham," Alec slurred and laughed at his own joke.

"His gun," I said and Shelly and Barbara both nodded.

John hadn't stopped talking. "So I hired one of your funny dinky little cars with the steering wheel on the wrong side and I guess I missed you at your house, Stewart. Missed you at the church too. But, hey, I'm here. Now, where's the bride? I've got some hugging and kissing to do. And I've got flowers." He held up an enormous bouquet.

In less than ten minutes everyone in the house got to know John; just about everyone liked him—and the ladies loved him. Margaret got him to bend down low enough so that she could whisper in his ear. He nodded, beamed at the lady in question and gave the flowers to her sister.

I looked across at Dad. He came over to me and said, "You can stop giving me that look. John would have been the only one who's helped you that hadn't been invited. So I invited him. Surprise, surprise."

I gave Dad one of the White family special hugs and pointed John to the food stacked up on the kitchen table. I couldn't believe that anyone would want to come four thousand miles because my dad had asked him to.

That wasn't the last of the surprises, though. One of the large downstairs rooms had been emptied of furnishings, and the rugs had been removed to reveal the polished wooden floor beneath. Before long the dancing started. I waltzed, quick-stepped, and jived with Shelly, Barbara, and Evangeline. The only dance I excused myself from was John teaching the eager women the boot-scootin' boogie.

During a lull in the proceedings John came and sat alongside of me and winked as he made another can of Budweiser disappear. He reached into his jacket pocket and pulled out a card.

"For you, Stewart, old friend. Hope it makes you feel good."

I pulled the card from its envelope and opened the picture of a fish leaping out of a lake. The writing I recognized; the words were new,

> *Hi Stewart,*
> *Thought you would like to know that after Robert died, I wasn't able to look at you without seeing him. It's a pity because we would probably have been good together, you and I. But I found another good man, never thought I would, but I did and I'm happy. Just wanted you to know that and to tell you that I wish you all the good things in life. Connie.*

I hadn't realized it until Shelly asked if I was all right but I had tears like a column of marching ants running down my cheek. "Something in my eye," I protested.

Alec Bell was passed out cold, the first time I had ever seen him drink too much. I thought about carrying him upstairs but Barbara said no and went on to say that they had had a lovely day but felt they should go home. She told me that Alec had given the driver a hundred pounds to drive us, told him he would be home in time for tea.

As it was now after eight I doubted he would make it, not even for a late one, so I gave our chauffeur fifty pounds as a tip and a bag full of goodies—mostly food with some tins of soda—and he seemed happy. John helped us load Alec into the car and gave the driver instructions to take them anywhere they wanted. I even gave Barbara a peck on the cheek, a big hug, and a promise to be in for work on Monday.

Dad and Margaret had already gone upstairs. John, who said he'd had no sleep for twenty-four hours ("Never could sleep on planes,") was more than happy to be led to a bed. I turned to look at Shelly.

"What are you looking at, Stew? I've waited all day for you; you don't think I am going to let you go now, do you?"

I was suddenly rather glad that I'd only had a couple of glasses.

Aldo Morgan had been on remand for four months and despite DI White and his team thinking they knew everything of importance about him, officers were fighting one another to squeeze into the observation room.

They brought a handcuffed Morgan into the room first and secured him to the table before Stewart White entered. Stewart had glanced into the observation room first and was knocked sideways by the number of people present. Even the Chief, easily recognized by his grey hair, was in the crowd.

Aldo and his father, the notorious and now deceased Mad Charlie Morgan, had been front-page news for weeks. Well, maybe today they could start putting the story to bed.

Smiling at Shelly, Stewart took his place at the table, set his folders down, and proceeded to do what policemen have done from time immemorial: question the suspect.

"Perhaps you would like to start, Mr. Morgan, by telling us exactly how you were involved in these crimes? And what part your accomplices played in them?"

Aldo shuffled his feet, looked Stewart straight in the face, and said. "I meant no one any harm, and the others are totally blameless. I used them and lied to them to raise money to free my father. Even the guns used were theatre props, glorified starter pistols."

"Is it correct the other five thought they were making a film?"

"Yes, aside from the last job when I took the money without any of them knowing. I had to twist Leonard's arm a little because he is very bright and was starting to put it together. That last job—the girls were working a genuine modeling job. I pulled a few strings, showed their portfolios to the agency I knew handled the Nicholson contract, and they were booked."

The interview played out, not surprisingly, as everyone expected. Aldo Morgan was heading to prison for a long time for doing what most of us do, really: loving his father.

His accomplices all had their day in court. The judge proved most lenient with the single exception of Paul LeDuc, who went down for seven years for stealing from a casino.

Al's phone rang and rang. It told Fizz that there was a problem, as the number was only used between themselves. She was planning on going back to the UK but if there were problems, it would be better to find out first before returning. Instead, she bought a ticket for a seat on a tour leaving Beirut and left it days later at Alexandria, having sailed past Israel and Gaza, places of her youth. It seemed more than improbable now that she might be traced.

Sometime soon, she would return to London. If anything bad had happened to Alan, she knew she could return to the hotel where Al had left the car parked in a paid-for private lot with her millions of dollars in the trunk. She had three months to get to the car, registered to "Dr. and Mrs. Farrah". Even if Al had blown it, the future still beckoned.

WATCH FOR THE RETURN

OF FIZZAH HAMMAD IN THE

OLD GOLD NEW MONEY SERIES

ACKNOWLEDGEMENTS

The authors would like to thank Barking Rain Press for their help and skill in bringing this book to market.

Ti Locke, as our primary editor, has helped to change English English to American English, and her eagle eyes have noted our lapses and improved the work. Hannah Martine has scrutinized the final proof of the manuscript.

Craig Jennion, whose cover artwork for the series has both individualized and unified each book cover as part of the whole.

We would also like to mention family and friends, both in the UK and the US, for their support and enthusiasm. In no particular order: Arty & Roberta, Joyce & John, Dan & Linda, Lynn, Jeanne & Mary, Bobby & Luada and Bob & Miriam. Also, our thanks to former members of the Double Triangle Club at Selby: Stewart White, Robert Cleghorn and Simon Crossland, for lending their names to characters in the DI White Capers.

And, finally, our thanks to Fizzah Hamad for permission to use her splendid name for our special character.

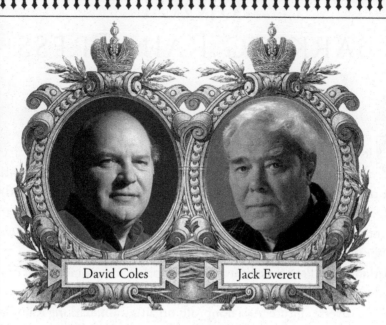

David Coles   Jack Everett

AUTHOR BIOGRAPHIES

DAVID COLES began writing fantasy and science fiction longer ago than he can now remember. His works have explored the local stars, killed off huge numbers of Roman legionaries, uncovered what happened to King Arthur and the Round Table—and hatched a few thriller plots. A founding member of the international Historical Novel Society, he has attended workshops run by Terry Pratchett and the late David Gemmel. David lives with his wife and a pet laptop in God's own county—Yorkshire in the UK—where he also designs and builds websites for friends and programs for fun.

JACK EVERETT is author and coauthor of a number of fantasy, science fiction, crime and thriller novels. Some are published, some are in progress and others are still in gestation. Jack also handcrafts stunning snooker cues and award-winning modern *objets d'art* from exotic and magnificently figured timbers. He collects books and playing cards though there is little space in a much overcrowded home. He dreams of having a bigger library, and hopes to one day have the extra room he dreams of.

WWW.ArchimedesPresseUK.com

ABOUT
BARKING RAIN PRESS

Did you know that five media conglomerates publish eighty percent of the books in the United States? As the publishing industry continues to contract, opportunities for emerging and mid-career authors are drying up. Who will write the literature of the twenty-first century if just a handful of profit-focused corporations are left to decide who—and what—is worthy of publication?

Barking Rain Press is dedicated to the creation and promotion of thoughtful and imaginative contemporary literature, which we believe is essential to a vital and diverse culture. As a nonprofit organization, Barking Rain Press is an independent publisher that seeks to cultivate relationships with new and mid-career writers over time, to be thorough in the editorial process, and to make the publishing process an experience that will add to an author's development—and ultimately enhance our literary heritage.

In selecting new titles for publication, Barking Rain Press considers authors at all points in their careers. Our goal is to support the development of emerging and mid-career authors—not just single books—as we know from experience that a writer's audience is cultivated over the course of several books.

Support for these efforts comes primarily from the sale of our publications; we also hope to attract grant funding and private donations. Whether you are a reader or a writer, we invite you to take a stand for independent publishing and become more involved with Barking Rain Press. With your support, we can make sure that talented writers thrive, and that their books reach the hands of spirited, curious readers. Find out more at our website.

WWW.BARKINGRAINPRESS.ORG

Barking Rain Press

Also from Barking Rain Press

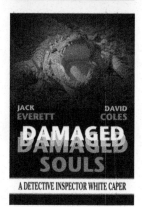

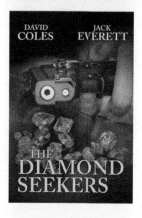

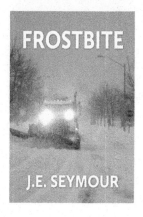

VIEW OUR COMPLETE CATALOG ONLINE:

WWW.BARKINGRAINPRESS.ORG

Lightning Source UK Ltd.
Milton Keynes UK
UKOW01f1559280218
318643UK00001B/41/P